MW01136177

THE PEOPLE'S BUSINESS

A Novel

MARK J. MOORE

"The men said to her, "This oath you made us swear will not be binding on us unless, when we enter the land, you have tied this scarlet cord in the window through which you let us down, and unless you have brought your father and mother, your brothers and all your family into the house. If anyone goes outside into the street, his blood will be on his own head; we will not be responsible. As for anyone who is in the house with you, his blood will be on our head if a hand is laid on him. But if you tell what we are doing, we will be released from the oath you made us swear."

"Agreed," she replied. "Let it be as you say." So she sent them away and they departed. And she tied the scarlet cord in the window.

- Joshua 2: 12, 14, 17-21

*There are those in the shadows
who relentlessly hunt evil.*

Now the wicked are afraid...

ACKNOWLEDGEMENTS

So many folks to thank for bringing this novel to fruition, so bear with me!

THANK YOU, to Jesus Christ, my Lord and Savior, for your favor, blessings and mercy in allowing me to put my story to paper. I also thank you for putting great people in my way to encourage and push me when I needed it.

THANK YOU, to my beautiful family – my wife Esther and my daughters Nyla and Arielle. You ladies have been my editor, my sounding board and my inspiration. This novel is just as much yours as it is mine.

THANK YOU, to my amazing parents, parents-in-law, family and friends. You all are my great support network who make me feel as if I can spin straw into gold. To Mom and Pop, I will forever be indebted to you both for surrounding me with great literature and nurturing my desire to expand my horizons.

THANK YOU, to my editors, Carol Taylor, Florence Brown, Arielle Moore and Ayesha Fraser. You brilliant ladies put your stamp on the novel each time you touched it. I am forever grateful.

THANK YOU, to Detectives Tracy Byard, Thorsten Lucke and Richard Harris of the Philadelphia Police Department for your expertise and insight in making Detectives Sisco and Luke genuine. Similarly, Thank you to my Sister-in-Christ Natasha Brown, veteran television anchor and broadcaster for CBS 3, Philadelphia, for your insight regarding Kelley Foster.

THANK YOU, to my good friend and best-selling author Nicole Bailey-Williams for your guidance and insight into this idea of writing for the masses.

THANK YOU, to Ms. Brenda Andrews, Leonard Colvin and the rest of the New Journal & Guide staff in Norfolk, Va., for giving me the chance to write, to make mistakes and then to write some more. Not only did you all teach me how to write, but how to build my story.

THANK YOU, to my good friend and personal trainer, James Tyler of TCore Fitness! I appreciate you pushing me to finish this book while pushing me to take my fitness to another level.

THANK YOU, to my good friend and barber, Jerry Williford of Mosaic Soul Barber Shop, for your advice and prodding to get the manuscript done. You always managed to keep me focused as we solved the world's problems during each haircut!

THANK YOU, to my church family, New Covenant Church of Philadelphia, my Brothers of Kappa Alpha Psi Fraternity, Inc., and my Hampton University family for all your love, support and encouragement on taking this huge step in releasing a novel. Special thanks to the G2 and Dynasty classes! I hope I make y'all proud.

THANK YOU, to all of my other friends, colleagues and associates who are too many to name, but far too important to forget. You moved me and didn't even realize it.

Now, please enjoy *"The People's Business"* …

Reddington, Mississippi – 1964

To the little brown-skinned boy, the plain white box was nothing special. To his grandmother, who gave it to him, however, the box's contents were priceless.

"What is it Grandma?" The box was too small to contain a Willie Mays baseball glove, yet too big to be a watch, he thought.

"Is it a toy?"

"Better than that, Alex," she answered. "Child, what's in this box will help you and give you wisdom. What's in this box will protect you and give you eternal life."

"Really?" The boy tried hard to mask his disappointment. While wisdom was nice, a new toy was what he really wanted.

He carried the box over to the worn sofa and sat down, nearly bumping into the black and white television on the rickety wooden stand. Another little black boy's picture filled the television screen. That little boy wore a nice hat and a friendly smile.

He looks like me, he thought. *A lot like me.* That frightened him. The boy, Emmett Till, was killed some years earlier in a nearby town. He'd been beaten, shot and then drowned. *Who would do something like that to a little kid?*

Shaking the box revealed nothing, because the box made no discernible noise when Alex shook it. His face wrinkled with disappointment.

The woman hummed an old gospel tune as she dried the dinner dishes and put away the rest of the smothered pork chops. She left the pitcher of lemonade on the table next to the plate of oatmeal cookies. The heavy southern air drifting through the kitchen window made the chilled glass pitcher appear to sweat.

"I know you wanted something you can play with for your birthday, baby, I know that," she said, wiping the counter with the used dishrag hanging from her apron. "But, you'll see one day that what's in that box will help you even more than you know."

Eager to see this newfound treasure, the boy tore open the cellophane wrapping and lifted off the box top. Inside were small white cards containing Scripture verses. Each card had a thin gold border and was laminated with plastic.

At six years old, Alex read very well for his

age. However, the cards contained many words too difficult for him to understand.

"If you read one of these every day, and keep those words in your heart, you'll know all about how God loves you," his grandmother said, drying her hands on the small dish rag.

"God's Word is life and power to those who obey Him, and death to those who do evil. Understand?"

"Yes, ma'am." He really did not understand, but he knew better than to say no.

"God has something special for you," she said, walking over to him and gently cradling his face in her hands.

"Yes, ma'am," he replied.

"Boy, I know it. I believe God put you on this earth to protect people." She patted his chest. "What do I always tell you?"

"Always love your neighbor?"

"That's right. And what else?

"Always hunt the devil and crush that serpent?"

"That's right, Alex. Always hunt the devil and crush that serpent," she repeated.

Then she bent over and kissed him on his forehead.

2018...

CHAPTER ONE

JANUARY 4th, 8:00 A.M.

The frigid early morning wind hit Zane full force as he opened his front door. Four days into the new year, and he could almost smell the Philadelphia cold.

"Where the Hell is Ron?" Zane said, as he glanced down at the watch on his left wrist. He was fully dressed, ready to go with laptop bag in hand.

From his home's wrap-around southern-style porch, he scanned the spacious front lawn and winding driveway. Come Spring, the lush greenery and budding trees would turn Zane's front yard into a vintage Norman Rockwell painting.

A black Crown Victoria with tinted windows soon appeared at the end of the driveway, as Ron Mason maneuvered the large car to Zane's front door.

"Sorry I'm late Zane," Ron said from the driver's side window. "The Schuylkill Expressway was backed up."

Zane hit the alarm button on the keypad just

inside the front door, closed the door and descended the short flight of stairs. He met the car just as it pulled up.

"Forget about it," Zane responded, easing his lean frame into the backseat. "Let's get moving. I need to be there early. I have a busy day."

As the big car wove its way through the small streets of Chestnut Hill headed toward downtown Philadelphia, Zane reflected on his life.

At 59 years old, Zane Alexander Russell looked anything but middle-aged. He was built like a gymnast: medium height, lean and angular. Between his extensive martial arts training and daily workout sessions, Zane had less body fat than some athletes half his age. His diet, healthy for the most part, kept his blood pressure down and his medium-brown complexion clear.

Zane kept his hair cut close to hide the just-beginning smattering of male pattern baldness on top of his head. He didn't smoke and rarely touched alcohol.

"You running again?" Ron asked as he turned onto another side street. "Next year is the election."

Zane opened his laptop and pressed the on button.

"I was thinking that same thing this morning," Zane replied as his laptop booted up. "My campaign manager called me last week and left me a voicemail about it. I was so busy that I put off calling him back."

"After this, you ain't got to run no more, right?" Ron asked.

"That's right. If I win, I stay on until I retire."

Zane gazed at runners making their way around the trail on Kelly drive. He marveled at the hearty souls who braved the frigid temps to get in their morning runs.

"Traffic is rollin' smoothly this morning," Ron said, breaking Zane's concentration. "We'll definitely get there well before nine."

Traffic was heavy all the way down Germantown Avenue.

However, once Ron turned right onto Mt. Pleasant Avenue, and then made his way onto Lincoln Drive, the drive became smoother.

"You know Ron, when I was in the military, I never thought that I would end up here," Zane said while scanning his laptop screen. "I just knew I wanted to help people."

"I know you got a lot of experience with criminals when you were in the U.S. Marshalls, right," Ron replied. "Hell, there you probably saw the worst of the worst." Ron shook his head.

"True," Zane agreed. "We definitely tracked down some of this country's most notorious fugitives."

In a Democratically-controlled city like Philadelphia, Zane was somewhat of an anomaly: a Black Republican. He felt the Democrats were too soft on crime. He hated welfare, thought teachers should be allowed to spank students, and felt juvenile killers should face the death penalty.

However, Zane broke ranks with his party on some key issues. He knew that racism was alive and well, and firmly believed affirmative action should be strengthened, not disbanded.

"Are you going to the Philly GOP ball this month, Zane?" Ron asked.

"Hadn't planned on it", Zane replied, scanning the morning news on his laptop. "I just can't deal with some of their foolishness."

Zane usually declined most of his party's offers, preferring instead to spend his most of his time pursuing his personal interests. Likewise, he turned down his party's campaign funds during his first election over ten years ago.

In fact, he used some of his own sizeable personal fortune during that campaign.

Zane built his wealth by starting a private security company after serving in the military and a stint as a United States Marshal.

He ultimately sold the company years later and made a considerable profit before entering law school. Many of the clients he guarded were well-paying high-profile diplomats, and some of his jobs were overseas. He wisely invested those funds, which had earned him a sizable return.

In addition, Zane owned several pronfitable properties in and around the city.

"I hate these fundraisers," Zane said. "I can't

stand having to suck up to some those corrupt donors. That's why I like using my own money."

Since running for publc office, Zane had become well-known for his strong political views. Because of this, he was a favorite target of many of the city's prominent liberals and some in the media. This was not surprising when a large number of criminal defendants in the city were minorities.

"Ron, I need you to visit our friends in the community this week," Zane said. "We have some new appointments to take care of."

"I'm headed out later tonight, Zane. I will keep you posted once I speak to my people."

"Good," Zane replied.

Zane had known Ron for over thirty years.

At 5-foot, 5-inches, 175 pounds, Ron was dark-skinned and well-muscled with a shaved head. He was a short but imposing figure. A former military man and fifth-degree black belt, Ron was Zane's oldest and most loyal friend.

A quiet man, Ron was known around the Criminal Justice Center as someone who greeted everyone, but mostly kept to himself.

Beyond that, little else was known about him.

Rumors, however, abounded.

Some claimed that he was a former hit-man. Others said he was an ex-con. Some even beleived Zane had saved Ron during one of his two combat tours in the military.

Only Zane and Ron knew the truth.

The rest of the morning drive through downtown Philadelphia was relaxing. Early-morning Philadelphia was like a massive bear stirring from hibernation. Storeowners put out carts, pulled up security grates on their storefronts, and readied themselves for another business day.

Ron had the car's radio tuned to the city's 24-hour gospel station per Zane. The leather interior of the big car was warm and cozy, shutting out the frosty morning. The hearty smell of coffee from his open thermos perked up Zane's senses just when the effects of his morning workout began to subside.

A computer freak, Zane had his ever-present laptop computer this morning. He was checking his voluminous e-mails.

"Zane, what time do you think you'll be done today?" Ron asked, navigating the car onto Lincoln Drive.

"Today's caseload is pretty busy, especially with the Norman case. He may demand a jury trial," Zane said without looking up from his computer.

He continued to type.

"I hope he doesn't request a jury," Zane continued, "because that case will probably take at least four days to try. Both sides have a large number of witnesses."

Ron maneuvered the car through the busy downtown traffic. There was little conversation between them for the remainder of the trip.

Ron was used to that.

Zane was a peculiar fellow: disciplined, rigid, maybe even a little fanatical. That didn't matter to Ron, though, because Zane was the closest thing he had to a brother.

That bond began in the military. After returning to the States, both men built upon that friendship. Ron was best man at Zane's wedding, while Zane helped Ron land several jobs over the years.

When Zane took the bench, he chose Ron to be his judicial tipstaff.

As the car cruised through the streets, Zane packed his files and laptop into his briefcase.

Zane looked out the tinted windows and noticed the many homeless people in the downtown area. Some slept on the sewer grates which warmed them by their steam.

Most, however, were mentally ill, cast into the street after budget cuts forced the state to close a number of mental health facilities a few years ago.

While private facilities treated as many patients as they could, they could not adequately treat the criminally insane. Thus, these people were released back into society to fend for themselves.

Or, to prey on others.

No wonder our streets aren't safe, Zane thought.

CHAPTER TWO

8:40 A.M.

"Good Morning, Judge."

Felice Paxton greeted Zane as he entered his chambers. She sat at the large conference table in the main room of the chambers. A number of case files in brown manila folders were stacked before her.

"How are you this morning Felice?"

"Fine, Judge. Did you hear?" she asked. "The 'Black Glove Rapist' got off. Not Guilty on all charges." She put aside the newspaper she was reading as Zane took off his coat.

Zane shook his head in disbelief.

"I can't believe a jury found that monster Not Guilty," Zane replied. "That's exactly why this city is so bad. These people here. . . I don't know what's wrong with some of them."

Felice handed Zane the day's case files from the table with her right hand. In her left she held a cup of hot green tea.

Felice had been one of a number of newly -graduated lawyers looking for work when she sent Zane her resume' over a year ago. When Zane discovered that he knew her pastor, he gave her an interview. After two minutes, it was apparent Felice possessed a quick legal mind. Zane offered her the job on the spot. Clearly, a number of law firms wooed her for her legal acumen, but she was also very pretty and very personable.

"I wonder how his lawyer pulled that one off," Zane said, sitting down his briefcase. He took the cup of green tea from Felice and nodded his thanks.

She left the room.

"Now, that demon will be back on the streets again." Zane shook his head and sat down behind the huge oak desk. He pulled a pen from his jacket pocket with his left hand and signed a few documents on his desk.

"I can't understand how they came back Not Guilty either," Felice said from the anteroom next to his office. "From what I saw of the trial, the Commonwealth's case was solid. Melnick, at one time, was on the Philadelphia Police Department's 'Most Wanted list.'"

Felice looked stunning today as she walked back into the room. Her navy blue business suit was cut perfectly, accentuating her curves. Her skirt was just long enough to be professional, yet tight enough to dare the eyes to investigate further. Her white silk blouse enhanced her mocha-colored skin, and her dark hair was pulled back casually into the working woman's ponytail.

"That animal deserves to be euthanized," Zane looked around and muttered under his breath. He wasn't sure if anyone heard him.

"I guess that's what happens sometimes when you try a case to a jury," Felice replied gathering the rest of the day's court files and setting them on his desk.

"That's *exactly* the risk when you have a Philadelphia jury," Zane countered. "When you have fourteen of those people in the box, all you need to do is raise enough reasonable doubt to just one of those bleeding-hearts - which isn't hard to find in this city - and you'll walk."

Zane's chambers were on the top floor of the Criminal Justice Center, fourteen floors above any prying eyes. The plush carpet, dark furniture and almost constant banter gave the chambers a country club atmosphere, rather than judicial chambers.

Ron came into the room with several sheets. He slipped out of his heavy coat and headed toward the coffee maker.

"Anyone else want coffee?" he called out to the rest of the Judge's staff.

"No, thanks," Felice said. "Ron, don't you know that stuff will kill you?"

"Felice," Ron said with a half-grin, "In the military, I drunk some things that would make a rat sick. So a little caffeine ain't doin' me no harm."

He continued.

"Besides, something's gonna eventually take you out of here anyway, right?"

Felice smiled and shook her head as she walked back to her cubicle.

As his staff went through their daily preparation, Zane readied himself for the day's list of cases.

Zane heard all types of cases, including Homicides. These were randomly assigned to him and a select few other Common Pleas Court judges in the court's Homicide program.

Today promised to be quite interesting. Among his list of ten cases were a gunpoint robbery, an aggravated assault, and a three co-defendant drug case. Any of these defendants could ask for a jury trial. If that happened, Zane would have to find a way to fit them into his already overloaded trial schedule.

"Judge, we have a defense continuance request from attorney Julian Vicente," Felice said. "He says he represents defendant Robert Scully in one of today's cases. Agg assault and gun charges."

"So, what's the Great Julian's excuse this time?" Zane asked sarcastically. "Meeting the Pope at the Vatican?"

"Not hardly," Felice responded. "He says he's on a federal trial down in Miami. He's representing a defendant named Paul Mercado. It's supposed to be some big drug case. I thought I saw something about it on CNN last week."

"I bet he'll show up for trial on time down there," Zane said. "Especially since the media's involved."

"You know private attorneys only play those games up here in Common Pleas Court," Felice said. "They know federal judges don't stand for any foolishness. They start at 9:00 a.m., and expect you to be seated in court with your witnesses by 8:59."

Zane nodded in agreement.

"The problem, Felice, is that these priave defense attorneys have little respect for the judges who actually want to keep our streets safe. If they can't fast-talk you, they don't need you. That's one of the main problems with our criminal justice system."

"Sure seems that way," Felice agreed as she reached for a stack of papers.

Zane moved toward the CD player sitting on his bookshelf when he heard a familiar voice outside in the waiting area of his chambers.

"I'm doing alright, Ron," said the cheerful male voice. "How are you doing?"

"Come on back, Beck," Zane called out to the waiting room.

"Good morning, Judge," Beck said, entering Zane's chambers. He reached out his right hand to grip Zane's.

Zane rose to greet the well-dressed young African-American man.

At 6-foot-1, Beck had to look down slightly to

face the judge. Beck was darker than Zane, with sharp cheekbones and a flat nose, courtesy of his boxing days. His hair, like Zane's, was cut close and well-kept. Beck's goatee and mustache were also closely trimmed.

Zane first met Beck – aka Darwin Beckley Stephens – nearly fifteen years ago when Beck was a first-year law student. Beck needed a mentor, and Zane needed a son. At least one who would talk to him. Beck was probably the closest thing Zane had to a protégé, and he'd eagerly taken him under his wing. Considering the tattered relationship with his ex-wife and two children, he may have even been the closest thing Zane had to a legacy at this point.

"How's your week look Judge?" Beck asked.

"Crazy," Zane replied. "The normal chaos."

Beck was a former professional boxer who had gained some local fame during his brief fighting career in Philadelphia. He managed to attend college part-time while pursuing a boxing career.

After he left the ring, Beck wanted to get into law enforcement or public service. He hated guns, however, so he thought about becoming a fireman. A chance meeting at a charity event for deceased firemen brought Beck and Zane together that first time.

Since then, Zane had watched Beck grow into a top-notch prosecutor, and an even better man.

Zane came around his desk and reeled Beck into a fatherly hug. Beck warmly returned the embrace. A constant admirer of Zane's keen knack for fashion, Beck caught a whiff of Zane's newest cologne.

"To what do I owe this honor, Counselor?" Zane asked. His broad grin was a mixture of pride and love.

"Judge, I know I should have called first," Beck said apologetically.

"Don't worry about it. I told you, Beck, you don't need to call before coming to see me. Just come on by."

"Thanks Judge," Beck said. "I really appreciate it."

"Sit down," Zane said, pointing to the chair across from his desk. "Coffee? Tea?"

"No, thanks, Judge. I'm fine."

Beck sat down in the comfortable armchair.

"I'm scheduled to start a jury trial this Thursday," Beck said. "I just dropped by to see if we could reschedule our lunch for that day."

Beck slipped his trial bag from his shoulder and sat it on the floor

"This case may go an extra week," he continued.

"Whatever works for you," Zane said. "We'll do it sometime after that. Alright?"

"That would be fine, Judge. Thanks."

"Where are you today?" Zane asked.

"Courtroom 819. I'm supposed to start the Rachman murder case in two weeks in front of Judge Manigault. We'll probably do pre-trial motions this week at least."

"Both of those guys are demons," Zane said.

"Rachman definitely needs to be off the streets, and Manigault… well, he is simply evil. Absolutely no redeeming qualities. He should be back at the ACLU, not on the bench."

"I know," Beck nodded. "It's like Manigault hates prosecutors just about as much as he hates cops." Beck checked his watch. "I think we have a good case, though. We even have a witness under police protection."

"Is this a death penalty case?"

"Yessir," Beck replied. "Hopefully we'll convict him, and then he'll get the needle. And, if anyone ever deserved it, he does. However, Rachman's so sleazy, he always seems to slip through the cracks."

"Rachman can run," Zane said, "but he won't be able to hide forever. Trust me when I tell you this."

"Hey, if you say so Judge. I hope you're right," Beck said, feeling reassured. He stood up and grabbed his trial bag then turned to leave.

He was thankful to Zane for the pep talk. Beck turned back.

"Oh yeah, Judge, Serene says Hi."

"How's she doing?" Zane asked. "You both really need to stop by so I can cook you dinner.

"That's a bet, Judge. I'll run it by her and call you later this week."

"You got it," Zane said.

Beck reached to shake Zane's hand. He appreciated

Zane's firm grip. Beck then turned toward the door and was out of chambers in a few moments.

The clock showed 8:55 as Zane slipped into his black judicial robe. He then walked out the door and down the hall to the private elevator, where Felice and Ron were waiting. There, they would take the elevator down to Zane's courtroom on the fifth floor.

"It was good to see Beck, wasn't it, Judge?" Felice said, as they waited for the elevator.

"Yes, Felice, it was." Zane seemed to be lost in thought as the elevator doors opened.

CHAPTER THREE

JANUARY 8th, 9:30 AM

Beck fought to control his voice as he rose from his seat behind the Commonwealth's table. He knew what the Judge would do when he told him. Still he had to make his argument anyway.

He cleared his throat nervously.

"Your Honor, the Commonwealth cannot proceed to trial at this time as our primary witness was found dead two days ago," Beck said. "Thus, we respectfully request a continuance in this case for further investigation and preparation."

Judge Irving Manigault wasted no time responding.

"This case is discharged. No witness, no case. I will not continue this case any longer! I hereby direct the quarter sessions clerk to mark the court file 'Dismissed' because the Commonwealth's witnesses failed to appear. Mr. Motley, you are free to go."

Beck was numb.

The other side of the court room instantly erupted

in joy. Raheem Motley, aka "Rachman", hugged his attorney and high-fived his many supporters nearby.

The witness' side of the room, by contrast, milled about not quite sure how to react.

Beck hoped the rest of the courtroom wouldn't see his shoulders sag. He knew the murder two days ago of the Commonwealth's star eyewitness gutted the capital murder case against Rachman.

He still thought, however, that there might be an outside chance Judge Manigault would grant a brief continuance. This might have given Beck time to try and find another witness, more evidence.

Something. Anything to make the case against Rachman.

Not a chance. Not with Judge Manigault, who seemed eager to dismiss the case.

"I said you was gonna beat this case, man," Baby Mike leaned down and whispered into Rachman's ear. The only reason Mike was still on the street was because Beck did not have enough evidence to link him to any of the murders – this time.

"I told you, ain't nobody comin' in to testify against you," Mike continued. "They know how you deal with snitches. The people in the street know that, and they scared. That's why the cops and the D.A.'s Office can't touch you."

'Baby' seemed an odd moniker for a man nearly six feet two, and three hundred-plus pounds. Mike, along with the rest of Rachman's family and supporters continued to mingle like it was Mardi

Gras. A number of them wore t-shirts with the slogan "Snitch Cure." There was a picture of a small gun underneath.

By contrast, the pall cast over the victim's side of the courtroom was visible. Beck shuffled and reshuffled the same papers in front of him on the table, not wanting to look up. Several sheriffs' deputies moved about the room, ready for any drama resulting from Manigault's decision.

Beck's head felt like it weighed a ton. Try as he might, he could not look at the victim's family. He felt he'd let them down.

Up until a week ago, the Commonwealth's evidence against "Rachman" was solid. The District Attorney's Office had finally built a strong case against the young drug dealer and murderer.

Rachman had terrorized South Philadelphia for years, leaving a string of bodies in his wake as he climbed the crime ladder. He and his associates always seemed to come out on top in the drug wars around the city. Likewise, he had beaten more than his share of murder cases.

In Beck's case, police believed Rachman had executed the elderly parents of a rival drug dealer to intimidate him. He allegedly shot both of them in the head with a .380 caliber semi-automatic weapon while they were tied up in their own beds.

Beck, newly-promoted to the Homicide Unit several months ago, had gotten the Rachman case from an older Assistant D.A. who was leaving the office. In fact, Beck had been in the unit for only two months, when Carlo Ricci, chief of the Homicide Unit, left the case on Beck's desk with a post-it note that said "See what you can do with this."

At the time, Beck looked at the assignment as a blessing.

Now, he wasn't so sure.

Since then, Beck had tenaciously prepared the case for trial. While the Commonwealth had some solid circumstantial evidence, the linchpin of their case was the testimony of Doretha Vann.

She lived on the victim's block, and heard gunshots as she came home late on the night of the murders. She clearly identified Rachman and another accomplice as they ran from the victims' home and into a car parked a few doors down. Her sworn statement was solid, and she had identified Rachman from mugshot photos.

Detectives subsequently searched Rachman's house after obtaining a warrant. Despite the fact that no .380-caliber guns were recovered, Detectives found .380-caliber ammunition in a shoebox in his room. The ammo matched at least two of the slugs removed from the victims' bodies.

Also, Rachman's cell phone records placed him in the vicinity of the murders near the estimated time of the crime. That, and Doretha's testimony gave the D.A.'s office a good chance at taking the notorious killer off the street. Beck remembered how proud he felt after Carlo signed off on Rachman's arrest warrant.

However, Doretha's staunch refusal to officially enter into the office's victim/witness protection program complicated matters.

"I ain't afraid of no Rachman," she said after meeting with Beck and some Detectives from the Victim/Witness unit. "Mister, I got the Lord on my side, that's all I need. What can man do to me?"

Even placing Doretha in custody to protect her as a material witness proved unsuitable. While Rachman was locked up, his tentacles still reached into the city's correctional facilities. There, her safety was no more guaranteed than if she were on the street. At least if she were out, she could have officers shadow her.

For nearly six months, Doretha and her family lived under the official protection of the District Attorney's office and the Philadelphia Police Department. Officers guarded her home and job as best as they could. Even when the police details lessened due to city budget cuts, Beck still felt she might make it to trial safely.

All of that changed after a jogger found Doretha Vann facedown in Fairmount Park two days ago with a hole in the back of her head. Ballistics showed the bullet in Doretha was a .22-caliber, unlike the ones taken from the rival drug-dealer's elderly parents and from Rachman's home. Even though Rachman was in custody, everyone involved knew he was behind the fifty year-old's cold-blooded murder. Her killer had apparently taken advantage of a security coverage lapse between the time she left work and arrived home that evening.

More chillingly, the killer had lulled everyone into a false sense of security by waiting until the eve of trial to take out the Commonwealth's star witness.

"Don't worry," Homicide Detective Evan Nash whispered into Beck's ear. "We'll find some more witnesses and rearrest this scumbag. He won't be smiling then."

"Damn it!" Beck said, slamming down the file folder he held. "This slimy bastard blows away two innocent people in their own bed, assassinates our star witness, and still gets to walk! With all the good, hard-working folks getting killed on our streets, how come one of those stray bullets hasn't found Judge Manigault and Rachman yet?"

"Now, that would be real justice," one of the uniformed officers in the room said.

Beck saw Rachman smirk at the victim's supporters as he left the courtroom. It was good that Beck didn't see him spit at another member of the victim's family in the hallway outside the courtroom.

If he had, Beck might have lost it.

"Is that bad man gonna go out and hurt somebody else like he did my nanna and pop-pop?" a little girl with a head full of brightly colored barettes asked no one in particular. She sat directly behind the DA's table in the first row of seats.

Don't lose it, man, Beck thought. *Maintain your character, even though you feel like exploding. You're not in the ring anymore.*

Beck walked over to the little girl and gently wiped the tears from her face with a tissue from his suit jacket pocket.

"We're not going to let that bad man hurt anyone else. Okay? Don't worry. We'll get him," Beck said with more confidence than he felt.

Turning away from the table, Beck took a deep breath. *Lord, forgive me for lying to that child.*

With all of the drama in the courtroom, no one noticed the older Black woman sitting in the far back seat nearest the door. Scribbling on a small yellow post-it note, she stuck it in her pocket book and slipped silently out the door. The sheriff's deputy stationed at the back door glanced at her as she passed him. He noticed the interesting burgundy braided cord on her right wrist.

CHAPTER FOUR

JANUARY 10TH, 12:00 noon

"Listen up, people! Today, you must make a choice!"

Gaylen Torres yelled into a bullhorn he held in his right hand as The Wailers' "Get Up, Stand Up!" blared from a small sound system set up nearby. He stood atop the stage and surveyed the crowd gathered in the City Hall courtyard.

Several uniformed Philadelphia Police bike officers milled among the crowd and kept an eye on the small, but vocal group of protesters.

The cops didn't faze Gaylen Torres. In fact, the look on his face dared anyone to challenge him.

"Either you're part of the solution, or you're part of the problem!" he said. "Simple as that."

"That's right!" yelled an old woman bundled up in a long trench coat and tattered ski cap. "I'm tired of these thugs getting off easy."

"Put 'em away for life!" shouted another woman.

"And, you need to throw some of them no-good judges away with them!" shouted a husky white man wearing a blue carpenter's union jacket. His words roused the small crowd.

Gaylen seemed oblivious to the harsh cold.

A big man with piercing eyes and a chipped front tooth, he was dressed in olive green army fatigues, a black ski cap and gloves. His neck tattoo boasted of gang affinity. He paced back and forth delivering his message.

The huge white banner emblazoned with R.O.C., RECLAIM OUR COMMUNITIES in red, hung from the front of the stage. The image of a roaring red lion was emblazoned above the slogan. The banner flailed in the frosty wind.

"Either you're gonna retake your streets and your lives, or you're gonna let the criminals have them! You decide."

"Hell, no!" shouted someone in the crowd, his fist in the air. "We tired of running! We ready to fight back!"

Gaylen pointed behind him across the street toward the Criminal Justice Center and continued his tirade.

"We have to go to war ourselves because those judges over there don't give a damn about us!" he shouted. "They don't walk down our streets, or live in our neighborhoods. You see they just let that demon Rachman walk free! Let him loose on our city!"

"They don't give a damn about us!" someone yelled.

Gaylen continued.

"Those judges don't have to live in fear of drug

dealers setting their houses on fire, or getting hit by stray bullets where they live!"

More applause from the crowd.

"That's why they don't think twice about letting these murderers and rapists back out onto our streets! Well, I ask you: if they don't care about us, and those criminals sure don't care about us, who does?"

"We gotta protect our own!" shouted a middle-aged man in a too-small brown parka that barely covered his stomach.

"That's right. That's exactly right," Gaylen responded, pacing once again. His words were punctuated by visibly-frosty air. "We gotta take back our own streets. We gotta make our streets a place where our kids can play safely."

"That's right," shouted several people in the crowd.

"Where our mothers and grandmothers and daughters can walk at night safely!"

"Amen!" the crowd responded.

"Where our young people can go to school without fear of gang violence or being kidnapped!"

"Tell the truth, man!" a man in the crowd shouted.

"But, let me say this, people," Gaylen lowered his voice, quieting the crowd. "Don't be fooled. We can't trust most of these cops, either."

"Man, forget them!" shouted a young man in a multicolored baseball hat. His upraised fist punctuated the cold air. "They part of the problem, too!"

"That's right. They never come to my street unless you lie and tell 911 there's a man with a gun," shouted a well-dressed African-American man wearing black-rimmed glasses. The crowd laughed and nodded in agreement.

"It's time, people! Time to stop begging others to save us," Gaylen said. "So what do we do?"

"We do it ourselves!" shouted an elderly man.

"Like Malcolm said," Gaylen paused to scan the crowd. "By any means necessary."

12:45 pm

Kelley Foster tried to put on her make-up, but the cold did not help. Neither did the tumultuous roar from the crowd, which startled her, or the fact that she saw Gaylen Torres as merely another so-called community activist trying to profit from beleaguered citizens.

Today, however, her employer, Channel 7, had sent her to cover the noon rally at City Hall despite the deep freeze. Kelley was determined to put her personal feelings for Torres aside and interview the mercurial activist.

"Kelley, you're on in five minutes," said her cameraman. A tall white man with perfect teeth, Rich Stansky was a ten-year veteran of local broadcast news. "Where do you want me to set up?"

"Let's do it here in front of the door to City

Hall," Kelley said. "Mr. Longwell, could you just stand over there until we're ready for you?"

"Sure, ma'am. No problem," he said. The middle-aged African-American man in the grey down jacket pulled the blue knit cap down over his ears, and stamped his feet for warmth. Jonas jammed his hands into his coat pockets and huddled near the side of the building.

Meanwhile, Kelley and Rich positioned the equipment in place for the broadcast as the crowd began to disperse. Off in the distance, Kelley saw Torres and two other men walking toward the far side of the small stage. She straightened her coat as Rich went back inside their news van. He checked the equipment inside to make sure the station was ready for the live feed. Kelley grabbed the microphone with the Channel 7 logo and a notepad as Rich gave her the countdown.

"You're on in five, four, three, two one..go." Kelley put on her newscaster smile and looked at the camera.

"Good afternoon. I'm Kelley Foster for Channel 7 news here at City Hall. The crowd you see behind me is not for some visiting rock star in town for a concert, but for Gaylen Torres, the self-proclaimed head of the community activist group, R.O.C., which stands for RECLAIM OUR COMMUNITIES. ROC has been gaining major support from many citizens in this city because of its strong anti-crime stance. While critics have denounced the group as nothing more than organized vigilantes, others have lauded them for energizing and empowering citizens in some of this city's worst areas."

Kelley fought to stand in the face of the cold wind. She used her left hand to warm her ear and hold in her earpiece. On cue, Jonas Longwell moved closer to Kelley and the camera.

"In fact," she continued, "I'm here with Mr. Jonas Longwell, one of the attendees of the rally. Sir, what brings you down here today?"

"Well, Kelley", replied Jonas, "I'm the block captain in my neighborhood, and we're having all kinds of problems with these drugs and killings. Kids, babies, old people, they don't care. They shoot each other all over that poison, and innocent people get hurt and killed. We need help badly, and we like what Mr. Torres and his people stand for."

"Does it bother you that some have called them vigilantes?" Kelley aked.

"Look ma'am, I bet you sure don't live in no neighborhood like mine," he answered calmly. "But if you did, you wouldn't care what other people called Torres and his group. If they can help us get rid of the crime and murder on our streets, I don't care what people say."

"Thank you, sir," Kelley said, wrapping up the interview. She turned back to the camera.

"This is Kelley Foster for Channel 7 News at City Hall."

It took about twenty minutes to completely pack

up the news van for the return trip to the station. Rich stood next to the truck finishing a cigarette, while Kelley sat inside sipping hot tea with lemon.

Once the rally ended, Torres and two of his associates made their way toward the news van. It appeared they would have to pass the van to get to their SUV, parked in front of the huge church next to City Hall.

Kelley quickly exited the van, hoping to make small talk with the mercurial Torres.

"Mr. Torres, I'm Kelley Foster of…"

"Channel 7, Philly Investigative News," Torres said calmly. He reached out a massive gloved hand toward her. "I know who you are."

She shook his hand. Her small hands seemed infantile compared to his.

It was then that she realized just how big Torres was. The other two men with him appeared to be cast from the same huge mold.

"Is this off the record?" Torres joked.

"Of course," Kelley responded playfully. "For now."

"Well, then I guess I better watch what I say." The other two men stood at his side. Neither cracked a smile.

"Mr. Torres, exactly what does your group do?"

"ROC is a community-based initiative that works with communities," Gaylen said. "We aim to help the people empower themselves in order to regain control of their neighborhoods."

"How?"

"We assist the community in planning rallies, drug marches, civil protest marches, whatever methods we can use to mobilize the neighborhood against the negative elements in their community."

"I understand that you also teach self-defense classes, and some people have even accused your organization of holding weapons training classes

Kelley paused for effect.

"Is this true Mr. Torres?" she asked.

Gaylen nodded.

"It is true. We offer self-defense classes for people in the community who want it. As for the weapons training, the Second Amendment gives us the right to legally arm ourselves."

"Isn't ROC afraid of some kind of retribution from the thugs that live in these neighborhoods?" Kelley asked.

"Not at all," Torres said. "We feel that when citizens are well-trained and well-equipped to resist the negative forces in their neighborhoods, those elements have no choice but to leave."

Torres took his time with the remainder of his answer.

"We also feel that when you, uh…*deal* with a problem the right way, it's taken care of. Understand what I'm saying?" Torres' tone indicated he didn't expect a response.

Kelley regretted she couldn't get their conversation on tape. Torres graciously thanked her, then slid his business card into her palm.

Kelley looked at it. It was a smaller version of the banner hanging from the stage.

"Why did your group choose the lion for its logo, Mr. Torres?"

"We chose the lion because they hunt together, they fight together, and they don't let anyone encroach on their territory," Torres responded.

Then, he paused and leaned close to Kelley.

"And, they will defend that territory to the death," he said. "Lions know how to handle their business."

"Can we get a story on you Mr. Torres", Kelley asked.

He smiled.

"Please call my Secretary," he responded. "She can set that up".

With a quick nod, Gaylen and his two silent companions turned and strode toward the street.

Rich and Kelley were left to ponder his words.

Kelley slid back into the van and fastened the top button of her heavy coat. She shuddered, but it wasn't totally due to the frigid air. Rich fastened his seat belt, adjusted the rear view mirror and then put the van in gear.

"What do you think?" he asked. "Is Torres legit?"

"After actually meeting him, I'm not sure," Kelly answered. "I think I'm still trying to decide whether he's part of the solution, or part of the problem."

CHAPTER FIVE

January 11th, 8:00 pm.

Zane had completed his legal reading for the evening, which consisted of some of the new search and seizure case law. He logged off the legal research website, satisfied with his work.

He then entered a password into another website which required Zane to enter several different security portals.

Finally, he typed the name "Raheem Motley" in the search screen. Instantly, columns of text appeared. In addition to various street addresses, the prompt spewed forth various nicknames and aliases such as "Rachman" and "Rock Money."

Delving further into the intel, Zane accessed a portal that showed photos of several homes on a variety of local streets. These, Zane reasoned, were some of Rachman's last known addresses. Since his murder case was thrown out recently, Rachman was reportedly back in the drug game.

Contacting him, however, was another story.

"This demon has been quite busy," he said, scrolling down the screens.

"However, he always knows how to make money. That's good." Zane finished reading the info, then logged off the website

"Greed kills," he said, grinning.

CHAPTER SIX

JANUARY 13TH, 10:45 PM

The man recognized the awkward gait and odd manner of the addict fumbling around on the corner. The addict stopped for a moment to use the street light pole to steady himself.

Sitting alone in the driver's seat of a battered car, the man had the tinted windows rolled up to avoid the cold and detection. He would wait until the addict got to the car before rolling them down. He wanted to make sure the addict was his contact.

It was late evening, and he'd made sure to park on the most desolate street in one of the city's worst neighborhoods. The cold, however, had driven most unsavory people indoors. The network website had given him enough intel on his target to make him feel secure that the mission would succeed.

He could always trust the network. It had never let him down.

As the addict approached, the driver saw his

shifty glazed eyes and shaking hands. The man was clearly losing the fight with his demons.

"Yo, you him?," the addict asked as he knocked on the window with a grimy hand.

"You see anyone else stupid enough to be out here this time of night?" the driver said through the small crack in the window as he rolled it down. "Tell me what I needs to know."

"Uh, uh. Give *me* what I need first," the addict commanded.

The driver exhaled slowly. While he hated bargaining with the addict, he felt he didn't lose any leverage if he played along. He knew he'd ultimately get what he wanted from the addict.

He fished into his pocket for the small plastic baggies with the glassine insert containing the brown powder. He let down his window just enough and offered them to the addict.

When the addict reached for them, the man quickly pulled them back.

"You think I'm stupid? I give you this stuff, and you'll be outta here," the man said. "And then I gotta kill you, which means I wouldn't get my information." He reached for the gearshift as if to put the car in gear.

It was the addict's turn to think. Quickly processing the dilemma as fast as his drug-addled mind could handle, the addict realized that he had to give up something first to get something. More importantly, he was afraid of the dark-skinned man with the sinister eyes threatening him.

"Okay, okay, Rachman be at 1291 Ross Street most times, but he also hangs out in the Northeast on Bennett Street," the addict confessed. "1900 block. That's his girl's house. They also call him "Rock Money," and he been out there a lot braggin' about how he beat that double murder case."

"How you know this?"

"My cousin lives on that block, and he sees him all the time," the addict replied.

"How can I get in contact with Rachman?" the driver asked.

"His cell is 267-555-2200. Tell him you know Mel. But, you better call him soon at that number, because he changes it all the time."

"That's it?" the man asked.

"That's all I know, man. That's all I know," the addict pleaded.

"Wait there, and be quiet," the driver commanded as he rolled up the window.

The driver quickly dialed and waited for a response. The male on the other end answered claiming he was Rachman. The driver told him Mel had sent him. After their brief drug-related conversation in which the driver asked to buy a large quantity of heroin, he ended the call and promised to meet the next night to complete the deal. Rachman agreed to the location of the meeting, then hung up.

The man rolled the window down.

"You gon' take care of me now, brotha?" the addict pleaded.

"Thanks for the info." The driver handed the small glassine packets to the addict, who greedily snatched them out of his hand.

"I hope this is that killer smack you promised me."

"Oh, it's definitely a killer, my man. Trust me."

The man put the car into drive and eased out of the parking space into the street.

He knew the addict would be dead before the car hit the top of the block.

CHAPTER SEVEN

JANUARY 15TH, 10:00 AM

After Manigault tosssed Rachman's double-murder case, Beck met with his superiors to determine their next move.

"Talk to the assigned detectives again," Carlo Ricci said. "See if there's any way to rearrest Rachman."

Ricci never raised his voice. But, he spoke fast. Like he was perpetually in a hurry. The only way you could tell he was upset was when he spoke slowly.

He spoke slowly to Beck.

"What did you expect, Carlo? We knew it was risky without Doretha," Beck said. "We were just taking a chance that Manigault would cut us some slack." He knew Carlo's response even before he spoke.

"I don't want to hear it", Carlo said, dismissing Beck's statement with a wave of his hand. He adjusted his rimless glasses. "Don't give me that. I don't care about what Manigault wants, Beck. Your job is to make *him* do what the Commonwealth wants."

The chief stood up from behind his desk and walked over to Beck. He handed him back the Rachman file.

"Keep on it," Carlo said. "Tell the assigned detectives to interview more witnesses, knock on some more doors. You have the skills to do well up here in Homicide, Beck. Use them. Get me Rachman back."

Carlo turned and walked toward the main door of the conference room.

"If we don't do something, the media and the public will look for someone else to blame," he continued. "The quicker we can get this monster off the streets, the better."

As Beck took the file and left the office, he felt like he was sitting in a ship that had run aground.

Beck didn't have much of an appetite, but managed to finish off the leftover meatloaf he brought for lunch. He took out his cell phone and speed-dialed a familiar number.

"Hey," answered a soft feminine voice. It was more statement than question.

"You busy?" Beck asked. He figured Serene was at lunch.

"Not too busy for you. How's your day going?"

Beck exhaled.

"You know this Rachman case is getting to me. Carlo wants me to see if we can rearrest him. I'm almost beginning to think this dude is invincible."

Serene let Beck stew before answering. They had been together for the past six years, so she knew what he was thinking.

"Honey, you know that's not the case. And you know that you'll ultimately bring this guy to justice. Just do what you can do. Let God do what He does."

Just let God do what He does.

Serene always seemed to solve his big problems with few words.

CHAPTER EIGHT

JANUARY 17th, 9:45 P.M.

It took nearly four hours for Rachman to get his hair braided. A good braid job could cost up to $500, but Rachman could easily afford one because of his thriving drug and prostitution business. He was hungry after sitting in the barbershop for so long. He wanted some Chinese food.

He dialed a number.

"Yeah, let me get some General Tso's chicken and two egg rolls," he said when a voice answered. "And, don't forget to give me some of those crispy noodles."

He gave the person his name and said he would pick up the food in about an hour.

His ultimate plan was to get some food and wait until his meeting with someone wanting to buy a large amount of heroin. This was not one of his regular customers, as he did not recognize the voice during their conversation last night.

No matter.

He was about to make another happy customer. Business had been booming for him ever since he wrested control of the corner from a rival drug dealer a few months ago. The double murder case he had recently beaten only caused a minor slowdown in business. His reputation on the street, however, had grown to mythic proportions as a result.

Rachman sold some of South Philly's best heroin, and he usually sold heavy weight. This evening's buyer had been very clear: he wanted to meet at 10 p.m. at 9th and Tasker Streets, and he wanted to buy two bundles of heroin.

That was heavyweight product.

Rachman usually told them where and when; that way he stayed in control. However, he made an exception this time due to the large quantity the buyer wanted.

"I know one thing, it's cold out there, so this nigga better be ready to hand me my money," Rachman said to one of his boys. "I ain't trying to freeze just so some fool can get high."

His phone buzzed. Rachman looked at the screen and saw he had a text: "will be waiting for you this evening after the deal."

It was Mike, his sidekick and loyal second-in-command.

Rachman turned suspicious.

What if this was a set up? The narcotics cops set up stings all the time where they use a confidential informant to contact a dealer. Once the informant makes the buy, the cops rush in and arrest the dealer. And, they get him holding the marked money.

"Cool. Will hit you up when I get to deal spot," Rachman responded with a text.

Rachman wasn't one to dwell on all the negatives, so he dismissed these thoughts when he calculated the money he'd make off the sale.

Hell, crime does pay, Rachman thought as he walked to meet the buyer. Actually it was the suburbanites who kept him in business because they had the money. He would've starved if he had to depend solely on the neighborhood junkies. Anyone who used drugs knew Philly had the purest heroin on the east coast. Rachman got his supply from his main connection overseas. Once he cut it and put it on the street, his superior product flowed like the Nile.

At 9:45 p.m., Rachman headed west toward the vacant lot to meet the customer. The meeting place was not so much a vacant lot, but the land upon where a row of homes once stood. Time, urban blight and a thriving drug trade had taken over the neighborhood and turned this once family-friendly block into a war zone.

In fact, Rachman was one of the main causes of the warfare, as he had personally driven rival dealers out of business – as well as out of existence – in this very neighborhood.

To Rachman violence was simply an occupational

hazard. He did what he had to do to survive and keep his business going. It was that simple.

Even killing his drug rival's parents didn't faze him. He didn't particularly like doing it, but he'd barely blinked when he'd pulled the trigger. Ordering Doretha Vann killed because she was the main eyewitness in that case had likewise caused him little anxiety. It was the price he was willing to pay for the life he had chosen to live.

"I told that fool I was taking his business," he'd bragged to his crew after the murders. Rachman killed his rival's parents in their own home to send a message to his competition. "Now he better recognize who running things."

Rachman reached the vacant lot at 9:55 p.m. He got there early to check it out, in case it was a setup. Rachman was a killer, but not a fool. He'd sent a couple of his soldiers to the area about a half an hour earlier to make some sales. If the cops arrested the buyers soon after, Rachman would know the area was under surveillance.

Everything seemed to be legitimate.

"Want me to make the sale?" Baby Mike asked Rachman earlier that evening. Mike was Rachman's most loyal soldier and right-hand man.

"Naw, I got it," Rachman said. "Besides, I need you to make a pick up from my man up near Allegheny, and then check on them stash houses down in West Philly. I'll get up with you in a few days. I'm gonna chill with my cousin in Delaware for a bit. You know, lie low. Don't worry, I know how to handle my business," Rachman said, patting the bulge in his waistband for effect.

"No problem," said Mike. "I'll be in the car down the block watching the street when you make the deal just to make sure everything is cool. Then I'll bounce afterwards. Text me when you get back."

Walking alone to meet the buyer, Rachman saw nothing unusual. With Baby Mike nearby, he felt comfortable letting his guard down a bit. This was still his neighborhood. Besides, the caller seemed legitimate. The fact that he had called him yesterday on his new cell number reassured him even more.

Normally, Rachman would have one of his corner boys make the sale. But, tonight, he was feeling good after having beat the double murder. He felt invincible. He wanted to handle this deal personally.

"Man, it's cold out here!" he said, stomping his feet to stay warm. His breath left his mouth as frosty bursts, and he still felt the artic chill through his expensive Timberland boots and heavy designer jacket. He thought about driving to the location, but figured if this was a setup, he could escape on foot faster than in a car. He would lose them in the vacant lot, which was filled with debris, trash, and overgrown weeds.

In addition, there were a number of abandoned homes in the rear of the lot. This ghetto maze would confuse the cops, but Rachman knew these buildings inside and out.

Plan B was his loaded .380.

Rachman was so preoccupied with his escape plan that he didn't even see the lean older man approach him. He was also completely unaware of the dented car with tinted windows parked nearby.

"Are you Rachman?" the man asked softly.

Startled, Rachman spun around, his hand on the .380. The brown-skinned man was dressed in a dingy medium-weight jacket, black jeans, boots, and leather gloves. He wore a weather-beaten ski cap pulled far down on his head. At 5-foot 10, the man was a good three inches taller than Rachman.

"Yeah old head, I'm Rachman," he answered, trying to control the nervousness in his voice. Rachman gave the man a quick glance up and down, sizing him up.

"What you want?"

The man's attire didn't alarm him. It was his calm attitude, however, that made the young kingpin shudder; a shudder that had nothing to do with the bitter cold. More compact than thin, the man moved with a sinister calm and confidence. He was buying drugs in one of the worst areas in Philly - from one of the City's Most Wanted criminals - but he could just as easily have been buying groceries at the local supermarket.

Rachman noticed that the man kept his hands in his pockets. *What's with this guy?* he thought. *He didn't even make a sound when he rolled up on me.* Rachman kept his hand close to the gun under his coat.

"I called you yesterday about two bundles of heroin," the man said.

"Well, where's my money?" Rachman asked, his cockiness coming back. "I ain't giving no product away."

"Oh, I have the money, but I'm not making deals here on the sidewalk," the man said. "Let's do this thing over there." He motioned Rachman toward a run-down building in the middle of the lot.

There he was again, thought Rachman: *making the rules*. Still, the lure of big money made him follow the man inside. The darkened building was dimly lit by the light coming in from the street.

Besides, this was still Rachman's turf.

Rachman led the way a few steps into the lot, with the man following close behind.

Rachman turned to face the man.

"Alright man, come out your pockets with the money," Rachman spat.

The man extended his gloved hand toward Rachman, holding what looked like several folded $50.00 bills. Rachman reached out to take the money.

Suddenly, in one swift motion, the man grabbed his hand and pulled Rachman toward him, turning him around so his back was against the man.

"You really thought you could run from justice, boy? You thought you were untouchable, didn't you?"

the man whispered into Rachman's ear. "Everybody knows you killed those old people. And, then you had the eyewitness killed to make sure you'd get off."

"What the…?" Rachman gasped. The man spoke with a professional tone.

"And don't worry," the man continued. "We will visit that demon Judge Manigault who let you back out on the streets. He will also answer to the people."

The man coiled his arms around Rachman's neck, putting him in a chokehold. He applied deadly pressure to Rachman's head and neck. All thought of his gun was lost as Rachman struggled to get air into his lungs.

"Without that witness," the man continued, "the D.A.'s office had no case."

Rachman's head spun as he struggled to get free. The man's grip was like a vise. One arm was wrapped around his neck, while the other was around the top of his head. Rachman's brain screamed at him to breathe.

His body, however, paid no attention.

As Rachman started to lose consciousness, the man continued, "See, justice never sleeps. It found you, fool. Now, the people demand you answer for your crimes."

The man's arms felt like two strands of twisted steel. As he squeezed harder, Rachman struggled violently, his legs jerking and flailing. The pressure around his neck was unbearable. Rachman clawed desperately at the arms twisting his head from the rest of his body. He started to pass out as his windpipe was slowly being crushed.

Despite Rachman's incessant struggling, the man continued to calmly apply pressure, as if he were simply holding two blocks together waiting for the glue to dry.

Soon, the young thug's neck broke with a muted snap. Rachman went limp as he died. His bowels emptying for the last time, staining his expensive jeans.

When the man finally released Rachman's body, it hit the ground with a dull thud, crunching the snow underneath.

The man looked around to make sure no one was on the street, then bent down and placed something in Rachman's jacket pocket. He then pulled a cell phone from his jacket pocket, sent a quick text message, then disappeared into the rear of the lot.

As the man left, an observer saw the action from inside a darkened second floor window of one of the homes bordering the lot. While he could not see faces, he saw enough to know that Rachman was no more.

Smiling, the elderly man checked his watch and slipped away from the back window. He wore a small purple bracelet on the same wrist. Everything had gone according to plan. The three working surveillance cameras on the block had been disabled, so no video evidence of the man or Rachman's murder existed.

He dialed a number from a worn cordless wall phone.

"Good riddance to bad rubbish," he chuckled to himself.

Snow began to fall and before long it quickly covered the lot. Soon Rachman's body was indistinguishable from the other snow-covered debris.

10:00 P.M.

Baby Mike sat in the heated driver's seat of his Range Rover, texting. He checked his watch as the powerful engine hummed. In five minutes he would text Rachman, then pick him up down the street. He figured the deal would be done by then.

Mike also had the vehicle's customized surround-sound system turned up so loud he never heard the man walk up to his car and tap lightly on the window.

Stunned, Mike nearly dropped his cell phone in mid-text. He gripped the rubber handle of the gun stuck in the console next to him. He hit the CD player's "Off" button.

"What the hell you want, old head?" Baby Mike growled, easing the window down. "I almost shot yo ass rollin' up on me like that."

From his car, Mike sized up the man with a quick glance. Mike figured him to be about 5-foot-6, dark-skinned, clean-shaven, mid to late 50's. He was dressed in a dingy lightweight jacket, black gloves, ski cap and worn jeans. His boots were like combat boots, but with a thinner sole, similar to the kind hikers wear.

He definitely wasn't a regular.

The short man appeared to puff on a cigarette he held in his left hand, although Mike couldn't tell if it was lit.

"Gimme two," the old man calmly said.

Mike had sold drugs to thousands of people, so he could easily spot a true junkie from a cop. While he didn't get a cop "vibe" from this guy, Mike wasn't convinced he was a heroin addict, either. The guy dressed like a neighborhood bum, but his eyes told another story. They looked right through Mike.

His eyes displayed the hardness of a true killer.

"Yo, old head, you better beat it before you catch a hot one," Mike warned him, trying to mask his unease. "I ain't got no time for you today." Mike turned to put the car in gear. Dismissing the man, he turned up the stereo again.

In the time it took Mike to hit the volume button, the man brought the cigarette to his lips for another puff.

However, the "cigarette" was actually a mini-blowdart with a small poison-laced tip. Mike also didn't notice the small hiss as the man blew into the blowdart aimed directly at the left side of Mike's meaty neck.

Instantly the dart found its mark.

"What the fu…..?" Mike exclaimed, grabbing at his neck with his left hand. He thought a bee had stung him.

Unfortunately for him, his muscles began to lock as the curae-tipped needle dart quickly released its powerful toxin into his bloodstream. The poison, from an exotic fish found in Central America, instantly attacked Mike's central nervous system, shutting it down. The toxin was so potent that a drop the size of a pinhead could take down a rhino.

Mike was having a massive stroke. While he could see and hear, his speech was gone. He began to sweat profusely. The paralysis spread to his limbs first, then moved toward his heart and lungs. They would shut down in less than a minute.

The man calmly stepped forward and looked up into the driver's side window. "See, you and your boy Rachman thought y'all could act a fool, selling them drugs and terrorizing innocent folks," he said in a low voice while glaring at Mike.

He could see Mike's breathing becoming labored.

"I can't imagine how them old people felt when Rachman shot them while they slept," the man said. "Shot 'em like they was dogs."

The man leaned even closer to Mike. He wanted to feel his last breath.

"You don't realize that out here in the streets, the Scarlet Chord rules. We hunt the predators and the serpents - just like you and Rachman - who do evil. Now, justice done found both of you fools. You and Rachman's time is up. Now, y'all goin' straight to hell."

The man then quckly pulled the small dart from Mike's neck, wiped it off with a tissue and placed it in a small metal case. He reached insde the car and, with a gloved hand, turned the car off. He placed a small plastic baggie on the dashboard, then held a finger to Mike's carotid artery to make sure he was really dead. The fat thug was slumped forward in the seat.

The man retrieved a cell phone from his jacket pocket and quickly read the text. Satisfied, the man walked briskly to his car nearby, and hummed an old jazz tune.

8:00 am the next day...

Homicide detectives swarmed over the large Black man slumped over the steering wheel inside the parked expensive SUV. Medical examiners had a difficult time getting him out of the vehicle as rigor mortus made him stiff and rigid.

A passerby two hours earlier saw him inside

the vehicle and was not sure if he was asleep or dead. When the man did not move after the person repeatedly knocked on the window, police were called in.

"ID says this dude is named Mike something," said the assigned detective on the case. He directed his comments to his colleague. "I can't read the last name or the address. The card looks worn and some of the writing is faded."

"I can't see any entry or exit wounds," said a female detective as she probed the large man in the drver's seat. She noticed the man's wallet appeared intact. She also noted there was no blood or visible wounds on the body.

The remaining law enforcement personnel attended to other aspects of the investigation. In addition, the police tow truck was already on the scene ready to take the deceased's truck to the police impound lot.

The detective, wearing latex gloves, retrieved various items from off the deceased and from inside the truck. Among them were a loaded 45-caliber weapon, car keys attached to a black alarm keyfob and several hundred dollars in United States currency. He placed each of these items inside of a separate stamped plastic baggie.

The remaining items he collected, including a small gold-bordered card inscribed with a Bible verse, he put into one large plastic evidence bag.

CHAPTER NINE

January 20th, 11:00 A.M.

The morning went smoothly for Zane. As usual, most of the cases on his list were continued. This was usually because the defense attorney was unavailable, the defendant was not brought down from state custody, or the Assistant D.A. was not ready to proceed because an important witness failed to appear.

It wasn't until 1:00 in the afternoon that Zane recessed Court for a lunch break.

"Breaking for lunch?" It was Judge Tom Coley, one of the city's oldest and most-respected judges. An older Irish man, his courtroom was next door to Zane's.

He popped his head in from the hallway behind the bench.

"Without a doubt," Zane answered. "If I hadn't, we might never have taken a break today."

"What are your lunch plans?" Judge Coley asked.

"It's not as cold today as it has been," Zane

replied, "so I'll probably just run out and grab a salad from the deli on Market Street. What about you?"

"Probably walk over to the Marketplace and get a bowl of chowder."

Zane smiled at the older judge as he put on his coat. He wondered what it was like to reach twenty-five years on the bench. Considering his troubles with Judge Friedmann, Zane wondered if he'd even make it through this year in his current assignment.

It was no secret that he and Judge Friedmann didn't get along. The problem was Jack Friedmann, the administrative judge of Philadelphia's Common Pleas Court. He was in charge of judicial assignments. As such, he could put his friends in line to hear the high-profile cases. Likewise, his enemies could find themselves stuck in Traffic Court, or other undesirable courtroom assignments.

Zane could not hide his dislike for the man who lorded his power over his judicial colleagues. To make matters worse, Friedmann's main priority was disposing cases, rather than doing justice. He openly advocated trial judges encourage lawyers to work out plea-bargains, even in the most heinous cases.

As such, a number of dangerous people were temporarily taken off the street. Zane felt they should be waiting for their turn in the state's electric chair.

Zane's get-tough, no-nonsense style was a direct challenge to Friedmann's lazy attitude and policy. Zane had no intention of encouraging violent criminals to take a plea. He thought the people needed to hear those cases. When the people actually managed to convict an especially dangerous thug, Zane loved handing down harsh sentences. His were some of the harshest around.

It was one way he felt that he helped keep Philly's streets safe.

Some believed that Zane's many wealthy Republican friends in Harrisburg kept Judge Friedmann at bay, despite the overwhelming local Democratic influence.

Because of his continued open defiance of Judge Friedmann, though, Zane knew it was only a matter of time before things between them would come to a head.

2:45 P.M.

The detective had barely finished his clam chowder when the phone on his desk rang. He knew that today's lunch would undoubtedly become tonight's dinner. Finishing a cracker, he picked up the phone.

"Homicide. Detective Siscowicz."

"Detective Siscowicz, this is Seargent Imperazzo at the 17th District," the male on the other end replied. "I got a body down here in a vacant lot off 9th and Tasker. Young black male. You know, the usual."

"Any positive ID?"

"Not yet," Sgt. Imperazzo said. "The body was frozen, so I can't get a good visual. We're still working on trying to find a wallet, driver's license, anything."

"Gunshot victim?" Sisco asked.

"Nah. At least I don't think so. Mobile Crimes is on the way, but from what I was able to tell, I don't think a firearm was used. Can't see any exit or entry wounds."

"Any witnesses?"

"None so far," said the Sergeant, "but you know how it is down here. No snitching. They don't talk to the cops."

"Thanks, Seargent. Hold the scene until we get there. We're on our way."

Siscowicz reached for his coat and put the lid back on his soup container,

"That's what you get for being up next on the wheel," said Nathan Jarrett, another veteran Homicide Detective in the office.

The "wheel" was the duty schedule the Homicide unit used to assign cases to Detectives. Jarrett, who was part of Three Squad, was completing the latest crossword puzzle while waiting to finish an arrest warrant.

"This seems to be a standard homicide job," Sisco said jokingly. "I should be back before

off 9th and Tasker.

dinner, Nate. I may even be back before you finish that crossword puzzle."

Det. Jarrett chuckled and leaned back in his chair.

"That's why they pay you the big bucks Sisco," Jarrett said.

Siscowicz headed for the door in search of his partner, Isaiah Lucas. Both worked in Five Squad, one of the unit's elite squads. Once he picked up Luke, they would be on their way to see what seemed like their one hundredth dead body this month.

Detective Gary Siscowicz, or "Sisco" as everyone called him, had just begun his twenty-fifth year as a Philadelphia Police Officer. At roughly six feet tall, one hundred ninety-five pounds, he bore little resemblance to the scrawny college second basemen he was over 30 years earlier. Despite his age, Sisco prided himself on still having a full head of dark hair and a 38-inch waistline. As soon he was promoted to Homicide Detective from Narcotics, he got rid of his small earring, as well as his trademark casual garb: jeans, loafers and some type of sweater. Suits and ties were mandatory for Homicide Detectives, and his full beard was gone.

Fifteen years ago, he'd been promoted to the Southwest Detectives Division. Ten years ago, he joined the Homicide Division. As far as he was concerned, that was when his career began.

As a kid growing up in the city's Fishtown section, Sisco remembered seeing the cops patrol his neighborhood in their shiny red and white police cars. The police shield emblazoned on the doors gave him chills every time he saw it. The fact that his father, grandfather and uncle served on the force certainly made his career choice easier.

"It's a good, honest living," his dad said when Sisco told the old man what he wanted to do with his life. "You can support your family, and help the community. That's what a man is supposed to do."

As in typical Polish households, Gary's father, John Wesley Siscowicz, was the head of the home. The ultimate alpha male, his father worked hard and played the same way. It was nothing to see his dad stagger through the front door, uniform shirt open, after a night out with the guys. Gary's mom dutifully left his father's dinner on a plate in the oven before she went to bed.

The guys with whom his dad mingled usually included some local politicians. Sometimes it was the police commissioner, himself a Polish/Irish mixture. John Siscowicz prided himself on being a cop's cop, when walking a beat was respected. Everyone knew his name, and his gun almost grew rusty from inactivity.

Times were different back then.

While the Siscowicz household would probably never be mistaken for the Cleaver's, love was not a scarce commodity. Food was put on the table, and you ate. You shut your mouth until the meal was done, and you washed behind your ears before you went to bed. You did wrong, you got a smack on the butt. You did right, you got a hug and pat on the back.

Serving your country was also expected.

So, when Sisco enlisted in the Marine Corps, his family knew the routine. They sent him care packages, wrote him letters, and made sure Father Wisnewski said a special Hail Mary for his safety at Sunday Mass.

The way the streets of Philadelphia were nowadays, sometimes the battlefields overseas seemed much safer.

"We got a live job," Sisco shouted to his partner. "Better tell the old lady to put the kids to bed early. It's gonna be a long day."

"On my way!" Isaiah yelled back.

At 52, Isaiah Lucas was a few years younger than Sisco, but the similarities ended there. Luke, as he was called – grew up in the heart of North Philadelphia's "badlands".

A chubby Black kid with asthma and crooked teeth, Luke took up boxing to protect himself and his sister at school. He became an adult almost overnight when their dad was killed during a holdup.

Luke was in middle school.

His time in the ring gradually built his muscles and his speed. Luke used those assets in football, hoisting himself out of Philly's notorious gang wars of the early seventies. In his senior year in high school, Luke made First-team All-Public League as a running back.

While football may have given him a pass from gang warring, it didn't totally shield him from the 'hood's other enterprises. When he found that part-time jobs were not helping him put food on his mother's table, or clothes on his and his sister's backs, Luke immersed himself in the thriving street pharmaceutical business in his neighborhood.

At first, Luke used his ill-gotten gains for useful things, like helping with the household, school supplies for his sister, and braces for his teeth. After enough brushes with the law, however, he figured it was time to stop playing with fire.

He quit seling drugs and earned his high school diploma.

A subsequent stint in the U.S. Army taught him discipline and took him around the world. He returned home, and through his uncle, got a factory job in West Philadelphia. He also attended a local junior college at night. After taking the Police Department entrance exam on a dare, Luke got one of the highest scores that year.

He was in the Police Academy six weeks later.

"I wasn't always a cop," was Luke's standard speech to young kids he met on the streets. "I could've gone either way. But, I figured, why should I spend my life looking over my shoulder, when I can make a positive difference."

Sometimes the speech helped. Some times, however, the kids he met needed more than just a little encouragement. Most, however, needed lawyers.

3:15 P.M.

After leaving the office, the detectives were met by the early afternoon sun. However, the arctic wind smothered any warmth the sun may have provided. Strong winds buffeted their unmarked squad car as they drove toward the crime scene.

"You and Helen going anywhere for vacation this year?" Luke asked as he unwrapped the scarf from his neck once inside the car.

"I don't know," Sisco answered as he drove. His eyes scanned the road ahead. "Her aunt has some timeshare in Vegas, and this is our year to get it. But, I don't know if I'm feeling real Vegas-y this year. You know what I mean?"

"No. Let me get a timeshare in Vegas, or anywhere there's a beach, a few drinks and some beautiful women in bikinis, and I'm there, bruh," Luke laughed.

Sisco laughed.

The ride into South Philly from Homicide headquarters was uneventful. As they arrived, they could see the marked police vehicles gathered together, dome lights twirling. A number of uniformed officers had already secured the location.

The huge mobile crime scene unit van was parked directly in front.

"Gentlemen," Sisco greeted the two uniformed officers as he and Luke got out of their vehicle.

"Good to see you guys," Sgt. Imperazzo returned the greeting, removing a hand from his bulky police jacket. He shook Sisco's hand, then Luke's. A simple head nod was Luke's greeting to the rest of the officers.

A short stocky officer took the detectives' names and entered them onto the crime scene log book, noting the exact date and time. After some small talk with the log book cop, the two detectives slipped on latex gloves and plastic booties over their shoes. They ducked under the yellow crime scene tape, and headed for an area toward an old light post in the lot.

Snow covered the numerous mounds of debris and junk strewn about. Luke and Sisco saw a number of people standing over a white sheet as they approached.

"I'll bet you guys were down at headquarters just waiting for another live job, right?" joked Officer Brian Mertz. "This one'll definitely get you guys in the papers tomorrow."

"I tell you, we need more press like we need a root canal," Luke joked as he shook the cop's hand.

"Well, you won't be able to avoid the press on this one, detectives. The stiff under the sheet is Raheem Motley. We finally located a state ID card stuffed inside some papers in one of his frozen pockets."

Luke and Sisco shot each other a look.

"You mean 'Rachman' Motley? The kid who just beat that double murder charge?" Luke asked incredulously. "Shot those old people in the head, right? We think he also killed the main witness in that case."

"Shoot, he's beaten at least three murder cases in the past two years alone," Sisco added.

"Yeah, well, that's him," the other officer said nodding toward the sheet. "We confirmed the state ID card inside the wallet. The kid's name and photo are on it." The officer handed the detective a small plastic bag with an expensive wallet inside. "I'm sure Mr. Motley has looked better."

Detective Siscowicz knelt down and peered under the sheet. He was careful not to get in the way of the Crime Scene photographer busily snapping photos of the body and the area. Another technician moved about the area with a video camera. The body was face up, but the head was cocked at a strange angle. The dark skin had an ashen blue hue, and the bulging inanimate eyes stared back.

It was the face, frozen in horror, however, that made the veteran detective uneasy.

"Looks like the kid died pretty violently," Siscowicz murmured. "His wallet looks intact. There's a wad of cash in there, and two bundles of heroin, so I think we can rule out Robbery as a motive."

Shaking his head, the detective pulled out a small pad and began taking notes.

"Sisco, I'm going to take a look around," Luke said. "I'll be back in a bit."

Sisco nodded without looking up from the body.

Despite their differing backgrounds, the two detectives were one of the best detective teams in Homicide. During their time as partners, they had solved some of the city's toughest murders. While they followed the normal police procedures (usually), their tactics were anything but conventional.

Both men had also grown close and were now good friends. After meeting the other's family at a detective division barbecue years earlier, each considered the other a brother. In fact, it was Sisco who persuaded Luke to seek counseling after his divorce. Over time, they had developed the kind of respect for each other that only comes from a common bond, which happened to be the death they regularly saw as cops.

Both were excellent investigators, but more importantly, they knew the streets. They were experts in information gathering and extracting.

Sisco stood up to survey the area after taking copious notes. He saw that a small crowd had gathered near the yellow tape at the entrance of the lot.

"Who found the body?" he asked an officer standing nearby.

"Anonymous radio call," another officer answered after flipping through his notes. "Came into the district at about ten this morning. Mobile Crimes figures Rachman was killed a few days ago, but was covered by all the snow we've had. The unusual warm spell we just had must have thawed him out enough to be ID'd."

"That's probably why he's so well-preserved", Sisco said. "All the cold and ice kept him nice and fresh. Like a damn popsicle."

"Oh, yeah, we also found this in his jacket pocket." Sergeant Imperazzo said, pulling out a plastic baggie. It contained a small white card with a gold border. He handed it to the detective.

"Rachman's business card?" Sisco said inquisitively. "He had nerve. I'll give him that."

The Sergeant shook his head.

"Seems Rachman was a religious man. The card has a passage from the Bible written on it."

Sisco eyed the card through the plastic. *God, the righteous one, knows what goes on in the homes of the wicked, and he will bring the wicked down to ruin. Proverbs 20:12.*"

"Maybe he carried this for inspiration. Heck, maybe he was trying to turn his life around," Sisco said, shrugging.

"Too late, now", the sergeant said. "It's funny,

though. Rachman died in a frozen lot. But, he's probably gonna spend eternity in flames."

Sisco looked up from the card to see two men in heavy jackets wheeling a stretcher towards the body. Sisco placed the bag with the card into the large evidence envelope.

"I bet they're not coming for you, sargent," Sisco joked.

"The M.E.'s show up just when things get fun," Imperazzo said.

"Good afternoon Detective", said Artemis Frazier, one of the technicians from the Medical Examiner's Office. Sisco had seen him on many of his jobs.

"How's it going Artemis," Sisco said, moving out of the technician's way. Turning to Imperazzo, he said, "I guess the show's over. Sergeant, take a walk with me."

As they headed toward the huge mobile crime scene truck, Sisco could hear the techs unzipping the plastic body bag into which they'd put Rachman. Pretty soon, he'd be taken to the city morgue to lie on some cold metal table, where only a toe tag would identify him. A few days ago, though, he had been one of Philly's most notorious criminals.

This is how it is supposed to end for the little thug, Sisco thought. Finally, justice had been served.

Street justice.

CHAPTER TEN

JANUARY 22nd, 2:30 P.M

By early that afternoon, Zane had wrapped up his day. A couple of guilty pleas, and a minor drug case completed the remainder of his case list. The jury trial was continued to next month because the defense attorney was unavailable.

By all accounts, this had been a slow day on the bench.

"This Court will recess until the call of the crier at 9:00 am tomorrow." With Lester's announcement, the remaining people in the galley began heading for the doors at the back of the courtroom.

"Judge, you have a message from Judge Friedmann, and a message from Beck," Felice said, gathering up the day's files.

"What did Beck want?" Zane asked.

"He wanted to know if you were going to watch the game this Sunday," Felice responded, "and if he could watch it with you. He thought you might be going out of town."

"I'll call him back and let him know I'll be checking out the game."

"What happened to the weekend with Judge Matthews?" Ron asked.

"She's got a sorority fundraiser this Saturday, and she claims she can't get out of it," Zane said.

"What do you mean 'claims?' You don't think she's bein' straight with you?"

"Terra has been up front with me since we started going out a few months ago," Zane said. "However, I think that she's pulling back a bit."

"You think you crowdin' her?" Ron asked.

"Never thought about it like that, Ron. I just thought my persistence showed her how serious I was about our relationship. Maybe I'm too intense."

Ron shook his head.

"Brother, you got a tough job. Dealing with these fools out here is serious business. Judge Matthews knows how you are. I'm sure everything is fine between you two."

As Zane sat down, he remembered the second message.

"Felice, what did Judge Freidmann want?" Zane yelled to Felice who was in the outer chambers.

"He didn't say, Judge. He just told me to have you call him as soon as you got in."

"He probably just wants to run his mouth again about how the defense bar is whining about your sentences or something like that," Ron said sarcastically.

"Yeah, well," Zane mumbled, slipping off his black judicial robe. "He doesn't pay my salary. The people of Philadelphia do. And when *they* complain, I'll listen."

He hung up his robe in the closet and turned on his laptop.

"Until then, I *will* do the people's business."

3:00 pm

Zane spotted the headline and picked up a copy of the *Philadelphia Clarion*, the city's daily newspaper, from the corner rack.

He was in Reading Terminal trying to decide on a late lunch.

"NOTORIOUS DRUG THUG FOUND MURDERED."

He read on.

"*Yesterday, police found the frozen body of one of the city's most notorious criminals in a vacant lot in South Philadelphia. The man, 27 year-old Raheem Motley, was discovered by a passerby in a vacant lot on near 9th and Tasker Streets. Police believe his neck was broken. Motley, also known as Rachman, had a long and violent criminal record, including murder.*"

He quickly flipped the page to read the rest of the story.

"*In fact, nearly two weeks ago, the District Attorney's Office was forced to drop Murder and related weapons charges against him in the deaths of Sylvester and Arletta Tate last May. Both were found shot to death in their home in what police describe as a drug turf revenge killing. At this time, police have no suspects in Motley's murder."*

Satisfied that he had read the entire article, Zane folded the paper closed, placed it back on the rack. He grabbed his cell phone from his jacket pocket, and quickly texted a message. Zane then headed for the nearby deli.

CHAPTER ELEVEN

January 22nd, 4:15 pm

While today's case schedule had been light, Zane still had work to complete off the bench. In addition to working on his upcoming trial schedule, Zane had several case opinions to write and publish. Felice helped him to write them, but Zane primarily did the legal analysis. This meant reading case law. This also meant working late on some days.

"Felice, I'm going upstairs to chambers if you need me. I'll be working on some opinions."

Zane gathered up the files on his desk, grabbed his briefcase and walked out of the small robing room. A few feet away was the private elevator for judges and their staff. Once inside, he pressed a button, closing the doors.

Zane took the elevator up to the Fourteenth floor to his chambers. Since the rest of his staff was still down in the courtroom preparing paperwork for upcoming cases, he'd have the chambers to himself for a while.

Once in chambers, he sat his briefcase on the big table next to his desk, took off his robe and hung it in his closet. He then stretched out on the long couch in his inner office and closed the door.

He touched a button the small remote control and gospel music wafted softly through the CD speakers. Zane closed his eyes and reminisced….

CHAPTER TWELVE

August 15, 1967

"Alex, baby, you stay close to Grandma, you hear?"

He scrambled down off the wooden bench.

"Yes'm."

"Not yes'm, Alex," His grandmother corrected him. "It's 'Yes Ma'am.' Always remember to speak correctly. People judge you by you your speech."

"Yes ma'am."

They walked toward the clearing where a large group of African-American people had gathered. He tried to keep up with her determined stride, but the crowd hampered his progress.. He heard singular voices in the distance which blended into a soft chorus as they got closer. They were singing an old hymn.

"I want to be at the meeting," the crowd sang. "I want to be at the meeting... I want to be at the meeting ... when all the saints get home. After separating, of the right and the wrong, I want to be at the meeting around the throne."

"*Come on Alex, you have to walk a little faster baby,*" his Grandmother said. "*I don't want you to get lost when the camp meeting starts.*"

Gloria Stewart was 5 feet 2 inches of pure mocha-colored dynamite.

Part Black, part Cherokee Indian and all rebel, she was Miss Black Mississippi Delta Queen back in 1933. She wore very little makeup, but even without it, her natural broad nose, wide hips and high cheekbones made men - black and white - take notice of her well into her 50's. She wore her hair pulled back in a long ponytail. She was also fiercely determined to fight racism and Jim Crow in Mississippi. She was well known around town to blacks as a crusader, to whites as "uppity", and to all of them a religious fanatic.

Alex heard the crunch of twigs in the distance. Probably deer, he thought. He wiped the sweat off his face with his t-shirt neck. The Mississipi summer heat was brutal, even at night.

Tonight, however, there was a hint of a cool breeze which made things bearable at least.

"*Those deer are about to mate,*" Gloria said. "*I'll bet we'll see some young calves soon. That should be right about the time the weather breaks.*"

"*Maybe we can have some deer for the fall, Grandma?*" Zane asked eagerly. He loved swamp deer stew.

"*Maybe we can,*" she replied, patting him on the head. "*Maybe we can.*"

Not many folks knew how to survive in this harsh land. Gloria Stewart, however, was an expert swamp woman. She could hunt and track animals, and live off the land better than most people; some say she could even survive there better than some of the animals. Alex believed that was because of the Cherokee Native American blood in her.

As good as she was, however, she wanted her only grandson to be better.

Alex heard the singing get louder as they neared the crowd. It was one of his grandmother's favorite songs.

"I want to be at the meeting around the throne." The crowd sang.

In the distance, Zane hard the incessant sound of the cicadas, and the occasional groan of the alligators in the nearby brush. Someone had built a small fire to keep the gigantic mosquitoes at bay.

It was a typical late summer night in Reddington, Mississippi. To be exact, it was near Poplarville, a small town just outside of Reddington. Last year, he came to live with his grandmother in Reddington after his parents were killed.

While most of Pearl River County, Mississippi, was all small towns, Reddington bordered on some of the several swamps that fed the mighty Mississippi River. His grandmother's house in Reddington was down Blue Stone Road about a mile from the mouth of the swamp.

He he was well versed in marsh life.

At seven years old, he was already an expert tracker. He could tell the difference between boar and deer tracks, and could kill and skin some small animals. He also knew how to start a fire with two dry twigs, and how to listen for the subtle sounds of snake movements in the mud.

He wielded a knife better than most kids his age, and his aim with a bow and arrow ws already impressive.

"God meant for you to defend yourself," Gloria always told him. "That way you can fight for others."

Alex heard a truck rumbling in the distance, its tires crunching the gravel off Piney Road. It pulled up into the clearing, as the crowd parted to let it through.

"We got that trash who killed Charles Dix!" Amos yelled, getting down from the cab of the dented pickup truck. The crowd gathered around the truck. Alex gripped his grandmother's hand tightly lest he get lost in the increasingly agitated crowd. He heard rustling coming from inside the truck's flatbed.

Alex was very observant. He was also very inquisitive, and his grandmother insisted he take note of everything around him. Thus, he wondered why all of the adults in the crowd, including his grandmother, wore those funny purple bracelets on their wrists.

"Me and Puckett caught these two fools around the back of the pool hall in town," Amos said, *reaching down into the flatbed. "The network said these are two of the demons who snatched Charles Dix out the jail a while ago, and took him away. Well, it may have taken some time, and we may not have gotten all of them fools, but we sure as hell gonna make these two demons pay for the rest of them!"*

"Bout time!" Granger Blake said. He was one of the local black barbers "Them damn crackers falsely charged and convicted him of raping that white woman last month. She lied on him! She finally told the Sheriff Charles never touched her!"

"Are Reggie and Deacon Willis guarding the entrance to this road?" Gloria asked. "Are they armed?"

"Yes ma'am," Amos replied. "And we also got old man Baker up in the tree house down there as a third gun."

"Well done," Gloria said. "Praise God!"

Alex remembered some of the grownups around town talking about a Black man named Charles Dix whose body was found in the Pearl River a few weeks ago. His grandmother said whoever killed him had beaten and shot him before throwing his body into the river. He had been falsely accused of a crime and then put in jail before a group of whites took him from the sheriff's office.

"Both of you crackas stand up!" Amos commanded. Two figures rose slowly out of the flatbed. Both of

their hands were tied, their mouths were duct-taped. Their feet, however, were not tied.

They were young white men in their early 20's. Their clothes were dirty, their hair matted with grass and mud. Both also had multiple bruises and dried blood on their faces.

Two muscular black men grabbed both white men and threw them out of the back of the truck onto the dirt. Amos reached down and ripped off their duct tape.

"Are y'all niggers crazy!" the first white male spat. "Do you know who we are?"

"Yeah, and as soon as we get out of here, we'll be back to string all your black pickaninny asses up like guitars!" The second male said. He had an oily beard.

"Ahhrggh!" the first man screamed as someone in the crowd kicked him hard in the ribs.

"Don't worry about that, demon!" another Black man said. "We don't plan on letting y'all out of here alive no way, cracka!. You both gon' die right here in this swamp."

"Take them over to the clearing," Gloria Stewart said, nodding to her left. "It's time to send these two fools home. It's time to get some justice for Charles."

"Yes, ma'am," Amos responded.

Amos and two other men quickly dragged the two bound men to the clearing where two large sturdy poles stood next to each other. The crown gathered round as the two men were brought to them.

"You gentlemen get those ropes and tie these demons up." Gloria commanded. "It's getting late and the gators around here are getting hungry!"

Like piranha feeding on a helpless fish, the crowd consumed the two white men. Men and women savagely beat them as they lashed each of them to a pole. Older women and children stood amid the crowd cheering. Alex stood among them and watched in awe.

When the crowd's bloodthirst subsided, both men vaguely resembled human beings. It was only the strong homemade hemp ropes and poles that kept them upright.

Barely conscious, one of the white men managed to speak. "Y'all ain't right! This ain't right!"

Gloria Stewart, holding a worn Bible, stepped forward and looked directly into the man's beaten eyes. She opened the book up to a passage and read: "The heathen are sunk down in the pit that they made; in the net which they hid is their own foot taken."

She stepped back and picked up a hose and nozzle, which was attached to a large canister. The crowd also stepped away from the men.

"You devils grabbed that young man from the jail after you falsely accused him of raping that white woman!" Gloria shouted. "No trial! No nothing! Then, you all, took him away and killed him like he was *nothing. Like he was trash! Well, it took some time for justice to find you. But, now you must pay for your crime. You'll go to meet Satan, your father, in the same way."*

She raised the hose and sprayed a pungent liquid on the men, who vainly tried to wriggle off the poles. They knew what was next.

One of the crowd struck a match and flicked it towards the men. Both ignited instantly.

Their screams were inhuman, but quickly subsided as they were engulfed in the lively flames. The crowd clapped and cheered, then began singing an old hymn, first in a low voice, then it grew louder as more people joined in:

"It's gon' rain. it's gon' rain. You better get ready, and bear this in mind. You see God showed Noah the rainbow sign, he said it won't be water, but fire next time!"

While the two men roasted alive, ironically, they were in no danger of being eaten by the various swamp creatures.

However, come daybreak, the fire would eventually burn itself out, leaving the wild swamp animals to feast off their remains.

CHAPTER THIRTEEN

JANUARY 25th, 11:35 A.M.

"Understand something, Zane," said the portly man in the tight suit, "I honestly don't have a problem with your work, or your views."

He took a drag on his cigarette before continuing. He let the smoke ease out of his mouth.

"But, you know how this city works. The defense bar's got a lot of clout, and they like to throw it around."

Zane could barely contain himself in his seat across from Friedmann's desk.

"What exactly do you want, Jack?" Zane had little use for small talk, and even less use for politics.

He had even less tolerance for Jack Friedmann, President Judge of the Court of Common Pleas. While he couldn't fire a judge, the President Judge could reassign him or her to unpleasant duties, such as Night Court.

"I know your beliefs and policies, Zane," Friedmann said, finishing off the cigarette, and stubbing it out in the ashtray. "Hell, I'm fed up with the crime in the city, too. But, you need to keep in mind that the defense bar carries clout with the judicial recommendations come election time."

"So?" Zane asked.

"So, you need to remember that. Zane you hand out these stiff sentences, and defense attorneys don't like appearing before you. How many of their clients do you think like facing the maximum sentence for an offense?"

"Then maybe their clients should stop breaking the damn law, Jack," Zane said. "This isn't a game."

"Know what they say about you, Zane?" Freidmann asked, switching gears. "They say you don't know how to say 'Not Guilty.' Is that the reputation you really want? When defense attorneys don't like a judge, they complain to the Bar Association. Then, they don't recommend you for re-election. Believe it or not, Zane, a lot of voters listen to the Bar Association," Friedmann sighed, and leaned back in his chair.

"Look, Zane, as your friend and colleague, you don't really need that kind of stress in your life," Jack said.

Zane leaned forward in his chair. He had heard enough.

"First off, Jack, we may be colleagues, but we're definitely not friends," Zane explained. "You are a sorry little Judas of a man who could care less about the citizens of Philadelphia. All you care about is putting your do-nothing friends in plum courtroom assignments and kissing up to defense attorneys."

Friedmann sat forward in his chair, a scowl on his face. "Zane, watch how you talk to me, "I could…"

"You could what?" Zane asked him calmly, cutting him off.

Zane raised his eyebrows inquisitively.

"Fire me? You don't have the power to pull that off, Jack. We both know that. The people of this city elected me. Not you or the criminal defense bar."

Then Zane got up and headed for the door.

"Don't ever think you can't be recalled, Zane," Jack reminded him. "I've seen it happen."

Zane walked back to the desk where the judge sat. Unsure of what Zane's intentions were, Freidmann straightened up.

Leaning over the desk, Zane looked directly into Jack's eyes.

"You know, the feds could indict you just on a fraction of the corruption I know you're involved in," Zane said. "Never threaten me, Jack. Never. When you threaten me, you make me an enemy."

Zane got up and walked toward the chambers door.

"Jack, trust me," Zane continued. "You really don't need *that* kind of stress in *your* life."

7:05 P.M.

Rita Gaines looked at her watch. The meeting was scheduled for 7:00 pm, and she was getting nervous. She always got that way whenever her girls ran late for one of their meetings.

Rita was a police dispatcher. She had the day off and was anxious to hear how things were going.

When the doorbell rang, Rita exhaled, and looked out her window.

They were here.

"Lord, y'all made it with five minutes to spare," she chided as they filed into her foyer. "Don't be giving me no heart attack up in here. I've had enough tragedy in my life."

The group of women, eight in all, ranged in age from early thirties to late sixties. They were just as diverse racially.

The one unifying element was the small scarlet bracelet each wore on their wrist. Each bracelet consisted of fine cords of braided silk.

"Girl, calm yourself down. We're all here and we're alright," said one of the women.

Rita directed the group downstairs. The stairway was narrow in the tiny house, which required the group to descend in single file.

"Let's start," Rita began, settling onto the end of the worn leather couch. "What's going on out there? Does anyone have anything to report?"

"Thank God that Rachman is history," said Dell Cottler, a small Black woman in her early sixties.

"The information we gave the network about that drug dealing murderer led them right to him. Beasely Morgan set it up, and he was there looking out his window and saw it all happen."

"The network's information was right on point once again," Rita said, jotting down some notes in a red notebook.

"Beasely even had Bishop Rawls take care of getting the stores on that block to turn off their surveillance cameras that night," Dell continued. "Of course, the Bishop's church is right across the steet from that lot. And, you know he turned their surveillance cameras off that night, too."

"Can we trust Beasely?" asked Linda Brown, an older White woman whose daughter, Abigail, was murdered two years earlier during a botched robbery near Rittenshouse Square.

"Is he a supporter? Has he ever done any work for the network?" she continued.

"He's trustworthy alright," Belinda Diaz, a local Hispanic store owner, replied. "Remember when Ricky Mambo beat those double murders last year, and how he got off when it was later discovered that some of the jurors were threatened?" She was the principal of one of the city's largest and most prestigious high schools.

"Yeah, I remember," Rita said. "His real name was Richard Lawson, and he lived up in Germantown. That bastard was smiling and giving a press conference outside the Criminal Justice Center right after the Not Guilty verdicts were announced. Like he was some damn rock star. He knew he set fire to that house with those two little girls inside."

Belinda continued.

"Beasely and another supporter ditched Ricky's body in that landfill after the enforcers took him out. Of course Beasely and them supporters didn't know who killed Ricky, so they couldn't tell the cops anything even if they had gotten caught."

"Well, that's another scumbag taken down," Rita said. "But, there's still so many of them thugs out there walking the streets. Who do we get next?"

"Listen, I hear what you are saying," Belinda responded. "But all we can do is just take it one criminal at a time. We just need to make sure our contacts around the city give the network as much good intel as they can, and let the enforcers do what they do."

"Ladies, Rome was not built in a day," Linda Brown reminded the group. She was a well-known local DJ whose radio name was "Phyllis Marlowe".

"Crime in this city is bad," she continued. "Lord knows, but we are making a difference. The network took a while to get traction, but ever since it got going a few years ago, it *has* made a difference on the streets. But, we can't get every criminal overnight."

"You right, girl," Rita said. "You right."

Linda's answer seemed to calm the fears of some of the members. After that, the conversation turned to the kind of small talk one would expect to find at a garden party or a community meeting.

When the meeting was finally adjourned, Rita began cleaning up the basement as the members slowly filed out. As she picked up some of the paper plates, Rita caught sight of the photo of her son Tre'. It was his high school graduation photo. Rita could not remember a happier moment, as she celebrated her only child's milestone.

Five years later, Tre' was dead. Shot in cold blood by a street thug whose criminal record was too long for one accordion file. It seems that Tre's wallet was worth his life that summer evening. Rita's heart still ached when she remembered the detective's call that night informing her that her son had been shot once in the chest during a robbery. The robber got away with $25.00.

Tre' died at the scene.

"Girl, what you doin' over there?" Melanie Paul asked. "I see you lost in thought. You all right?" Melanie was a bank executive whose nephew had been paralyzed from the neck down after being shot by a drug dealer who'd mistaken him for a rival.

Rita sat down heavily on the small sofa, then leaned back and rubbed her face with both hands.

"Mel, it hurts," she replied. "It still hurts. God knows my baby shouldn't be laying in some cold grave in his best suit. He should be using that brilliant mind and his degree for some big corporation. He shouldn't be dead."

She sobbed into her hands.

Melanie put her arm around her friend, and let her cry. Rita could take all the time she needed.

A few moments later Rita wiped her face with the backs of her hands.

"You think we're right to be doing this?" Rita asked, looking up at Mel. "Is God going to punish us for this?"

"Girl, I don't know," Melanie answered. "I often ask myself the same question. Maybe I can rationalize it because we're not the ones killing these criminals. We just give information to the network and keep our mouths shut. Hell, we don't even know who actually kills these scumbags. Is it one or two killers? Is it a male or a female? Are the killers Black, White, Asian? Look, the less we know, the better."

Melanie paused and looked away for a minute, then continued.

"All I know is how good it feels when we find out that these fools die horribly. Like my son did," she said.

Melanie took Rita's chin and looked down into her eyes.

"Look, Rita," she said. "This ain't no time to get soft now. We didn't start this fight. God's got enough forgiveness for us, girl."

"I hear you," Rita said. "Remember when Mrs.

Cordelia told me she knew how to get Tre's killer? I was so eager to get involved. The only condition was that I didn't ask questions and kept quiet. She said if I just gathered info I got from the street, and then enter it into this secret website, my family and I would be protected."

"When you recruited me two weeks later, I couldn't wait to be part of the network," Mel said. "I just wanted to get folks riled up enough that they would fight back."

Rita dabbed her eyes with a tissue.

"But, somewhere along the line, Rita, it became about getting revenge," Mel said. "And, now the network is getting bigger than we ever imagined. There are network cells all over the city. We aren't the only ones who want to get even."

Rita shook her head.

"I don't look at it that way," Rita said. "To me, all we're doing is getting some peace of mind. Honey, in the end, that may be all we can hope for."

CHAPTER FOURTEEN

JANUARY 28th, 10:30 A.M.

Zane's new entertainment center took shape quicker than either he or Beck had expected.

"Beck," Zane said with a huge grin, "we are going to be checking out the fights on the new widescreen television set before you know it. This thing is taking no time to put up."

"You definitely got a great hook up on the tv, Judge," Beck said as he sat down.

The large rec room floor was covered with instructions and styrofoam packaging. "I may need your to help to negotiate a deal for me when I finally upgrade my old CD and sound system," Beck said.

"Ahh, you don't need me," Zane said. "Just go and make your deal. You're a lawyer, man. A good lawyer, remember that," Zane said gathering all the trash into one big pile.

"Thanks, Judge. I'll keep that in mind," Beck replied.

While the judge could be stubborn and rigid at times, Beck loved him and respected him like a father. Considering Beck's own dad, his love for the Judge may have been even greater than that.

This made it hard for Beck not to defend Zane to others who criticized the judge for his views on crime, no matter how antiquated they may be. In fact, Beck found himself on the Judge's side more often than not.

Plus, Zane was always there for Beck; at his law school graduation, Zane was in the front row beaming like a proud papa; When his mom died, Zane shed tears of his own, all the while being a pillar of support for him. When the Phladelphia D.A.'s office was looking for young prosecutors, Zane personally lobbied the D.A. to give the one-time local middleweight a job.

By the time Zane and Beck had cleaned up the recreation room, it was nearly noon. Beck gathered up the trash, and headed for the stairs leading up to the living room.

"Judge, thanks for the hearty lunch."

"Anytime. Thanks for all of your help. Your timing is great because Ron is on his way over. We need to talk. We actually have another one of those, uh, charity meetings to go to late this evening. You know, one of those citizen's panels."

What kind of charity group meets late on a Saturday night? Beck thought to himself, but quickly dismissed the thought. He knew the judge well enough to know that he would attend any kind of community meeting anywhere, from the city's richest areas to some of the absolute worst neighborhoods. As long as folks had problems with crime and criminals, Zane was there. Beck knew Zane had little fear, which Beck attributed to his martial arts and military training.

Ron was cut from the same mold. Even as hard to read as Ron was, however, Beck had grown fond of the man around whom so many rumors revolved. Chief among them was that Ron had not always operated on the right side of the law.

CHAPTER FIFTEEN

12:00 P.M.

"Okay. Let's get this meeting started. It's Saturday, and some of us have things to do. Y'all know I like to start on time, so we don't have to be here all day."

The speaker was Dorothy Haynes, president of the Concerned Neighbors Coalition, (CNC). The Coalition, at one time, had been one of the largest community organizations in Philadelphia with nearly 300 members on its roster.

How many members actually showed up to meetings these days, however, was another matter.

While the drug trade was evident all over the city, drugs were hammering the North Philadelphia area represented by the CNC. "Beleagured" was the word one newspaper used in describing the area. While the group's clout enabled it to gain the ear of some of the city's most prominent politicians, inevitably all the CNC managed to do to was secure a few more police officers and some well-meaning promises. That hardly made a dent in the crime and violence in the area.

Today was the CNC's monthly meeting. Most members had stopped coming altogether. Tired of the broken promises, they resigned themselves to simply coping with their declining neighborhoods. Now, all that was left of this once-proud group was a few faithful neighbors. The chatter among them faded as Dorothy began the meeting.

"Thank you members," Dorothy said, looking down at her one-page meeting agenda. "I first want to welcome all Coalition members who turned out for today's afternoon meeting".

A smattering of applause went through the room. "We have quite a bit to cover today, and we're going to try to keep things moving," she said adjusting her glasses.

As Dorothy moved down the agenda, the group hardly noticed a large brown man dressed in an army fatigue jacket, dark jeans and an olive ski cap enter the room through the rear entrance. Two other similarly-dressed men followed him and took seats near the back doors. The man's size belied his agility as he gently folded himself into a chair. He removed his black leather gloves and placed them in his pockets, then rubbed his hands together to warm them.

"Our special guest speaker has arrived. Would you come up, Mr. Torres?" Dorothy said, motioning him toward the stage.

Gaylen Torres rose, took off his skull cap, and walked toward the front of the room. More than a few audience members shuddered slightly as he took his place at the front of the room, and it was not only due to the room's faulty heater.

"Thank you Mrs. Haynes," Torres said as Dorothy took a seat behind him at the table.

"Good morning to everyone," he continued. "And to my Muslim brothers and sisters I say 'Al Salaam a'alaykum.'"

Various members greeted him in English and in Arabic.

"As many of you know, my name is Gaylen Torres, and I am founder and executive director of the R.O.C. – RECLAIM OUR COMMUNITIES Initiative here in Philadelphia. We are a non-profit organization that is dedicated to helping our communities take back our streets from drugs, violence and the negative elements that endanger our children and the safety of our neighborhoods."

"I saw you on T.V.," said an older black man in a plaid shirt. "You and your group were out in front of City Hall about two weeks ago, right?"

"Yes, sir, that was us."

"What y'all want with us?" another member asked.

"We're concerned with uplifting neighborhoods, and we work with neighbors like you to accomplish our mission," Gaylen replied.

Walter Ford, one of the older residents on the block stood up.

"Well, Mr. Torres, exactly how will you help us eliminate the drugs in our neighborhood? It all sounds nice, but we call the cops night and day about these damn drugs, but they don't do squat. These little hoodlums sell that poison right out on the corner in broad daylight, and then they curse you out and threaten to shoot you if you say something to them about it. If you ain't no cop, how you gonna help us?"

A chorus of "yeah," "that's right," and "tell me about it," went up from the crowd.

Unfazed, Gaylen let the murmuring die down before answering.

"Sir, I understand your frustration, I really do," Gaylen said calmly. "I grew up on these streets, and I still live not far from here. I know about having to step over crackheads asleep in front of your home. I know about not being able to sleep because of the heavy traffic in and out of the crack house across the street from your home. I know about confronting the drug dealers day in and day out because you are tired of their foolishness."

The room was silent.

Gaylen continued.

"One thing I also know, however, is I got tired of having to fight for my right to live in peace. I got tired of begging scumbags to stop dealing their death on my block, in front of my home, in front of the kids." Torres's voice was louder now.

"So you know what I did?"

It might as well have been a rhetorical question as no one had the courage to answer the big man who had become very angry in just a few short moments.

"I decided to stop running and complaining and I decided to play offense. I decided that I wasn't gonna take it anymore, and I knew there had to be others who felt the same. So, when I got out of prison a few years ago, me and a few other neighbors – most of them are ex-cons like me – formed ROC and asked to have a meeting with the head of the drug gang operating in our area. We let him know in no uncertain terms that he and his operation had to leave our neighborhood."

"Did they leave?" asked Mrs. Van Rose, another one of the elderly residents, who was seated in the back.

"Well, ma'am," Gaylen replied coolly, "let's just say they found out we meant business."

"Mister Torres, no offense," Walter Ford said, standing up, "but we've had all the drug marches we need here. Besides the only thing them marches do is let the dealers know who's against them. If that's all you can do for us, we already done plenty of that."

"Drug marches are a part of our arsenal because they show the drug dealers we aren't afraid of them," Gaylen answered. "We also feel marches show the community and the rest of the city that we're not backing down anymore."

A buzz went through the crowd.

"However, sir," Gaylen continued, "ROC's strength lies in our ability to *persuade* them to leave after they see how serious we are. Drug dealers don't like it when people fight for their neighborhoods."

"Do you work with the police to help clean up a neighborhood," asked a neighbor.

"Sometimes," Gaylen answered. "But, the police aren't always willing to embrace our objectives or our methods."

"Are any of your group's tactics illegal?" someone called out from the back.

Gaylen paused before answering.

"We're not trying to work against the cops," he said. "We only want to help people live peaceably, so they can enjoy their homes and their neighborhoods. We respect the laws of this city, and encourage others to do so, whenever possible. We believe in the right to free speech, and in the Constitution. Our main weapon is our mouth."

The room went silent.

"However, ROC also believes in the Second Amendment. Our neighborhoods have become battlefields. And when you are at war, the only law that truly counts is the law of survival."

Gaylen was preaching now.

"And, if you really think about it, folks, no court on this planet can find any innocent man guilty of breaking *that* law."

Gaylen's message was beginning to resonate with

some of the crowd. Many people were murmuring their approval and nodding in agreement.

"Just think about it," Gaylen challenged. "No more having to sleep on the floor because you're afraid of a stray bullet. No more worrying about your children, or your parents or grandparents getting caught in the crossfire."

"I hear you, brother. I hear you," shouted Edwin Malloy, one of the group's younger members. "That's what I'm talkin' about," he said clapping loudly.

"What's in it for you, Mr. Torres?"

The question quickly quieted the crowd.

Lurline Pendleton, one of the more skeptical members of the group, asked, "I mean, why do you and ROC care if our neighborhood is safe?"

"Ma'am," began Gaylen, looking directly at Lurline, "I am a convicted felon. But, I educated myself when I was in prison. Even got my degree online. Still, I can't vote, or own a firearm. I can't even get a job some places."

He paused and looked around before he continued.

"While I did my time, I had a chance to think about all the things I did wrong. I thought about the people I hurt, the things I took. A few years ago, I was one of those criminals shooting, selling dope and stealing on these same streets. I felt it was my right to take stuff that wasn't mine," he shrugged. "Hey, only the strong survive, so I felt that if you were weak, you deserved to be preyed on."

Gaylen paused to let his words sink in.

"While I was locked up, I changed. I got with some true Muslim brothers, and I started reading the Qu'ran. These brothers showed me the error of my ways. I promised Allah that if He would let me out of prison, I would do everything I could to help people, not hurt them."

The room was completely silent as Gaylen spoke.

"I made up my mind that instead of preying on innocent people, I'd prey on those who are guilty. Then, he turned back to Lurline. "That's where I'm coming from, ma'am."

Despite his words, Lurline Pendleton was still skeptical.

"We need to move on with this meeting." It was Dorothy, the group president. "Let's all thank Mr. Torres for his time, and for sharing with us this afternoon. We have his business card if we need to contact him."

A small round of applause went up as she shook Gaylen's hand. He nodded at the president and left the stage.

A few moments later, he and his associates were out the door.

The group murmured among themselves almost as soon as Torres left.

"I believe he can help us," remarked Grady Stokes, a long-time resident of the area.

"I *believe*," said Lurline Pendleton, "that man is nothing but an ill wind that blows no good."

2:30 P.M.

With the old entertainment center taken apart and stacked in the garage for trash day, the new one fit the space in Zane's recreation room perfectly.

"How's Judge Matthews doing?" Beck felt like he was moving in slow motion as he tried to hoist himself from the big lounge chair in the rec room. This was the aftermath of having eaten his fill of the grilled jumbo shrimp, potato wedges and crab cakes that Zane had ordered from Big Leslie's on Chew Avenue. If there was a better seafood place in Philly, Beck wanted to know where. As if that wasn't enough, the pecan caramel pie Beck brought over had been reduced to a mere sliver long ago.

Most days the Judge ate "clean"; no sugar, lots of greens, little or no carbs, lean meats and fish. However, Zane had a cheat day occasionally to break up the monotony. He often invited Beck to join him.

Today was one of those days.

"She's alright. I want to take her to opening night of that new play downtown next week." Zane had to yell from upstairs where he was loading the dishwasher.

"Terra Matthews is one fine woman, and she keeps her business, our business, I should say, to herself," he continued. "Ironically, the only problem is that she's a judge."

"How's that a problem?" Beck asked. "I mean, she knows what you go through, and the stresses you face. I'd think that would be a plus. Besides she's over at City Hall in civil, while you're at the Criminal Justice Center."

"You might think that, but it's not always so, Beck," Zane replied. "Philly is a small *big* city, so everybody knows *something* about everyone. Keep that in mind. Second, the judge and I butt heads politically; she's a liberal, and I'm definitely not. She's still salty with me over the Andrew Meadows thing."

The Andrew Meadows murders were some of the biggest cases the city had seen in a while. Nicknamed "Madman" by the press, Meadows had brutally murdered more than fifteen people in Philly over a decade. His specialty was torture. One of the most heinous attacks involved Cara Porter. Meadows hacked off one of her hands before duct-taping her, then repeatedly raped her before shooting her twice in the back of the head.

He managed to elude cops for nearly ten years, until he got sloppy. Solid police work by Homicide detectives ultimately traced the scant evidence to Meadows about a year and a haf ago. Upon his arrest, he gave a rambling, sometimes incoherent, confession, in which he told detectives things about the victims and evidence only the real rapist would know.

Things seemed sewed up, until defense psychologists claimed Meadows had a fifth grade education and mentality. After examining him, even some neutral mental health pros agreed that the man had some serious psychological issues. He was barely found to be competent to stand trial.

Ultimately, Zane was assigned the case. The Public Defender's Office, Meadows' lawyer, opted for a jury trial rather than have Zane hear the case as a bench trial. Zane was known as a harsh sentencer, but in a death penalty case, the jury, not Zane, would decide Meadows' guilt and punishment. Some even felt they might get at least get one bleeding-heart juror who couldn't make up their mind, or at least acquit him on one of the multiple charges.

While the trial took three weeks, the verdict took less than three days. The jury unanimously found the defendant guilty on all charges. A death sentence seemed a foregone conclusion, until the media began calling for the jury to give Meadows life in prison, instead of lethal injection because of his arguably-diminished capacity. Everyone assumed that once the jury heard the overwhelming evidence of Meadows' horrible childhood and mental issues, they'd vote for him to get life in prison.

That is, until Zane refused to let the defense present that mitigating evidence. In a ruling that astounded even some prosecutors, Zane claimed the evidence was merely "cumulative," and therefore irrelevant. Not one to kowtow to pressure, Zane in fact, seemed to relish the criticism. The more defiant he became about his decision, the more Beck admired him.

"Beck, somebody's got to speak for his victims like Cara Porter," Zane told Beck.

Zane's ruling was ultimately overturned by the Pennsylvania Supreme Court. However, Meadows' supporters gained only a hollow victory because he hung himself in prison awaiting a new sentencing hearing.

"When she gets back in town, I'll take her to dinner so we can hash things out," Zane continued.

"That should work, Judge," Beck replied.

Beck noticed the frost between Zane and Judge Terra Matthews after the Meadows case. She was one of the most-respected, and most-loved judges on the bench.

An avowed liberal, Judge Matthews made no attempt to hide her distaste for the death penalty.

"I think don't think the state should be in the business of revenge," she had said during an interview regarding the case.

It was no surprise, that Terra was more than a bit upset with Zane's ruling. His continued stubbornness to reconsider also didn't win him any points with her, either.

"Look, I think I have managed to smooth things over, so far," Zane said, gathering up the remaining spare parts for the entertainment center. He placed them in one of the center's compartments.

"However, I think she is starting to get the picture about me."

"How so, Judge?"

"I am very serious – deadly serious – about keeping these streets clean of criminals."

CHAPTER SIXTEEN

JANUARY 31ˢᵗ, 10:00 A.M.

Sisco turned up the heat in the car as he drove southbound on Broad Street. It had been nearly two weeks since Rachman had been found dead, and the case was beginning to get colder than the weather. If they didn't find Rachman's killer soon, the department's Cold Case Squad would take over the investigation.

In hopes of jump-starting the investigation, Sergeant Marinovitch sent Sisco and Luke out to question some more neighbors in the area where Rachman was killed. They would also re-visit some people they had already interviewed.

This morning, Luke sat silently in the passenger seat going over previously-done Activity Sheets in the case. His head was down, and he squinted as he read them just inches from his face.

"I don't understand," Sisco said as he turned off Broad Street onto Federal Street, "why don't you just wear your glasses? I bet you'd stop squinting like Mr. Magoo if you did."

"Sisco, I told you before, I don't need no glasses," Luke said, squinting even more. "My eyes are fine. The print is too small, that's all. Besides, my glasses fog up when I get mad or nervous. Can't have my glasses all fogged up when I'm questioning someone, or if I have to testify in court."

Sisco laughed as he eased the car down a side street.

"I'd rather know that my partner can see who the hell he's talking to or shooting at," Sisco replied.

"Don't you worry about me, Sisco," Luke chuckled. "You just take care of you, I'll take care of me. And, we'll both take care of each other."

"I hear you brother," Sisco said. "I hear you."

It was close to 11:00 a.m. when Sisco pulled the car into a parking spot in front of The Corner Café, a tidy little deli on the corner of 11th and Tasker Streets. The building stood amid mostly renovated structures, which were part of the recent gentrification in that part of Tasker Street. The other end of Tasker, however, was another matter. The vacant lot where Rachman was found earlier in the month was a few blocks away.

The owner, Clarence Peterson, was an elderly black gentleman with thick bifocal glasses and a sharp tongue.

"Well, well, if it ain't Moe and Larry," Peterson

remarked as the two detectives entered the store. He was in the process of cutting ham for the lunch menu. The ever-present aroma of onions and lunchmeat greeted the detectives.

"All y'all need now is Curly and you boys will be back in business!" With that, the older man laughed heartily and clapped his hands, oblivious to the fact that the joke was not very funny.

Slightly bigger than a small garage, The Corner Cafe was a "café" in name only. There were no tables or chairs, just a long counter with a few stools for customers. Clarence and his wife Freda prepared the sandwiches from behind the counter, and rang up the customers from the cash register at the end of it.

"Morning, Mr. Peterson," Sisco said as he extended his gloved hand toward the older man. "Good to see you again." Peterson wiped his hand on his apron and half-heartedly shook the detective's hand.

"Good morning, detectives," said a small sweet voice from the back. It was Freda, Clarence's wife. She was a large affable woman with a gap between her front teeth and a pleasant disposition.

"How are you this morning, ma'am," Luke asked. Sisco smiled, then nodded his greeting to the woman as she entered the store. She was holding a large rectangular block of cheese wrapped in plastic.

"Thanks for the cheese, honey", said her husband.

Clarence turned his attention back to the Detectives.

"What y'all want now?" Peterson asked.

He went back to cutting the ham.

"Don't tell me you still tryin' to find out who killed Rachman?" he continued. "Why y'all wastin' taxpayer's money tracking down that murderer's killer, anyway?"

"We don't make judgements about our victims, sir," Luke said, giving Peterson the textbook answer.

"What y'all need to do when you find this guy is give him a damn medal, that's what you need to do," Clarence replied.

"Don't talk like that Clarence," Freda said in a sharp tone. "No matter what that boy did, he's still God's child, and his momma's son. Even he deserves mercy. God is the only one who's gonna judge him."

Clarence mumbled something under his breath, but never stopped his cutting. The whir of the electric meat-cutter was the only sound in the room.

"When was the last time either of you saw Rachman before he was killed?" Sisco asked when neither Freda nor Clarence spoke for several seconds.

"Probably about two weeks before ya'll found him in that lot," replied Clarence. "I seen him and that other boy, big fella, what's his name Freda? Mick, Mike, something like that. Anyway, they was sitting in a car down near the Chinese store."

"What were they doing?" Luke asked.

"Probably something they wasn't supposed to be doin'" Clarence said. "Every time you saw that boy, he just looked like bad news. And the people he hung around was just as evil."

"Mrs. Peterson, did Rachman or his boys usually come into the store?" Luke asked Freda.

"Hardly ever, Detective," Freda answered. "These people around here know about us, and they know what kind of store we run. We don't tolerate any foolishness. No drugs, no liquor, no fighting. Nothing. Rachman and his boys knew that, too," she finished proudly.

Sisco checked his watch and saw that the store would be open soon for lunch. He was not keen on having anyone see him and Luke questioning the couple, especially not any of Rachman's crew.

"Tell me something, Detectives," Freda asked, "how was that boy able to walk the streets? I mean, everyone around here knew he'd killed those poor folks. Didn't the courts know?"

Clarence stopped the meat cutter and looked at the detectives, waiting for an answer.

"The Commonwealth's main witness was murdered right before trial," Sisco answered. "Without that witness, they had no case."

"But you know Rachman had that lady killed, right?" Clarence said, barely containing his anger. "Y'all don't have to have no degree or no badge to figure that one out!"

"We knew that the witness had been shot," Sisco responded, "but there was no evidence as to who, so there was nothing we could do. The case had to be discharged because there were no other witnesses. At least, none willing to come forward to testify against Rachman."

"So that's it?" Clarence asked, throwing his hands up in the air. "See, that's why this city is so damn bad! That's why these thugs think they can do whatever they want."

"Now, Clarence…"

Clarence interrupted Freda in mid-sentence.

"Don't you try to hush me Freda! You know I'm right. Right as rain."

Turning to the detectives, Clarence resumed his oratory.

"I know y'all got a job to do, and you probably tryin' to do your best. But that ain't good enough! The judges here are rotten to their bones. All except Judge Russell. He's the only one who cares about punishing those criminals. He locks them fools up and throws away the key, and that's why they don't like him."

"Maybe if he'd been the Judge, Rachman wouldn't have been out on the street," Freda added.

Sisco realized they were far off track now, and tried to redirect them back to their investigation.

"Can either of you think of anyone who might have information on who killed Rachman?" Sisco asked.

When neither of them answered, Sisco and Luke looked at each other and then reached into their suit jackets for their cards.

"Please take our cards and give us a call if you get any more information, OK?" Luke said.

"Save them, detective," Clarence said, dismissing them with a wave of his hand. Luke noticed the burgundy bracelet on Clarence's wrist next to his watch. Freda wore a matching one on her wrist.

"Save them 'cause nobody round here wants to see his killer go to jail. What they need to do is give him a medal, 'cause he did us a real favor. Most folks feel that his death wasn't really no crime, anyway. The only real tragedy is that somebody didn't take that thug out sooner."

12:35 P.M.

Valerie McIntosh stood at the podium and waited for the lunchtime crowd's clamor to subside while she scanned the room for signs of the press. She recognized a few print journalists, but wasn't sure if any of the television networks were represented.

After a few moments, she raised her hands for silence.

"I'd like to take this time introduce the speaker of the hour," McIntosh began. "One of our own, a man who needs no introduction. Please welcome, the Honorable Aubrey Pratt, mayor of the City of Philadelphia!"

The crowd rose in unison, filling the large hall with applause.

While the Mayor walked to the stage, the crowd stayed on their feet.

All except for Gaylen Torres, who sat in the back of the hall. He and two other men occupied a small table, their lunches untouched in front of them.

"Thank you and good afternoon ladies and gentlemen," Mayor Pratt said. "I am honored and humbled to be before you today."

The applause subsided as the crowd sat down.

"On this the twenty-second annual Philadelphia Crime Victims Coalition Luncheon, it gives me great pleasure to recognize the group for its outstanding work on behalf of crime victims. Furthermore, it gives the city a chance to show what we are doing to stem the tide of crime in our City of Brotherly Love and Sisterly affection."

"And exactly what is it that you're doing, Mr. Mayor?" Gaylen Torres asked, rising from his chair.

All heads turned towards Torres, who was now standing. His dark suit stood in stark contrast to his fiery demeanor.

"We still lead the nation in homicides, we have the purest heroin and opiods on the east coast, our mothers and fathers are being slaughtered in the streets, and our judges are still as rotten as ever," Gaylen said.

"Mr. Torres, I don't think this is the right forum for -"

"Mr. Mayor, this is the *perfect* forum for this discussion!" Gaylen challenged. "How can you spout that crap to the people who give their lives to help crime victims knowing you and your administration cut funds to organizations like these? And then, you have the nerve to put off the investigation into some of these corrupt judges."

The well-dressed crowd murmured among themselves waiting to see what happened next. Though his face was bright red, the Mayor seemed to regain his composure.

"Sir, if you have a question, you can direct it to my staff, and we'll look into the problem. Otherwise, please sit down and shut up!"

Some in the crowd clapped at the Mayor's rebuke, while others seemed to want Torres to respond.

"Mr. Mayor, I'm a taxpayer, and a constituent! You work for me," Torres responded. "So, no I'm NOT shutting up. And if you cared more about us constituents than how your sorry career was going, maybe our streets would be safer!"

To the mayor's chagrin, some more people clapped at Torres' response.

By this time, the Mayor's security detail, which consisted of three Philadelphia cops, headed for Gaylen's table.

"You don't have to send your boys to remove us. We're leaving." Gaylen said, walking toward the doors. His two-man entourage followed closely behind him. When he reached the double doors, he turned back to the Mayor.

"Even though we're leaving, Mr. Mayor, your

problems are still out there," Torres said. "You still ain't gonna make this city better until you clean up the criminal justice system. And you can't run from that!"

On his way out the hall, Gaylen smiled to himself as he caught a glimpse of Channel Seven's reporter scribbling furiously in a notebook.

Mission accomplished, he thought to himself.

6:00 P.M.

"Good evening Philadelphia and Delaware Valley, this is Channel 7 Investigative News at 6!"

Kelly Foster sat behind the news desk next to her co-anchor Clark Reed. During the opening segments, both took turns doing various news segments.

Kelly took the lead, however, after the commercial beak.

"And in local politics, it seems that everyone is a critic of the Mayor," Kelley reported. "This afternoon at the city's annual Crime Victim's Coalition Luncheon downtown, it was Gaylen Torres' turn to roast Mayor Pratt."

Soon after, the station cued up video from the afternoon's luncheon. Specifically, Gaylen's confrontation with the mayor filled the screen, complete with audio.

The camera cut back to Kelley after the 20-second video played.

"Could we be seeing a challenger to Mayor Pratt's reelection bid next year?" Kelley intoned. "Could this be Gaylen Torres' message to voters fed up with crime? We shall see."

* * *

Gaylen Torres sat down in his favorite living room chair. His day had just ended after a full schedule of activities.

He saw the full story on the luncheon.

He grinned as he switched his television to another channel. He leaned back in the lounge chair and whistled a salsa tune.

CHAPTER SEVENTEEN

February 1ˢᵗ, 10:35 P.M.

Since Luke and Sisco were working the standard 8am - 4pm shift that week, Luke had his evenings off. Tonight, however, he would still be working – sort of.

He was going downtown to meet Jada.

She was not his girlfriend, but an exotic dancer at one of the city's most popular strip clubs, or "gentlemann's clubs" as they were called.

She was also his main informant, and it was her beauty that made her so effective. Jada got into all kinds of places and collected choice street information mostly because most men told her things and dropped names trying to impress her.

So, as she drank their free drinks, flirted with them, and made them feel like they had a chance to be with her, she also soaked up their confessions and other key street intel like a sponge. Her information had helped Luke and Sisco solve some of their toughest cases.

Luke arrived downtown shortly past 10:30 p.m. and pulled into an empty parking space on a small side street close to Chestnut Street. While the lighting was not the best, it was enough to keep away most of the predators who inhabited downtown Philadelphia after dark. Luke wasn't worried about anyone stealing his truck – that's what insurance was for.

Besides, if anyone could get past the truck's expensive security system and steering wheel locking device, they deserved to have it.

He definitely wasn't worried about getting mugged. His Glock 9 milimeter was always with him, locked, loaded and ready for any situation.

Luke walked toward Market Street and pulled his hat down over his ears. As he got closer to the corner, he could hear the large crowd gathered in front, even on a frigid night like this.

Luke had gotten his first taste of the club a few years back, and had mixed feelings about it. The food was good, but the crowd consisted largely of bourgeoise blacks and professional whites interested in sports and drinking. They would not be caught dead, however, in a bar in the 'hood, where the food was less expensive and definitely much better.

When Luke walked in, he could feel the energy from the crowd. He scanned the front waiting area and moved past the bar to the stairs leading to the upper level. At 6-foot-1, and 210 pounds, Luke still carried his college running back bulk well.

He reached the top of the stairs and glanced toward the far wall where the large lights gave way to softer recessed lighting. While the crowd up here was still fairly large, they had a more singular purpose in mind.

As he approached the small booth, Luke recognized the pretty young woman who sat there. She wore a beige sweater and black jeans, which hugged her fabulously. The burgundy lipstick perfectly complemented Jada's auburn eyes and her dark brown skin.

"You need to get a better watch, detective," she greeted him sassily, but with a smile that accentuated her left cheek dimple.

Luke eased into the booth. He took a seat across from her and pulled a menu toward him.

"So, tell me what I need to know." Luke pretended to study the menu as Jada spoke.

"Where you want me to start?"

"Tell me about Torres," he replied.

"Torres and his boys been busy," Jada said. "Ever since he got out of prison a few years back, he been on a crusade to take back the streets."

"I heard," Luke responded.

"He also stepped to Mayor Pratt at yesterday's Crime Victim's Luncheon," she continued. "He came at the Mayor in front of the whole crowd, and basically called him out because of all the crime in the city. Some say Tores may run for mayor next year."

"Go on," Luke said.

Jada looked at him and continued.

"I hear he and his group may have even taken out Richard Lawson last year."

"Ricky Mambo?" Luke was surprised. "From West Philly? We thought that Lawson's murder may have been gang-related. All the evidence, at least what we could gather, pointed to that."

Jada shrugged.

"That's why you pay me, baby," she replied. "To show you how much you don't know," she said.

"Did he do Rachman, too?" Luke asked.

"I can't say for sure, but I wouldn't put it past him. Torres and some of Rachman's boys had some beef a few weeks earlier. Rachman was still in custody at that time. Then, of course they found your boy Rachman frozen in that lot after he beat that double murder case."

Luke listened as he quickly scanned the dimly-lit room.

Jada continued.

"You know, as bad as Rachman was, though, there was still people in the hood who had love for him," she said. "He handed out turkeys at Thanksgiving, gave young mothers money for baby formula. You know, the whole ghetto Santa thing."

"What I want to know is Torres and his gang into snapping necks?" Luke responded. He noticed the crowd near the stairs starting to disperse.

"You ever seen Torres?" Jada asked in a low

voice. "He's so big he damn near blocks out the sun. And the two guys he always rolls with are just as big. They could probably break a few necks and arms and whatever else they want. They may even be bigger than you sweetheart. Although you pretty big yourself."

She gave Luke a playful glance.

He ignored her look.

"What I don't get is this: Torres did time for armed robbery – not murder," Luke said. "Even during that crime, there was no real assault. He and another guy apparently hit a store owner making a night drop at an ATM. Torres flashed a weapon, the guy handed over the cash. No injury. Hell, Torres' gun wasn't even loaded. Now, you telling me he does bodies? What would make him go from stick-up man to murderer?"

"That's what you gotta find out. You the detective," Jada answered, patting the back of her hair. She pulled out her cell phone and checked a text message.

"Go and detect," she added.

Luke checked his watch, then went back to scanning the club.

"You got my new cell number, so hit me up if you get anything new, okay?" Luke passed several folded $50.00 bills to Jada under the table.

"Good work, Jada. I appreciate it."

Her hand met his. Luke noticed how long she let her fingers linger on his before taking the bills.

She leaned in close and whispered into Luke's ear. He tried to maintain his composure, but her light perfume was inviting. While he tried hard not to blur the lines between business and pleasure with Jada, he found himself spending more "business" time with her. He tried to justify it as simply obtaining more intel for the job, and things had not gotten physical – yet.

Luke knew it was only a matter of time, however.

She got up to leave, and leaned over the table toward Luke. He got a full view of Jada's tight curves and sexiness.

"Baby, keep spending time with me, and I'll do whatever you want." Jada purred.

11:35 P.M.

Sisco had dozed off somewhere between watching the Sixers game and the eleven o'clock news. The fact that he fell asleep on the couch meant that everyone else was asleep upstairs. Beast was in his usual spot – curled up next to the sofa.

His cell phone on the coffee table buzzed, breaking his nap. He fumbled for a few seconds before answering the phone.

"This is Sisco," he answered. "Can I help you?" Sisco was too tired to answer with his standard professional greeting.

"Hey Sisco, this is Detective Frank Bonner."

"Frankie from Three Squad?" Sisco asked.

"Yeah, it's me. Sorry to call you so late, but I wanted to give you some info."

Sisco sat up.

"I'm working on the case of a large young Black male found dead about two weeks ago. Somebody found him slumped over his steering wheel down in South Philly. From what we have found so far, he apparently died of natural causes. Couldn't find any gunshots wounds, stab wounds, or anything."

"Why would you think I'd be interested in that case?" Sisco asked.

"Well, he was basically a John Doe until a few days ago. When they found him in his car, the only ID he had on him was a faded state ID card. Said his name was "Mike," but we couldn't make out his last name. The medical examiner's office had to eventually use dental records to ID him. Turns out he was Mike Watkins, also known as Baby Mike."

"You mean Baby Mike who was Rachman's second in command?" Sisco answered.

"Yep, that's him. We know you and Luke are working Rachman's murder."

Sisco was wide awake now. He needed to call Luke with this.

"I am still waiting for the medical examiner's office to call me with an official cause of death," Bonner said. "I'll keep you posted as soon as I hear from the ME's Office. I will let the medical examiner's office know they can call you about Mike's autopsy results as well."

"Hey thanks Frank. I appreciate it," Sisco said, ending the call.

He hoped Luke was awake.

CHAPTER EIGHTEEN

February 2ⁿᵈ, 12:15 A.M.

"Girl, it's too cold out there to be taking the bus."

Nicola Williams offered her opinion as she finished washing her hands. Most of the regular Friday night customers had left Julian Piccolo's, a small restaurant nestled on one of the many small side streets in South Philly.

"Honey, don't worry about me." Denise Mignucci answered. "I'm an Italian girl with five brothers. I'm not worried. I can take care of myself."

She zipped up her heavy jacket, wrapped her wool scarf around her neck and headed toward the door.

"Besides, my brother is working the late shift at his job, and I'm not waiting for him to get off to come get me."

"Well, you need to be careful. You know the "Black Glove Rapist" is still out there," Nicola said, arranging clean dishtowels for the early morning breakfast rush. "The guy they arrested for all of those violent rapes was found not guilty last month on some technicality. They just let him out."

At twenty-three, Denise Mignucci was an attractive brunette who listed "aspiring actress" on her resume'. However, until Hollywood called, she supported herself as a waitress at the restaurant.

Denise glanced at her watch and slung the large pocketbook across her shoulder. She gripped the small canister of mace in her coat pocket. She had it so long she wasn't even sure it still worked.

It was 12:30 a.m.

"See you tomorrow, Nicky. You can tell me all about your new date." Denise hugged the short African-American woman with dreadlocks and headed out into the wintry night.

Denise had walked almost two blocks when she turned down a small street.

The man saw her as she turned the corner. Positioned a block and a half down the street on the same side, he sat huddled beneath a grimy blanket in the doorway of an abandoned warehouse.

His homeless disguise worked perfectly, as more than a few passersby earlier in the evening had even stopped and dropped spare change into the plastic cup at his feet.

"Alpha One, this is Alpha Two," the man whispered into the neck microphone connected to his light walkie talkie equipment. "I got a visual on the target."

"Copy that, Alpha Two. I read you loud and clear," a voice responded in his earpiece.

At one time, this was a thriving street which was home to a number of small businesses. From mom-and-pop stores, to bodegas, to auto repair shops, this street was one of the city's small business meccas.

That was a long time ago.

Since then, Philadelphia's economy changed as the small shops gave way to the mega-stores, draining the life and business out of the corner stores. Now, after dark, this street was largely quiet and deserted.

While Denise had talked tough in the restaurant, she felt different as she walked toward her bus stop.

She barely noticed the homeless man to her left in dark clothes crumpled in the doorway of a small bookshop. A dingy blanket covered his lower body.

Under the blanket, the man was dressed warmly in layers. These fit close to his body, allowing him to be flexible and mobile. His face was painted with camouflage grease and he carried a k-bar fighting knife in the sheath strapped to his right side. He wore soft-soled boots, which sturdy, yet comfortable. He'd sat in this same spot every night for a few hours the past week.

She walked briskly past him, increasing her stride as she moved down the street.

Studying and watching.

"Alpha One, we still on J Band for communications?"

"Roger that Alpha Two".

The men made sure their communications were on a radio band wave not normally used by the police or other law enforcement. Stealth was crucial, as anyone with a police scanner could monitor the airwaves. On this channel, the men could hear police activity, but no one could hear their conversations. The small radio receiver unit was clipped to his belt on the right side.

The man in the homeless garb set up his surveillance nearly two hours ago, and outside of a single patrol car passing through, he could count the traffic on the street on one hand.

As Denise Mignucci crossed the small intersection, the man under the blanket spotted a dark-colored Jeep Cherokee turn the corner going in her direction.

The Jeep followed her at a slow pace.

"Alpha One, bogey spotted. 12:00." Alpha Two reported.

"Copy that, Alpha Two."

The man sprang into a standing position, and moved toward the woman who walked a few feet ahead of him. Years of training enabled him to move with cat-like quickness, his feet barely making a sound on the pavement.

The Jeep drew alongside Denise Mignucci.

"Excuse me Miss," said the driver after he rolled down his window. His facial features looked distorted through the pantyhose stocking covering it. From what Denise could tell, he was a white male, between 30 and 40 years old. He also wore a dark- colored baseball cap, and a dark sweatshirt. "Can you help me?"

Denise's heart began to pound as she stepped back from the jeep.

"I'm s-sorry, but I'm late for my bus," she said, and quickened her pace. A major street lay half a block away, and she figured she'd be all right if she could get there.

The Jeep sped up past her on her right. It then pulled up partially on the curb, blocking her path. In her nervousness, she didn't notice the dented sedan that was parked across the street. The sedan's driver opened the door and eased out unnoticed.

"Oh my God!" Denise yelled, trying to maneuver around the Jeep.

The homeless man sprinted toward Denise, quickly covering large chunks of ground.

"On the move toward you Alpha Two!" the homeless man said as he ran and pressed the small microphone piece onto his neck.

The jeep's driver jumped out. He wielded a large hunting knife in his right hand. He wore a heavy parka and black leather gloves.

"Get into the car – now!" the man ordered, rushing toward Denise. He was certain her screams would go unnoticed. Soon she'd be like rest of his women. He'd fooled the jury. That, and the harassing letters his friends had sent to some of the jurors scared them into finding him not guilty. He was sure of it. Then, he'd kept a low profile, and went off the grid.

Now his wait was over, and he was back in business.

The homeless man was now in a full run, crouching low, but covering the distance between him and Denise quickly. At the same time, the sedan driver crossed the street and positioned himself behind the Jeep. He waited, scanning the area for potential witnesses or the police.

"Help! Someone help me please!" Denise screamed, as she tried to run the away from the attacker.

In her haste, she barely saw the homeless man behind her. The man hurtled past her toward her attacker with the knife. In less than the time it took for her to turn around and see what was happening, the homeless man was on the attacker in front of her.

Surprised, the man with the knife tried to slash the homeless man who sprinted toward him.

Easily avoiding the knife, the homeless man sent a perfect front kick with his right leg to the knife-wielder's left knee. His knee snapped at a grotesque angle, bone and tearing tendons. The knife-wielder shrieked in agony and grabbed his knee as he hit the pavement.

He dropped the knife.

The homeless man easily disarmed the attacker after that.

"We knew you'd be here tonight, Melnick, the homeless man said."

He then grabbed the crumpled attacker by the back of his parka and dragged him toward the Jeep.

"Computer spyware on your laptop, and good old fashioned surveillance led us to you!" the man said crouching over Melnick's prone form. "You may have fooled the system, but you did not fool justice! Tonight, you will know what it's like to feel real pain. After that, you will pray to die."

The sedan driver, a smaller compact man, was now outside the truck standing by the open trunk hatch. He scanned the block once more to see if anyone was coming.

The homeless man lugged the would-be rapist from the sidewalk into the street. "What are you gonna do with me?" the injured man groaned.

Despite the injured attacker's struggles, the homeless man was surprisingly strong. The sedan driver met them both at the back of the attacker's jeep.

"We got ya now, fool," the man at the Jeep said as he helped lift the attacker inside. The smaller man seemed to be made of iron and had the strength of two men.

"You gon' answer for yo' crimes, fool!" he said as he quickly hog-tied the injured man's hands and feet with some duct tape he carried. Both men hoisted the injured man up and into the back of the jeep.

Then the smaller man slammed the rear hatch shut and jumped into the sedan, while the taller man got into the driver's side of Melnick's Jeep.

A few moments later, they were all gone. The entire ordeal took less than a few minutes.

Denise Mignucci stood shaking against a nearby wall during the entire episode. She heard sirens in the distance, but doubted they were coming her way.

* * *

The street was just as deserted as before.

Shaken, she made her way back to the diner, suddenly needing some hot coffee.

She dialed her brother's number.

CHAPTER NINETEEN

FEBRUARY 3rd, 9:15 A.M.

"The M.E.'s Office estimated the time of death at approximately 5:25 a.m. some time yesterday," said the uniformed officer with the crew cut. He glanced down at the report he held.

"However," he continued, "from the looks of the body, I'll bet the guy wished he'd died earlier than that. Somebody really brutalized him."

Luke and Sisco were working the 8 a.m. – 4 p.m. shift today, when Luke took the radio call a half hour ago of a dead body found down at the city's sports complex. The morning maintenance crew had found it in a dumpster behind the arena during a shift change. At first, the maintenance worker thought it was rotting meat because of all the black flies that buzzed near the lid.

When he opened the dumpster, however, he knew otherwise.

After processing the scene, Sisco and Luke came to several conclusions. First, whoever dumped the body had unusual access to the arena's lot – which was normally off limits to non-employees. Second, none of the victim's personal items had been taken. This ruled out robbery as a possible motive. Third, the body appeared to have been tortured extensively. Both detectives noted the visibly-broken limbs on the body.

Later, the medical examiner would discover the victim's testicles had been crushed, apparently while the victim was still alive. Considering the condition of the body, this was definitely not a routine homicide.

Motive became a bit clearer after the body was ID'd as Richard Melnick, the man recently charged as the Black Glove Rapist. His driver's license and other identification were in his wallet when his body was found.

"Maybe one of the victim's family members caught up with him and paid him back," Luke said as he examined the crime scene.

"After that so-called 'trial', it's a wonder some of the victim's families haven't tried to take out some of those jurors as well," Sisco replied.

In Melnick's most recent case, a jury came back with a 'Not Guilty' verdict after a two week trial where there was no solid identification of the rapist because he allegedly wore pantyhose or some type of mask over his face. Furthermore, there was no DNA evidence linking him to the five brutal rapes.

He also allegedly wore black leather gloves during the rapes.

Prosecutors, however, appeared to have an overwhelming amount of circumstantial evidence linking Melnick to the crimes.

First, all the attacks occurred in South Philadelphia not far from Melnick's apartment.

Second, Melnick matched the physical description of the rapist – a tall Caucasian male with a jagged scar on the left side of his neck.

Third, an SUV matching Melnick's was seen in the area at the time of the crimes. The Commonwealth also presented evidence to the jury that Melnick had a prior sexual assault conviction.

The jury deliberated for only two hours after seeing two weeks' worth of evidence. This led some to wonder if they had been tampered with. Both Sisco and Luke had heard rumors that several female jurors had received death threats.

Whatever the reason, Melnick ultimately beat the cases.

"Is that his truck," Luke asked, pointing to the Jeep parked a few yards from the dumpster. "I'll check it out."

Uniformed officers secured the perimeter around the dumpster, but did not have the authority to search the vehicle. That was Homicide's domain, along with Mobile Crimes, which was on its way. The two officers stationed at the Jeep moved aside to allow Luke access.

A tall uniformed officer took down Luke's name and badge number and entered them into the Crime Scene Log book. Luke scribbled his signature on the empty line next to the date and time.

Slipping on latex gloves and plastic booties, Luke duked under the crime scene tape and walked over to the vehicle. He noticed the doors were unlocked. Outside of some visible minor front-end damage, the vehicle was in pretty good physical condition.

Luke opened the driver side door and scanned the interior for any obvious visible evidence. The full interior search and dust for fingerprints would be done later, after the Jeep was towed to the police impound garage.

He was amazed at how clean the vehicle was. There was no trash on the floor, no visible smudges on the windows. Even the seats looked recently polished. It was so pristine inside that Luke was almost certain the car had recently been professionally cleaned.

Most disturbing, though, was the small plastic baggie Luke discovered on the passenger side floor. It contained a small white card with a gold border.

He gently lifted the bag by the corner with his left index finger and thumb, he placed it inside a larger plastic baggie with an property receipt number sticker on it.

He read the card.

"*Upon the wicked He shall rain snares, fire and*

brimstone and an horrible tempest; this shall be the portion of their cup. Psalm 11:6."

He placed the bag in his coat pocket and headed toward the dumpster.

"So, maybe someone just carjacked him for the joyride, and then took him out to prevent any witnesses," Sisco said after Luke came over. "Serves him right for brutalizing, excuse me *allegedly* brutalizing, those women."

"Normally, that wouldn't be a bad guess," Luke said, pulling the bag from his coat and handing it to Sisco. "But riddle me this Batman: You think those carjackers would be diligent enough to wipe the inside clean and leave a small card with a bible verse on the floor?"

Sisco took off his hat and rubbed the back of his head. He didn't even need to ask if the card had a gold border on it.

CHAPTER TWENTY

February 4ᵗʰ, 11:30 AM...

Beck had been in Homicide for nearly six months. Unlike the Major Trials Unit, where the Courtroom action was almost daily, Homicide was much slower.

While there were hundreds of murder cases, these cases usually only went to trial, if at all, after lengthy investigations. Outside of the few cases he had brought with him from the Major Trials Unit, Beck's caseload in Homicide so far had been light.

So, when he received the Raheem Motley casefile, Beck wasn't surprised. He had already handled a few of Rachman's cronies' cases, and now he'd have to determine who actually killed Rachman.

In the Homicide Unit, the Assistant District Attorneys normally handled two types of cases: cases with actual suspects, and cases where a suspect had not been arrested. The latter required the ADA to basically babysit the file and work along with the Homicide Detectives assigned to the case.

Beck scoured the Rachman file carefully, reading

each document inside several times and taking notes. He had been in touch with Siscowicz and Lucas, the Homicide Detectives assigned to the case. From what he'd heard, they were two of the best homicide detectives around. So far, all they had was general information on the case.

The most confusing aspect of the Rachman murder was the discovery of a small white card with a Bible verse found inside his jacket. What confounded Beck the most about the card was that Rachman didn't appear to be religious at all. So, it was odd that he'd have a verse from the Bible in his pocket.

Beck reviewed the Rachman file so many times, that he knew the case cold. While motives and suspects seemed abundant, evidence of the killer (or killers) was almost non-existent.

Here is what evidence they did have: a dead body, a small card inscribed with a scripture verse and any number of people who wanted to kill Rachman. The assigned Detectives had talked to some people in the area of the murder, but no one wanted to give them a statement. In fact, a few neighbors even expressed a sense of relief when they heard Rachman was dead.

Beck had gleaned some choice information on what little evidence he had in the file.

For example, whoever killed Rachman was a strong individual, as evidenced by the cause of death: a broken neck. The killer or killers left almost no clues because there was no weapon used. All the detectives managed to get from the body were a few coat fibers, which were sent to the crime lab.

So far, the fibers led to nothing.

In fact, the murder was so quick and efficient that Beck thought the killer might be a professional. The killer also apparently knew Rachman, or at least made the drug dealer feel comfortable enough to get close to him.

"Maybe it was a drug deal gone bad, or an assassination?" Beck talked to himself as he flipped through the casefile documents for what seemed like the hundredth time.

Since there was no evidence of an entry or an exit wound on Rachman's body, Beck was confident that a broken neck was the primary cause of his death.

According to the medical examiner, the damage done to the body indicated the killer was left-handed. He'd deduced this from the angle of the neck and the vertebrate damage. This was a key detail, since there were no fingerprints to lift.

The assigned detectives had pulled Rachman's phone records from the day of his murder, as well as a few days prior. In addition to recurring calls to and from his family and crew, detectives discovered calls from legitimate sources.

However, one call placed to Rachman a day before, piqued their interest. It was the only unregistered number, likely from a "burner" phone, or throwaway phone. People used these unregistered phones so their calls cannot be traced.

Could this call have been from Rachan's killer?

The phone rang, breaking Beck's concentration.

"District Attorney's Office. This is Assistant D.A. Beck Stephens."

"Counselor, this is Detective Siscowicz. We got some more info on the Rachman job. It could be a possible link".

"How so?" Beck asked.

"Well, you know we found that Bible verse card in one of his jackets?" Sisco reminded. "That card was wrapped inside a small sandwich baggie."

"I remember," Beck responded.

"So, The Black Glove Rapist killing is our job, too. And, when we processed that crime scene, we found another white card inside a plastic baggie. This time with a verse from the Book of Psalms. Found it on the passenger seat of the Jeep. We traced the Jeep back to Richard Melnick."

Beck was silent. *Two cards, two bodies*, he thought. *Awfully similar to be a coincidence*

"You still there?" Sisco asked.

"Yeah, I'm here?" Beck said. His head swirled with the significance of this new find. "Any prints on the card?"

"None," said Sisco. "The laminated cardstock doesn't seem to hold a good print. Not only that, if the killer wore gloves, we wouldn't get a print anyway. Besides, the inside of Melnick's jeep was cleaner than a hospital operating room."

"Thanks for the call, detective," Beck replied. "Let's talk tomorrow so I can make arrangements to take a look at the new evidence."

FEBRUARY 5TH
4:30 pm

Sisco and Luke had ended their shift, but they wanted to make sure they reviewed the evidence file on Baby Mike before they left for the day. While his death was still being ruled as "Natural Causes", both detectives had a nagging feeling that there was more to it.

"Was this dude a drug dealer or a pack rat?" Luke remarked as he cut open the large sealed plastic bag from inside the box. "Didn't he have a home?"

He and Sisco tracked down Det. Bosco, the assigned Detective on Baby Mike's case, earlier in the evening to get his evidence file. Once Bosco learned of the medical examner's findings, he was all too happy to let Luke and Sisco take a look.

Both sat down at a long table in one of the unit's conference rooms. They began to go through the large box.

The gun, ammunition and money were all stored in separate units in the evidence room on the 12th

Floor of the Philadelphia Police Administration Building.

Luke carefully took the items out making sure to account for each of the items listed on the lengthy poperty receipt inside.

"Mike must have also been the money man for Rachman," Sisco said as the combed through the documents. "Look at all of these tally sheets."

He flipped through several handwritten notes and calculations which appeard to document drug weights and prices. Luke concentrated on a smaller pile of papers.

He stopped as he came to a small laminated card with a gold border the size of a business card. It was inadvertently sandwiched between two other pieces of paper.

It was inscribed with a Bible verse.

"For the wrath of God is revealed from Heaven against all ungodliness and unrighteousness of men, who by their unrighteousness suppress the truth. – Romans 1:18."

Luke flipped the card over and saw the familiar serial numbers in bottom left corner.

"Damn," Sisco said. "They match the ones we took off Melnick and Rachman. And no one found a bullet hole, knife wound or nothing on Mike?"

Luke leaned back in his chair and continued to study the card.

"Hell," Luke said, clearly frustrated, "maybe they just scared him to death."

11:30 p.m.

"Miriam, please call your mother back. She called when I was on the other line."

Judge Manigault put the cordless phone on the sink, then squeezed some toothpaste onto his toothbrush.

"Did she say what she wanted?" his wife yelled from down the hall.

"Just call her. Then you won't have to cross examine me," he yelled back.

The Manigaults had been in their home for the past thirty years. The Judge, then a tough civil rights attorney, had scooped up the property quickly after a realtor friend told him about it. The fact that it was in the Germantown section of Philadelphia didn't hurt, either. One of the city's most diverse neighborhoods, Germantown offered Manigault a chance to establish city residence in his run for a judgeship.

The sturdy brick and stone home was one of the largest on the block. It also had an ample back yard and enclosed front porch. Manigault and his wife liked the home's old country feel.

In addition, Manigault liked the fact that the street bordered on some questionable neighborhoods.

He felt he was a man of the people; thus, he eschewed a home alarm, or even bars on his windows. Manigault felt his reputation for "being down" with some of the more unsavory elements in the community was enough the keep him and his family safe.

Manigault heard the old hallway stairs creak as his wife ambled up with his milk.

Taking the mug from Miriam, Manigault nodded his thanks. She settled into bed next to him and turned off the nightstand lamp.

"Irving," she said, "you ever think that maybe it's time to consider retiring? I mean, you can always go back to teaching."

Manigault shook his head in the dark.

"Retiring isn't even on the radar for me right now, Miriam. Not even close."

"It's just that you're always under so much pressure," said fluffing her pillow. "Whether it's the media, or the DA's Office, it's like they blame you for all the crime and evil out there. You're only doing your job."

"I'll be fine, dear," he said. "I'm the hedge out there preventing these damn cops from running amok. The citizens need me on the bench. I'm not afraid of anything or anybody at work or on the street."

"How can you be so sure?" she asked.

"Trust me, Miriam. Rest easy, dear. Just rest easy."

****

FEBRUARY 6TH, 1:15 AM

Without a doubt, Judge Irving Manigault's house was one of the largest and most beautiful homes on the block. Built during the 1950s, its architecture was astounding. Solid stone foundation, brick structure, the home spoke of a simpler time in Philadelphia's history.

The old Victorian-style home had no central air conditioning, nor an alarm system. Manigault however, had window unit air condtioners in several rooms. The homes was also heated the old-fashioned way: a system of radiator pipes and ducts.

Manigault saw no need for a home alarm security system since no one had ever tried to break into the home since they bought it.

Prior to entering the home, the short, but compact intruder cut the phone lines by disabling the phone box outside. The intel from the network said Manigault still used landlines in his home despite having a cell phone.

The intruder carefully picked the lock on the basement window. He had to take his time disabling the painted-shut latch. He was careful not to let the large window creak when he finally opened it.

The intruder quickly shined his pencil-thin flashlight into the opening to see what lay below inside the basement. He carefully slipped into the open window and landed softly on the cheap carpet which covered the basement floor.

From what he could see with the night-vision goggles, the basement appeared to fully-finished. Furniture was spread out in the basement, which was fairly large.

"I'm in. Copy that Alpha Two," he whispered into the small thin microphone alongside his cheek. This was attached to his walkie-talkie headset which fit over his night-vision goggles.

"Copy that Alpha One," replied a voice from inside his headset. "The block out here is quiet. No police activity."

In reality, the intruder's partner was sitting outside in a black car with tinted windows a few houses away. He monitored the police activity with the sophisticated laptop he had in front of him.

The intruder inside Manigault's home scanned his surroundings. He crouched inside the foyer for a few minutes and hoped the residents were hard sleepers.

He felt the slim knife in the sheath strapped to his thigh.

In addition to the goggles and headset mic, the intruder was dressed in a black half ski mask, all black fatigues and soft-soled black boots. He blended in well with the home's shadows. He also wanted to make sure no one was in the living room.

The intruder paused to pick up the house's *feel*. All homes had one. From the creaks in the door, to the settling of the foundation, each building has its own life.

All one had to do was listen to it.

Letting his vision adjust to the dark, the intruder eased the back window closed, then scanned the layout.

He ascended up the carpeted basement stairs quickly, and ended up in the kitchen. Luckily he didn't have to worry about a door, as there was no door separating the kitchen from the basement.

He left the kitchen and entered the large dining room.

The information he'd gotten from the network on the layout of the house was correct.

The front door of Manigault's home led into the main foyer, with the living room on the left, and the dining room on the right. Directly in front was the huge winding staircase, leading up to the other two levels of the three-story home.

In the back was the kitchen and a small playroom.

Even in the dark, the intruder could make out the expensive antique furniture.

The intruder moved nimbly across the oriental throw rug on the floor, resting his weight on the balls of his feet.

He reached the stairs and silently made his way up to the second floor. Fortunately, the stairs were carpeted. Still, there was no way to avoid the stairs creaking entirely. He made sure to test each stair, feeling where the wood was weakest and then treading elsewhere.

The intruder froze when a police car's siren blared outside. He fought to keep his breathing regulated as the piercing wail reached its crescendo, then subsided as the car passed by the home and sped down Lincoln Drive.

After a few minutes, he made his way to the main bedroom.

Once at the landing, the intruder faced four doors. The main bathroom and a hall closet were on the left, while a small bedroom and the master bedroom were on the right.

The door to the master bedroom was ajar.

Silently entering, he saw the king-size bed in the middle of the room. His boots seemed to sink into the thick carpet. A nightstand to the left of the bed held a small alarm clock and phone. On the right stood a large armoire. A loveseat hugged the far left corner farthest from the door.

The figures on the bed barely moved as the intruder silently made his way toward them.

He was careful not to touch anything on the nightstand as he bent down and placed a small plastic bag next to the clock. Then, kneeling next to the sleeping figure, the intruder slid a small, but very sharp knife, from his thigh sheath and raised it over the sleeping man's head.

"You done perverted God's laws," he whispered. "You think justice is a joke, letting them murderers free."

He worked quickly and expertly, barely touching the pillow.

"Now, Judge Manigault, hear the Word of the Lord."

4:45 A.M.

"Now tell me this again, Judge. Somebody broke into your home and did what?"

Detective Maurice Candelaria asked Judge Irving Manigault for what seemed like the tenth time. Both were seated at Candelaria's desk inside Northwest Detectives Headquarters.

"Are all you cops dumb?" said the Judge. "I just told you what happened! Some nut broke into my house and cut off my phone and some of my hair. I found it about two hours ago when I got up to use the bathroom. It was taped to the mirror inside an envelope."

"What else did you find?" The Detective asked, writing down what the judge said.

"Like I told you, for the eighth time, I found an envelope taped to our bathroom mirror. When I opened it, I found a white card and some of my hair," he repeated.

Fingering the card again through the plastic bag, the Detective Candelaria read the verse: *"Acquitting the guilty, and condemning the innocent, God detests them both. Proverbs 17:5."*

"Either you or Mrs. Manigault hurt?" The Detective asked.

"No, but we're still a bit shaken up," Manigault relied. "Who would do something like this? Maybe it's one of your fellow cops with a grudge against me for doing my job."

Or, maybe it's some distraught victim's family member out for vengeance, the detective thought. *They probably watched you let their loved one's scumbag killer walk free.*

"Judge, just a few more questions, and I'll be done."

"Just do whatever you need to, detective," Manigault replied. "Just know that I am not going to let this bastard run me from my home. I've lived there for over thirty years!"

"I understand, sir," the Detective said.

"I want whoever did this to pay. You hear me!"

Yeah, well if he had you hearing his case, he'd never have to worry about that, the Detective thought.

Detective Candelaria completed some paperwork on the case, put the paperwork into the case evidence file and glanced at the clock on the far wall.

It read 4:45 A.M.

It was about an hour ago when Judge Manigault called 911, hysterical over an alleged home invasion that had just occurred. Detectives subsequently brought him and his wife down to Northwest Detectives to talk further about what had happened to them.

Other officers were back at Manigault's home combing it for possible clues.

While none of the officers moved with haste in taking Manigault's report, one of them, Lieutenant Hassan Knight, took special interest after hearing the judge's story.

"Judge, that's all the information I need right now. Mobile Crimes should be finishing up its investigation at your house," Detective Candelaria said.

Candelaria put the notepad in his drawer and capped his pen. He placed the white card back into a plastic baggie, and then into his official case file envelope.

"Why don't you and your wife go on home and try to relax," Candelaria suggested. "Maybe take some time off? If I need any more information from you, I'll call you."

Mangault dismissed the Detective.

"I have no intention of taking any time off. I'll be back on the bench come Monday morning," Manigault vowed.

Same day
3:45 P.M.

"Detective Siscowicz, please call Dr. Vishnu Makrat from the Medical Examiner's office at

215-683-8999 regarding the case of Michael Todd Watkins, case # 28914."

Sisco hit the "Repeat" button on his desk phone again just to make sure he heard it correctly.

"I think they got something on Baby Mike," Sisco said to Luke.

"Maybe the fat boy just fell out with a heart attack," Luke relied. "Hell, he was like 6'2'' and 400 and something pounds. It was probably inevitable." Luke reached into his desk drawer and retrieved his service weapon and holster.

"Had to be some medical condition," Sisco replied. "It's like he just keeled over and died."

"On the same night his boss was being strangled down the block?" Luke responded. "And the cops just happen to find the same type of card on him like Rachmn? That's a helluva coincidence my brother," Luke responded.

Sisco sat down and hit the speed dial button on his cell phone. He didn't bother with the office phone when he had the doctor's number on his cell phone.

Two rings later, Sisco made contact.

"Office of the Medical Examiner, may I help you?" a female voice inquired.

"This is Detective Siscowicz returning Dr. Makrat's call about Michael Watkins."

"I'll get him. Hold on a second."

A few minutes later, the doctor answered.

"Doc?" Sisco asked. "Detective Siscowicz here. I got your message. What's up?"

"Detective, I just finished my autopsy on Mr. Michael Watkins," the doctor replied. Sisco heard papers shuffling in the background.

"I just wanted to go over the report with you before I released it," he continued. "It appears this rather large gentleman was poisoned. Whoever killed him apparently used some type of poisonous dart, needle or something. I place the time of death between 10:30 and 10:40 p.m. on January 17th."

Sisco didn't answer. He decided to let it all sink in first.

He moved the phone away from his ear for a second and motioned for Luke to come over.

"Go on Doc."

The doctor continued.

"Someone managed to pierce the man's neck with this needle or some very sharp object; This was no easy task considering Mr. Watkins' considerable bulk," said Dr. Makrat. "The killer specifically knew that the skin on his neck was likely to be the quickest pathway to his bloodstream. I almost missed it; the hole on the carotid artery was size of a pinprick, but the area started to turn purple and swell slightly after rigor mortis set in."

Sisco held his free hand over the cell phone mouthpiece and whispered to Luke what Dr. Makrat had just said.

"So, apparently two different killers did Mike

and Rachman," Luke mouthed in response. He held up two fingers to Sisco as he talked to the doctor.

Sisco gave him an uncertain look and resumed his conversation with the doctor.

"Doc, any idea what kind of poison killed him?"

"We are still working on that, Detective," Dr. Makrat said. "I sent some samples to our lab, as well as the FBI crime lab for testing. What I can tell you is that whatever the substance, it was very powerful and took Mr. Watkins out quickly. It doesn't look like anything I have really seen around here. The preferred weapon of destruction in this town seems to be the good old-fashioned firearm."

Sisco scratched the back of his head; his mind swirled with questions.

"What do you mean when you say 'around here', Doc?" Sisco asked. "Have you ever treated patients poisoned with this stuff before?"

"As I said before, I don't know exactly what the poison is, but I have treated patients with similar wounds. Years ago, I spent time as a missionary doctor overseas. I dealt with all sorts of people. I remember being in the bush country in Central America where the civil war was fierce. In addition to guns, many soldiers still used poisonous blowdarts on their enemies. These are quick, silent and deadly, and those who use them are usually highly trained. These are no amateurs."

Sisco thanked the doctor and ended the call. The doctor promised to make the report ready for review by the end of the week.

"So, what else did he say," Luke asked.

Sisco sat down heavily.

"This is getting crazy," he said.

CHAPTER TWENTY-ONE

FEBRUARY 6TH, 11:50 P.M...

"Hammond Corp,..Buckley & Bradford, LLC..Wister Pharmacy..."

Sisco went down the list of companies from the Reddington, Mississippi Chamber of Commerce that he had pulled off the Chamber's website.

The card from Melnick's jeep, the card from Baby Mike's vehicle along with the card in Rachman's jacket pocket made Sisco and Luke realize that they may be looking for a serial killer.

The three cards appeared to be similar in size, shape and style. Sisco was determined to find where they were printed in hopes they might shed some light on the killer, or killers.

On the back of each card, written in small print, was the name, "Hastings Religious Specialties, Inc", 2100 White Flower Road, Reddington, Mississippi."

In the bottom far right hand corner on the back of each card was a series of numbers and letters. Sisco guessed it was some sort of serial or volume number. There was no phone number for the company listed on the cards.

Sisco decided to use his evening off to track down this company. Hopefully, it was still in business, and if so, he hoped to find out if anyone had made any recent orders for the cards.

Unfortunately, after scouring the internet for nearly two hours, Sisco found no sign of a business named Hastings Religious Specialties.

He pushed himself from the computer screen, leaned back and put his hands behinds his head.

The house was quiet. His wife Helen had called it a night hours ago. Sisco's teenage daughter Marte' was sleeping over her girlfriend's house for the night.

Their dog Beast settled down in the small space between the refrigerator and the wall. The warmth it generated, combined with the low hum of the worn refrigerator motor made it the perfect spot for the beagle.

Sisco closed his eyes for a minute to reminisce. He had been fighting crime for twenty two years.

Twenty-two long years of late nights, cold take-out, rousting drunks, and crawling into putrid places looking for the bad guys.

Not to mention the two times he was nearly killed.

Along the way, he had managed to find the time to get married, raise a family (and a beagle), and do all the other things that go along with being an adult. From Lieutenant to Detective in less than ten years, Siscowicz had seen the passage of time from behind a badge.

He returned his attention back to the Scripture cards.

What am I missing? He wondered.

Sisco looked down at the brown accordion folder open on the table. Papers and documents spilled forth from it like some disemboweled file cabinet.

He picked up the small white cards and examined them again for what seemed like the thousandth time.

As far as murders went, these seemed anything but garden variety: a dangerous drug dealer found dead in an abandoned field with his neck broken. A brutal rapist beaten, tortured and left dead in a dumpster. No fingerprints, no shell casings, no blood.

No real evidence, except for small white cards placed at the crime scenes.

In their time on the force, Sisco and Luke had encountered few serial killers. Historically, Philadelphia had not been a breeding ground for them. After talking to Detectives from other cities, Sisco knew one thing for certain: Serial killers were meticulous and methodical.

If so, he and Luke had some tough cases on their hands.

CHAPTER TWENTY-TWO

FEBUARY 8th, 1:05 A.M.

The wind was vicious as Beck turned the corner to Serene's block.

Beck was lucky this evening, as if by some miracle, a choice parking space awaited them almost directly in front of Serene's door. Beck eased his car into the spot with room to spare in the front and back.

Beck turned off the vehicle and walked around to help Serene out. He struggled to keep the door from whipping about in the wind.

"You coming in?" asked Serene as she pulled her scarf tighter around her neck.

"Of course," Beck said. He took her hand and walked her up the short stairway to her front door.

Dark-skinned with an inviting smile and flawless complexion, Serene Amber Douglas first caught Beck's eye at a church function six years ago. At 5 feet 4 inches, slim and toned, she was the Keystone State Gymnastics champion in several events years ago while in college. Her intelligence made her even more beautiful.

Serene noticed some hestation in Beck.

"What's up Beck?" Serene asked.

He stood behind her as she opened the door.

"This Rachman file is getting to me," he said. "I know it's late, but I think I need to compare it against some of this new evidence the detectives found."

Once inside the small, but cozy row-house, Serene disarmed the home security system. She dropped her keys on the table next to the small lamp by the door, then took off her heavy coat.

She turned on the CD player on the small entertainment center near the door. Classic R&B ballads flowed softly through the speakers.

"You have to go now?" she whispered.

Beck gave Serene another good-bye hug. Beck vacillated between staying and going.

While they had been seeing each other exclusively for almost three years, they'd promised each other they'd remain celibate until they got married. Neither were virgins, but they decided to do things differently and challenge themselves to concentrate on other aspects of their relationship.

They knew sex would eventually come.

Lately, however, Beck was struggling to keep his end of the bargain.

Beck gently pulled Serene toward him and she offered no resistance. Her feminine softness and alluring scent was intoxicating. Minnie Ripperton's "Inside My Love" played on the radio station's "Mellow Midnight" segment, which featured classic old-school R&B slow jams.

"I really should be going," Beck whispered. Even in the darkness, Beck could feel Serene's longing gaze as she snuggled closer to him.

"I'd rather you stayed," Serene said softly.

"Serene, you know what we promised…"

Her kiss silenced him. He had his hands firmly around her hips, fully embracing Serene's warm curves.

With each kiss, Beck knew he was getting farther and farther from the office that evening.

CHAPTER TWENTY-THREE

6:45 A.M.

"Good morning."

Beck felt a pair of soft lips brush his own and heard Serene's sensuous voice. He was almost awake, but the rest of his body took it's time catching up.

"Good morning," Beck responded. He managed to sit upright amid the huge pillows. Serene's couch was as soft as any bed he'd ever slept in.

"What time is it?" he asked.

"Almost seven," she said. "How'd you sleep?" Serene asked, turning on the coffeemaker on the counter.

Her kitchen was small, but spotless. She was dressed in shorts and an old college sweatshirt. Beck's gaze lingered on her hips and slowly moved down the back of Serene's well-developed legs and calves.

"Slept like a baby," Beck said as he joined Serene in the kitchen. He was glad she still kept a pair of her dad's oversize sweatpants around because they fit him perfectly.

"Honey, you know I was not going to let you go back out into that cold last night," Serene said.

Beck stood behind Serene as she cracked some eggs. He gently hugged her around the waist.

Serene was gorgeous. Her hair, cut short on the back and sides, fuller on top, tickled his nose.

Beck gently nuzzled her neck. "And we even behaved ourselves."

"Honey, we made it this time," Serene chuckled. "But we can't keep flying too close to the sun. Eventually, we're going to get burned."

She was right, of course.

Beck felt the same way. Still, he was glad (though he had a hard time admitting it at first), that their promise was still intact after last night. Watching Serene go up to her bedroom alone was bittersweet, but, he knew they'd made the right decision.

"How is your case coming?" Serene asked between sips of green tea. Beck, seated across the dining room table from her, fipped though a magazine.

"Still gathering evidence," he replied. "I have a little bit of evidence, but a lot of possible suspects. There are a whole bunch of folks who probably wanted this fool dead."

Serene put down her cup and walked over to Beck. She kneeled down next to him.

"Honey, do you ever pray before you work on these cases?" she asked. "I mean, do you ask God for guidance when you deal with this stuff?

Beck pondered the question before answering. He felt a heavy issue on the horizon.

"Look. I pray, Serene," Beck replied. "I talk to God enough. I mean, don't always get on my knees, but I know how to pray."

She stood up.

"Beck, whether you realize it or not, you are dealing with more than just people doing bad things," Serene said. "A lot of this is spiritual warfare, and you need guidance to do the right things. Godly guidance to treat everyone fairly, even those who do ungodly things."

8:35 A.M.

Zane had been training for about two hours. On Saturdays, he liked to get up early and work out after his morning prayer and strectching. Today he got up at about 6 a.m., prayed, then stretched for about 30 minutes.

Zane always had a fascination with the martial arts. However, few places in the segregated south offered karate classes – especially Blacks. Whites were not keen on African-Americans practicing ways to defend themselves.

Zane first became aware of the martial arts one

summer morning after seeing Vince, his neighbor's cousin from California, training. Vince was doing what looked like ballet in his cousin Drew's backyard. Drew was practicing with him. Fourteen year-old Zane was entranced as Vince and Drew moved effortlessly through the rhythmic patterns.

"What's that?" Zane asked as he yelled across his grandmother's fence. "I've never seen a boy do ballet. Thought that was for girls."

"It's called karate, man," Vince answered without breaking his routine. "I've been taking karate classes back home in Los Angeles. My dad says a real man should always be able to defend himself."

"Yeah, but you don't have any weapons," Zane yelled back.

"My *body* is a weapon, man," Vince said. "Dig this."

Vince got into a stance, and kicked his right foot into the wall of an old shed. The wall cracked in a spray of wooden shards. It all happened in the blink of an eye. Zane had never seen another human move that fast.

He was hooked.

It wasn't until he joined the military, however, that he was able to learn martial arts.

Once he started, Zane soaked up the training like a sponge. He made it a point to learn many different styles during his military tours overseas, especially in Asia. By the time he left the military, he had earned black belts in various martial arts styles like wing chung, jujitsu and ken-po.

He also became an expert in many "underground" styles that served only one purpose: to efficiently kill another human being.

Zane was also an expert with weapons.

To quality for the U.S. Army Special Forces, Zane had to be able to identify, break down, assemble and use any weapon faster than most soldiers. He was also an expert sniper and was deadly with a knife.

While guns were nice, Zane loved hand-to-hand combat the most. To him, there was something gratifying, almost primal, about close quarter combat. Zane became an expert in inflicting severe pain on the human body with his hands. As a soldier, he took great pleasure in that skill.

Zane was practicing Shotokan Karate today, and was well into the 20th kata, or form, when he heard the door bell ring. He pressed a button on the intercom near the stairs.

"Who is it?" Zane asked into he speaker.

"It's me, Ron."

Zane saw Ron's image through the small video monitor on the far wall of the workout room. This monitor was attached to the hidden surveillance camera mounted over the front door. Zane grinned as he hit another button on the speaker, unlocking the door.

Zane barely heard Ron's light footsteps overheard

as he made his way across the living room toward the basement.

"I see you started without me," Ron said, dropped his gym bag. After removing his heavy parka, he began to stretch. Ron wore his karate gi pants, but had on a tank top under a sweatshirt.

"Man, these days, I need a whole session just to stretch," Zane said. "To get my body ready to train on Saturday, I darn near have to begin warming up on Thursday."

Though his t-shirt was soaked with sweat, Zane resumed his katas. Before long, he and Ron would start sparring. An integral part of their workout, sparring tested their skill against an opponent. Even though they used fake weapons, and pulled their punches, both men still fought hard, honing each other's skills in the process.

A half hour later, Ron finished stretching. He picked up a genuine-looking plastic dagger from a table nearby and approached Zane.

Both men faced each other, then bowed. Zane quickly moved into his opening defensive stance, while Ron assumed an offensive stance with the replica knife held close with his arm across his chest and the knife blade pointed at Zane. This was how a skilled assassin would employ his weapon, and Zane readied himself to parry the attack.

At 58, Zane's reflexes were still incredibly quick. Years of training and combat had honed his skills to a point where his body moved instinctively. For nearly 45 minutes, Ron thrusted and Zane parried with blocks and various punches. The actions were so quick and precise, it looked like they had choreographed the routine.

Ron was no less a skilled martial arts expert. His short stature and wiry frame caused many a bigger man to challenge him, much to their detriment. In his time, Ron had filled up many an Emergency Room, and those were the lucky ones.

The morgue held the unlucky ones.

Ron was nearly all sinewy muscle, and his pain threshold was incredibly high. "I tell my body what to do, not the other way around," is how he explained it.

After an extended session where each man fought blindfolded with the fake knives, both concluded their vigorous training with a series of cool-down exercises.

"Good workout, Zane," Ron said, catching his breath.

"Thanks. You too, Ron. Seems like we're getting better with age, my friend." Zane said, wrapping a towel around his shoulders.

"And, with all that's going on out here, Zane, we'd better be," Ron added. "We don't want none of these fools to catch us slippin'."

9:30 A.M.

After leaving Serene's house, Beck knew he needed to burn off some energy. He headed home to change clothes, feed his dog Hannibal and hit the gym.

Pounding leather was always his escape.

He made his way through West Mt. Airy to The Slaughterhouse, the gym where he learned to box. He couldn't help but be envious every time he drove past the huge Victorian homes along Lincoln Drive, one of Philadelphia's oldest and wealthiest neighborhoods.

A short time later, he cut through 38th Street, then hit Market, driving past Drexel University. Before long he was driving under the elevated train tracks and into West Philadelphia.

The neighborhood had changed since he was a kid. What used to be a thriving marketplace was now merely a strip of run-down liquor stores, fast-food restaurants and check-cashing places.

Beck cruised into a parking space right in front of a weather-beaten building with a worn black sign emblazoned with 60th Street GYM in faded white letters. The Elevated train, or "El", roared overhead.

Beck turned off the engine and zipped up his heavy jacket. He grabbed his gym bag from the back seat and exited the vehicle, locking it remotely from his keyfob.

Numerous black-and-white photos of men in various

boxing poses adorned the walls of the building's lobby. Each bore the autograph of the fighter pictured. They were all there on the wall: Freddie "Haines Street" Bennett, Andrew "The Gangster" Monzatti, and Benilde "Butcher" Ramirez. They were all, at one time, some of the best boxers in the city.

At one time, they had also trained at 60th Street Gym, or more commonly known as "The Slaughterhouse".

Back in the 1930's and 40's, local meat packers used to roll the beef directly off the El overhead into the building, which was known then as the Greater Philadelphia Meat Processing Plant. At one time, it employed nearly 200 people. Tons of chicken and cattle met their demise daily during the Slaughterhouse's heyday.

After World War II, meat processing became more technologically-advanced, and the plant eventually closed. Eager to make whatever he could off the building, owner Edgar Steinman, a local Jewish businessman, began renting out the back of the plant to local youth for their boxing matches. Before long, the Slaughterhouse became the place for budding fighters to test their mettle. Any Philly fighter worth his salt, had, at one time, gone to battle against a Slaughterhouse fighter.

Beck was proud to be a part of that fraternity.

"Stand there too long, son, and you'll never leave." Beck instantly recognized the voice.

"Oh, I can leave, Mojo, trust me," Beck said smiling. "My boxing days are long gone."

Beck turned to the older Black man and gave him a hearty handshake. Mojo was completely bald, clean-shaven and had a small dimple in his chin. Dressed in a gray sweatshirt, jeans and sneakers, he looked like a high school gym teacher.

"You still looking pretty, Mojo", Beck said. "Better leave those young girls alone, man. Your old heart can't keep up!"

"Look, son," Mojo said with a lecherous grin, "you can't get outta life alive, so you might as well die doin' what you love."

"You still a crazy old man."

They both laughed, and headed down the hallway. In his heyday, Morris A. Phillip Randolph Jones, aka Mojo, was one of the toughest and best trainers in the city. In his youth, he was a pretty solid fighter, compiling a career record of 50 wins and 15 losses, with a number of knockouts. After his boxing career was done, he moved into training up-and-coming fighters.

Mojo met Beck nearly three decades ago, when Beck was just a skinny kid who fought too much at school. Because the kid fought daily, he spent more time in the principal's office than the principal. Beck's gym teacher, a buddy of Mojo's, sent Beck to the Slaughterhouse. He figured that if the kid had an outlet for his energy, he'd fight less at school.

He was right.

Over time, Morris developed Beck into a tough southpaw with quick hands, good enough in fact to win a Golden Gloves championship, and even go on to a brief pro career.

Years later, he and Beck still remained close.

In the gym there was a huge boxing ring built in the center of the room. Off to the side was a wall of mirrors. In front of the mirrors were long punching bags, suspended from individual metal hooks. Not long ago, the hooks were used to hang up pieces of freshly-killed beef. Beyond the ring on the other side was a large space for skipping rope, and next to that were three smaller punching bags. These were used for practicing speed and agility.

"Hey Mo, you hear anything else about the Rachman killing?" Beck asked, slipping off his sweatshirt, and tossing it on his gym bag sitting on the empty bench next to him.

Mojo just shrugged and climbed into the ring.

"You gonna let me know if you do, right?" Beck said pulling on his t-shirt. "Whatever you can dig up would be appreciated."

Beck took a long elastic cloth strip from his bag and began to wrap his hands. His hands were unusually large for his size and fast. They kept him competitive during his boxing career.

While not totally scarred, his hands, especially his knuckles, had noticeable dark spots where callouses had formed after years of training and boxing.

"Them hands, man. Them hands." The old trainer beamed at Becks' hands as though they were works of art.

Beck grinned and kept wrapping his hands.

"Whew! Them hands is what made you," Mojo said. I tell you, son, you sho' knew how to throw that left hook."

"You taught me well," Beck replied.

The old trainer had taught Beck all the tricks of the trade to give him an extra edge: like keeping his hands tight at all times, keeping a little extra tape bunched up in Beck's palms to give him a better grip inside the gloves and dipping his taped hands in icewater to harden the tape just before putting on the gloves.

He even taught him how to step on an opponent's toes during a fight to keep them off balance. The techniques may not have all been exactly legal, but that was why boxing was not for the fainthearted.

Beck took a worn jump rope out of his bag and started to slowly skip rope. The light staccato tapping of the rope made it's own melody.

"Ever miss it?" Mojo asked, leaning on the ring's ropes. He looked down at Beck. "I mean, do you ever think what might have been if you had stayed in the fight game?"

"Nope", Beck said. "Don't get me wrong, I loved boxing, I truly did. But I knew when I walked away it was the right thing to do."

Beck inceased the tempo of his rope skipping.

"Besides, Mo," Beck continued, "you were there at my last fight with June Bug. You remember what happened."

Mojo grunted.

"Let it go Beck," Mojo said. "Just let it go. Things like that happen in the ring! Boxing is a dangerous sport. You need to make peace with that thing, son."

The old trainer shook his head, turned and climbed down from the ring. He walked toward his office a few feet away.

He suddenly stopped short and turned back to Beck.

"Take some advice from an old man! Put that thing to rest, son and do it soon," Mojo said, lowering his voice.

He shook his finger at Beck.

"Them demons don't stop once you let 'em in," he continued. "I know. They put down roots in your soul, and once that happens, you ain't never gonna have no peace."

CHAPTER TWENTY-FOUR

11:00 a.m.

By the time Beck had finished skipping rope and finishing his abdominal workout, the gym was alive with activity. Fighters hit the heavy bag, some skipped rope, while others worked on their footwork. The odor of sweat and ointment hung in the gym like the various banners on the walls.

Beck found an open heavy bag and began to practice his punches. Working slowly, he alternated between right jabs and overhand left combinations. While it had been years since Beck last stepped into the ring, he still maintained some of his boxing skills.

As he settled into his workout, Beck felt a comfort wash over him. Try as he might to distance himself from this world, Beck missed the sport even more than he'd realized.

"You look like you can still go a few rounds, Beck," said a husky voice behind him.

Beck turned to see a heavyset man in sweats and

boxing shoes walk toward him. At 6 foot 4, and a strapping two-hundred and thirty pounds, he looked as if he could bend steel with his bare hands.

Shirtless, the man had the kind of muscle tone only obtained through hard labor. Prison labor, to be exact.

"My man Beck!" he said.

"What's going on Tito? Beck replied, stopping his workout.

Both fighters then stood facing each other and shook hands. Beck gave up more than a few inches in height to Tito.

"How you been T?" Beck asked, wiping his face with the back of his hand.

"I'm good," Tito replied. "I just got out of Camp Hill a while ago, and I'm staying positive, know what I mean?"

"That's good, Tito. I'm glad to hear that." Beck put his hand on the big boxer's shoulder. "We don't need brothers like you locked up. We need you out in the community doing positive things and showing these young kids how to live right."

"I hear you in Homicide now," Tito said. It was more of statement than a question. "I bet you like that, huh?"

"Well, you know, it's alright," Beck said. "It's a chance for me to try some bigger cases. Get some of these real fools off the streets."

Tito began to pound a heavy bag next to Beck's. Each of his punches seemed harder than the last.

Beck lowered his voice and moved closer to Tito. "If you hear anything on Rachman, you'll let me know, right? I'm handling his murder case."

Tito stopped abruptly and looked around to see if anyone had heard Beck.

"You trying to get me killed?" Tito asked, nearly whispering. "I ain't no damn snitch. And even if I was, I wouldn't care two cents who killed Rachman."

Then, he leaned in closer to Beck.

"Beck, Me and you is cool,'cause we from the Slaughterhouse," Tito said. "So I will drop this on you: Some crimes can be solved. Others don't need to be."

He paused momentarily, glanced around quickly ad continued.

"Word on the street is that Rachman was taken out by some cats that you D.A.'s have no clue exist. They called the Scarlet Cord, and believe me these mofos are scarier and more dangerous than Rachman could ever be. Dudes in prison used to talk about this like underground vigilante network operating in the city."

"Did you ever hear any specific names?" Beck asked.

Standing so close, Tito towered over Beck.

"Nah, no names," he replied. "Hell, dudes too scared to even talk about the Cord. Like they afraid there may be some members inside the prison."

"The Cord?" Beck asked. "What the hell is that?"

Tito glanced around again, then leaned down to Beck.

"Part urban myth, part urban truth, no one is really sure. But what is true is that a number of those unsolved murders of some of these thugs ain't all neighborhood beefs. Word has it that the Cord is looking to do what these sorry cops and prosecutors can't: clean up the streets by any way possible. No offense."

Beck stepped back and blew air through his cheeks. His mind spun with the ramifications of this news.

11:30 A.M.

"They look like the same cards. Same size, shape, style," Sisco said, turning over the plastic baggies containing the two cards.

Luke sat across from Sisco who was hunched over his desk examining the evidence. The fact that this was the weekend meant nothing to the Homicide Unit, which was already buzzing with activity.

"I wonder if the company still even exists?" Luke asked.

Sisco looked up at his partner.

"The $64,000 question is 'What are we dealing with? Religious serial killer? Spiritual vigilante? Or just some nut who wants media attention?"

"Probably a little bit of all the above," Luke

said. "Let's look at what we do have. Three dead thugs, who were: A notorious drug lord, his bodyguard and a serial rapist. None of them were shot, so no fired cartridge casings to compare."

Sisco fingered the cards in front of him.

"And, aside from the different Scripture verses, three nearly identical cards found at each crime scene," Sisco added. "Was Rachman ever in front of Judge Manigault?"

"Who do you think discharged his case?" Luke said.

Sisco thumbed through Rachman's case file. He reviewed the dead thug's lengthy criminal record.

"How in the world did that psychopath avoid doing any hard time?" he asked.

"Slick lawyers, inefficient judges and dead witnesses, my brother," replied Luke. "Rachman had Wayne Cummings for one of his murder trials. When Cummings was through picking apart the Commonwealth's witnesses - who were all drug dealers themselves - the jury wasted little time finding him Not Guilty."

Luke got up to pour a cup of coffee.

"Sisco, where's the sugar? You fasting or something?" Luke asked, scrounging around on the desk next to the coffee maker.

Sisco shrugged.

"Helen's been on this healthy foods thing," Sisco said. "No processed sugar, no white bread, none of that."

"And the problem with that would be what?" Luke responded. "She's trying to keep you around, old man," Luke joked. "I'm gonna grab some raw sugar from down the hall. I'll be right back."

After Luke left, Sisco picked up the cards again. Comparing the cards, he noticed each serial number ended with the letter J. No matter how different the serial numbers were, the "J" remained constant. He copied them down.

A moment later, Luke strode into the office holding his coffee cup.

"If we have a genuine serial killer, the Captain may have to call in the feds. You know that, right Sisco?"

"I know," Sisco said. "I told Sarge about the cards. He also knows that if this goes upstairs, the feds will get involved. But, I get the feeling that the department isn't trying to rush that step."

"Why not?" Luke asked. He leaned across Sisco's desk and picked up one of the cards.

"Because the press has been killing us on crime lately," Sisco replied. "As bad as the city's crime rate is, the media is making us out to be the bad guys because they feel we haven't solved as many murders as they'd like."

Sisco drummed his fingers on his desk.

"The department is taking the bad press on the chin, and we're doing all we can, but you know this is an election year, and -"

"And the Mayor doesn't want to look like he needs outside help handling business in his own city," Luke finished.

"So calling in the feds won't happen anytime soon. Unless things really start to get crazy."

"Which they just might, Bruh," Luke added. "They just might."

* * *

It was nearly noon when Beck got home from the Slaughterhouse. Windswept gray clouds dotted the sky, ushering in a sharp cold wind. Beck wanted to look over the Rachman file, and use the court database, otherwise he would have taken the day to rest.

His parents moved to West Mt. Airy from West Philly when he and his sister Delacy were teenagers. After his dad went to jail, and his mom died, Beck wasn't sure if he should keep the house or sell it. Between the good memories of his mother, and the bad ones of his father, he wasn't sure if the house was worth the emotional effort needed to maintain it. In the end, Beck decided to move in.

Delacy did not object. She subsequently moved to Atlanta after graduating college.

Unlocking the front door, Beck heard the sharp bark from behind the house.

Hannibal knows when I'm home, that's for sure,

Beck thought as the familiar warmth and smell of home greeted him.

He moved through the house to the back window. There, Beck saw his dog running frantically back and forth. More Belgian Mallinois than Rottweiler, Hannibal was big and solid for his breed. Beck remembered when he saw the dog two years ago at the animal shelter. He was the smallest pup in the place, but the most active. Beck was drawn to him when he looked into the pup's eyes and saw a fire that matched his own. He took him home that day. Hannibal was one of the smartest dogs Beck had ever met.

Today, though, Hannibal was also one of the hungriest.

Beck made the short walk downstairs to the basement, and to the back door leading to the yard.

"I know, boy, I know. Where's breakfast, right?

Beck knelt down and scratched behind Hannibal's ears. "I should have fed you before I left. I didn't think you'd be hungry. I guess I was wrong."

Beck let the dog in, and followed him into the small, sparsely-furnished basement. Grabbing a huge bag of dog food, Beck poured out a solid mound into Hannibal's bowl.

"Start on this 'til I get back," he said.

Beck bounded up the stairs into the kitchen and located the half-open can of high-protein chunky dog food. Grabbing that and a huge wooden spoon from the top of the cabinet, he walked back downstairs. Beck found Hannibal following the bowl around the room as he ate ravenously.

Beck managed to move Hannibal's face out of the way long enough to pour in the remaining contents of the can.

"I'm going to shower, Hannibal," Beck said, as he made his way up the basement stairs to the bathroom. "And stay off the couch!"

The dog made no indication he'd heard, or even cared, as he continued to feast on breakfast.

Beck stowed his sweaty gym clothes in the hamper, then stood in front of the bathroom mirror.

He took stock of himself.

Although he was largely fit, Beck wasn't proud of his ever-so-slightly expanding midsection. While he was far from fat, he realized that age and a sedentary job had added some inches to his waist. His once-chiseled six-pack was now a moderate four pack.

It wasn't long ago, however, that his abs stood out like a hood ornament. He was so shredded, he could clearly see the veins criss-crossing his biceps and arms. Running ten miles a day and boxing countless rounds certainly kept him in top shape.

After stepping into the shower and soaping up, Beck studied the design on his left bicep. It was the oriental symbol Yin and Yang representing balance. Once a source of pride, the tattoo had lost its luster long ago after Beck began to seriously study God's word.

"You were bought with a price," Pastor Floyd had preached years ago. "That means you have no right marking up your body, because it is not yours."

Beck felt even more guilt as the Pastor's message came the week after he had gotten the tattoo. It cost him four hundred dollars, but, at the time, it was worth it because Taleah Robinson liked it.

She was the hottest girl in his neighborhood. Beck remembered the swing in her hips as she walked past his house to go to the store. After playing hard to get, she finally agreed to go out with Beck to a Keith Sweat concert after two months of his playful flirting. He nearly lost his composure when he saw her in the crowd at one of his fights.

"I bet you'd look fine with a tattoo, especially something exotic like a Chinese symbol," Taleah had cooed to Beck one night after they had been very naughty.

Beck couldn't wait to get one after that. He asked some of the other Slaughterhouse fighters the next day about theirs. The consensus pick was Toronnado's Den, an extotic tattoo shop in Northern Liberties.

He went the next week. His chest swelled with pride as he watched the tattoo artist work on his arm with the electric needle. He thought it was well worth the money.

Turns out Taleah loved it. However, it couldn't save their relationship. They broke up a few weeks later.

I wish mama was here, Beck thought as he stood under the warm shower water. *Lord, it's hard, and even though I try not to, I miss her.* Beck's silent prayer was a plea with which he knew God was very familiar.

CHAPTER TWENTY-FIVE

2:30 P.M.

After examining the Scripture cards, Sisco and Luke hit the streets. The cold kept most folks inside, but all that meant was that people would simply kill each other indoors. The detectives fully expected their Saturday night to be ripe with nightclub shootings, a deadly drug deals or domestic-violence-related killings.

Sisco had just finished off his coffee when his cell phone chirped.

"Detective Sisco. Homicide," he answered.

"Detective, this is Lieutenant Hassan Knight from the Fourteenth," said the voice on the other end. "I got something here that you might be interested in."

"Hey Lieutenant," Sisco said, turning up the worn car heater. "Talk to me."

"Early yesterday Judge Manigault and his wife came barging into the district with a story about a break-in at their home last night."

"Anybody hurt?" Sisco asked.

"Naw, no one was hurt, and nothing was taken," the Lieutenant said. "Scared the mess outta Manigault and his old lady, though. But, the person, or persons left a little present: a small white card with a gold trim. It has a passage from the Bible on the front."

"You're kidding," Sisco said looking over at Luke.

"I'm serious as a heart attack, Sisco. It was taped to Manigault's bedroom mirror, along with some of the Judge's hair."

"You show it to anyone else?" Sisco replied. His mind was racing.

"Only Seargent Gentry was at the front desk when Manigault came in, but he's cool," the Lieutenant said. "Soon as I saw the card, I thought about the one you found on Rachman a few weeks ago."

"How'd you hear about that?" Sisco asked.

"Detectives, you know nothing stays a secret with cops," the Lieutenant said.

"How long will you be down there, Lieutenant?"

"I'm eight to four today," the Lieutenant responded. "I have to serve some warrants in about an hour, but I'll be back by five."

"We're already on our way to you," Sisc said, then hung up.

He turned to Luke.

"We need to go up to the Fourteenth, Luke. They got something for us."

"What is it," Luke asked.

"Another white card with a Bible verse. Luckily no dead body this time."

4:00 pm.

Afternoon naps always brought out the best in Beck.

Beck got home from the gym, showered and then slept for about two hours. While he had initially intended to go into work to review some files, he was glad he had brought the Rachman file home with him. Even though he planned to work on that case, for the most part this Saturday would be a rest day.

The nap refreshed him. He headed downstairs to the living room and clicked on the television.

He eased himself into the recliner. He continued to go over in his mind the Rachman killing and scripture cards. He hoped the television would divert his attention.

All in all, Beck had to admit that life was good so far. His career was going well, his love life was, well, stable, and his spiritual life was getting better. Especially now that he had joined his friend Ozzie's church. Ozzie was the pastor, and Beck liked it so much he was even thinking of joining the men's choir.

It wasn't long before Beck was in a comfortable almost-prone position. As he leaned back, he caught a glimpse of a picture on the mantle that made him smile. It was a faded picture of him with a big jacket draped over his arm, a big backpack on his back, and an even bigger smile.

Beck had just started the fifth grade at Hooper Bates Elementary School in West Philly, and he'd had to fight almost every day that he was there.

* * *

"Welcome to the Hoop, punk."

Beck braced himself on his heels as the older boy pushed him. Gerald Wistrom, also known as June Bug, was the school bully. When Beck stepped back slightly, June Bug got in his face.

"Aw, man, you ain't gonna fight back? You ain't gonna do nothing? You is a punk!" June Bug's gang had fnow surrounded him in the schoolyard. It had been leading up to this all month, his first at the school. While he knew being the new kid was going to be tough, he wasn't expecting this.

"Punch him in the face, June!" It was Paul "P-Nut" Noland, June Bug's second-in-command.

The crowd tightened around Beck. He saw a car pull up to the curb next to the school-yard entrance. The car's radio blared one of the latest urban hits, "It Takes Two," by Rob Bass and DJ Eazy Rock.

Two older boys got out and came toward the crowd. Since June Bug wasn't backing down, Beck accepted the fact that the only way out was to fight. Once he decided that, he tightened his fists and focused on June Bug's big mouth, which was grinning so wide he could see the gap between his two front teeth.

All Beck remembered after that was punching the bigger boy repeatedly, hitting eye sockets, nose and whatever else he could reach. While he was sure June Bug managed to hit him a few times, Beck couldn't feel any pain. That would probably come later.

It always did.

After what seemed like an eternity, Mr. Parsons, the gym teacher, separated the two boys. "Alright! Alright! Both of you, to the principal's office! And, you best believe I'm calling your parents!"

His arms ached and his fists were bruised. Beck assessed the total damage. Outside of the pain in his arms, he had a swollen lip and some cuts on his knuckles.

Overall, he was fine.

June Bug was a different story. His mouth was bloody, and both his eyes were nearly swollen. Beck did all he could not to grin.

"Man, the new guy snuck you June! It wasn't no fair fight!" said another weasley youth who was just happy that June Bug didn't beat him up. By this time, some of the older boys had come over. Two of them inspected June Bug like he was an ancient artifact.

"Aw, cuz, you caught a serious beat down!" one

of the boys said. "Was it that little skinny kid! Aw, man, he ate you up!"

June Bug avoided Beck's eyes. He probably would have cried had no one else been around. His remaining crew dusted him off, mouthing weak words of encouragement.

June Bug finally managed to get up enough courage to speak to Beck as they headed for the principal's office.

"You and me got another fair one going after school tomorrow, punk," he said. "And, this time, I ain't gonna let you sucker punch me."

Beck just smiled to himself. He didn't need to respond. His fists did all the necessary talking.

CHAPTER TWENTY-SIX

FEBRUARY 9TH, 8:00 P.M.

It was early evening when Sisco and Luke left the Fourteenth Police District. They returned to Homicide headquarters to get some additional paperwork and warrants.

Once they picked up the scripture card from Lt. Knight, the detectives knew it matched the three they had already recovered.

Since this new card was evidence in the Manigault case, which was not a Homicide, technically the Detectives could only borrow the card. Then they could compare it to the ones taken from Rachman, Melnick and Baby Mike kilings.

While examining this new evidence in the Scipture Slayings was a priority, the Detectives had other cases to solve. Thus, their top priority this evening was serving various warrants in those cases.

Getting a judge to sign them was another matter.

Normally, it was impossible to find anyone other than the emergency weekend judge to sign an arrest warrant on a Saturday night. However, Luke and Sisco knew Zane was always willing to help out law enforcement, day or night.

Sisco had spoken to Zane earlier that evening and confirmed his availability.

Luke appeared from the small storage closet next to the main office floor. "You got the warrants for Judge Russell to sign?"

"In the envelope," Luke nodded.

* * *

Cruising up Germantown Avenue toward Chestnut Hill was more difficult this evening because of traffic near Mt. Airy Avenue. With all the new jazz clubs and dinner spots in that area, getting past it on a Saturday night was no easy task.

"I would've taken the back way up to the Judge's house. We'd be there already," Luke said.

"Relax, buddy," Sisco said. "I got it. It's a nice evening, so I figured we'd swing by Chew Avenue to see what was going on. Besides, Judge Russell said he'd be in after 9 pm. We've got some time to kill."

At one of the main intersections on Germantown Avenue, Sisco turned left onto a small side street. On the corner about a block away sat D's Sizzle Spot.

A hole in the wall bar with the original neon

sign from the 70's still hanging off the roof, D's was known as a cop's bar. It was run by Lavelle Newby, a former numbers runner who had turned his life around years ago. He ultimately used the proceeds from his numbers-running racket to buy the bar nearly 40 years ago.

Lavelle was also one of the detectives' confidential sources of intel in that area.

Sisco pulled up across the street from the bar. Luke buttoned his overcoat and went inside, while Sisco kept the car running.

The music was loud inside D's as a few patrons milled about around the bar. Stale cigarette smoke mixed with the smell of fried chicken wings from the small kitchen in the back gave the place a basement party feel.

Danny was tending bar. He was a dwarf who looked older than his 50 years. He stood on a padded crate, which raised him up so his torso cleared the bar.

"Big Luke!" Danny greeted the detective. He reached out his right hand to Luke, and continued stacking some glasses with his left hand.

"W'sup Danny?" Luke returned the handshake. "Looks like you getting taller, my brotha," he smiled.

Danny snickered at Luke's comment.

"He ain't here, man," Danny said.

Luke knew he meant Lavelle.

"Ain't come in at all today. Said he had a doctor's appointment."

Luke scanned the bar, then turned toward the door. The regular crowd milled about as the sound system played a mix of contemporary and old-school funk and R&B. As best as Luke could tell, nothing seemed out of order.

"Just tell him we stopped by," Luke said. He reached out and gave Danny a fist pound.

"I'll let him know. Tell my man Sisco I said W'sup."

"Will do," Luke said and headed out the door.

Luke thought for a second, then turned back. He motioned for Danny to meet him in the empty room at the other end of the bar. Dan complied.

He closed the door as soon as Luke got inside.

"Got anything on either the Rachman or Menick murders?" Luke asked.

"Not much," Danny said. "The streets is kinda quiet on these. I don't know for sure, but I don't think no local thug took Rachman out. Same with Melnick. It's like folks too afraid to even talk. Some body, or some people, got these folks spooked."

"Appreciate it," Luke responded by giving Dan a firm handshake and slipped him a twenty dollar bill in the process. "Just let Lavelle know I came by."

Luke left the bar and got back into the passenger side of the uunmarked squad car.

Sisco took off almost simultaneously. As he maneuvered the car through traffic, he noticed how alive the city was at night, especially along the main corridor of Germantown Avenue.

By contrast, the neighborhoods he and Luke usually worked were thriving with drugs and illegal activity. It was if there were two Philadelphias, each one ignoring the other's existence.

* * *

By the time they'd gotten clear of traffic, it was nearly 9:00 p.m. The neighborhood changed considerably as they moved up to Chestnut Hill, an area known for multi-million dollar homes.

Before long, Sisco had guided the car to a spacious home at the end of a quiet cul-de-sac.

Luke rang the bell on the side of the front door.

Zane answered the door within minutes.

"Detectives, come in." Zane shook their hands and ushered them inside. Dressed in a heavy sweater, jeans and soft-soled workboots, Zane closed the door behind them.

"Good evening Judge," Sisco replied. "Thanks for approving these warrants for us. We got a tip that Myron Parker, our favorite arsonist and murderer, may finally be back in town. We wanted to hit him quick before he -,"

"No problem, Detective," Zane said, cutting Sisco off. "Always glad to help take another fool off my streets." He directed them to sit in the living room, then he took the documents to his study.

Inside the spacious living room, Sisco and Luke unbuttoned their overcoats. The detectives were impressed by the exotic Asian and African artwork and expensive furniture. A number of the items looked Oriental. In addition, both couldn't help but notice the number of awards and photos.

Sisco noticed what appeared to be a high school diploma on the trophy case in the far right corner.

"How you guys doin'?" Ron said, rising from the couch to greet them. Ron was clad in a heavy flannel shirt and corduroy pants. He, like Zane, wore soft-soled workboots.

Ron shook Luke's hand then shook Sisco's. Ron was at least a foot shorter than both detectives, but his handshake was vise-like. Luke took note of just how large the smaller man's hands were.

Just then, Zane walked back in and handed the folder to Sisco.

"Thanks again, Judge. We really appreciate it," Sisco said as he and Luke headed for the door.

"Glad to help out. Let me know if you need me to sign any more," Zane said, then he shut the door behind them.

"Did you check out the judge's crib?" Luke asked as he walked down the porch stairs.

"Must be nice to have that kind of money," Sisco said, nodding. "Now you see why people spend so much money trying to get elected to the bench."

"Not to mention that free lifetime parking spot," Luke joked.

Sisco and Luke reached their car parked at the end of the short driveway.

"Did you check out Ron's tattoo?" Sisco asked. "A mongoose with the words 'Serpent Killers' underneath."

"Yeah I saw it as he mangled my hand," Luke replied. "That dude has a grip like a steel trap."

"I've seen it before," Sisco said, pointing the car in the direction of the street, and easing his foot onto the gas.

"It's military."

"How do you know that?" Luke asked.

"When I was overseas, I ran across some guys with that same tattoo," Sisco said.

"Marines?"

"No. We had different tattoos," Sisco responded. "Each platoon and company had their own. My unit had a blazing shovel on our arms. We were the 'Gravediggers'."

"We had tattoos in my unit in the Army, but nothing like that," mused Luke.

"I think it was a Black Ops tattoo," Sisco said.

"Special Forces? Luke asked.

Sisco nodded.

"Those guys are no joke, man," he said. "Stealth killers. Navy Seals, Rangers, Recon Marines, Special Forces. Those guys are all deadly."

Sisco turned the car onto a small back street which ultimately emptied out onto Lincoln Drive.

"So Judge Russell is a Green Beret, huh" Luke said. "That figures. He seems like that type of guy."

"Those guys are trained to infiltrate and live behind enemy lines" Sisco said. "And they could be dug in deep for years, operating with little or no radio contact with the outside. They are expert killers, with or without weapons."

Luke nodded. "I had a buddy in my platoon who told me about some Special Forces soldiers who stayed in Southeast Asia after their tours. They mostly served as bodyguards and security for government officials. Some were mercenaries. Got paid pretty well, too. Apparently many are trained in a lot of underground martial arts and techniques unheard of in this country."

"Mercenaries?" Sisco asked.

"You got it."

"Well, that makes sense," Sisco replied. "Hell, if I needed bodyguards, or needed someone taken out, I'd hire them in a minute."

CHAPTER TWENTY-SEVEN

FEBRUARY 10TH, 3:00 P.M.

Beck took an extra long nap after Church this morning. He might have slept straight through to Monday morning had it not been for Hannibal's incessant bark.

He walked into the bathroom still wearing his sweatpants, t-shirt and robe.

The wall clock read 3:00 P.M.

If he hurried, Beck figured he could shower, change and still make it over to Judge Russell's house by game time. The game started at 4:30.

He remembered that Judge Russell had invited him over today to watch the Eagles-Cowboys football game.

It took Beck less than 30 minutes to shower and slip on his clothes. He pulled on his heavy coat and headed down to the basement.

"Hannibal, come on in buddy." Beck held open the basement door as the big dog scampered inside.

Hannibal found his worn blanket near the heater

and settled in. Beck had filled his bowl with food and his dish with clean water. A warm place to sleep, and plenty of food and drink and Hannibal was good for the night.

Once outside, Beck moved quickly in the the cold afternoon air. As he walked down the steps toward his SUV, he aimed a small black keyfob at the vehicle and clicked it twice. Seconds later, the interior light flickered on, and the engine hummed to life.

* * *

"You have got to be kidding me," Zane said. All three men were lounging in Zane's recreation room munching on pizza.

"Ron, Dallas is nowhere near the best team in the NFC. Are you forgetting about our hometown Eagles?" Zane said between bites of pizza.

"Zane, you crazy!. Philly is okay, but they ain't no Cowboys," Ron chimed in. "Ain't that right?" Ron reached for his can of root beer.

His mouth was full of meat-lover's pizza, so all Beck could do was nod. He wasn't a big football fan. In fact, Beck did not much care for team sports. That's why he preferred boxing.

Zane laughed. "Ron, you always root for the underdog."

"Hey, that's me," Ron nodded. "I'm always like David fighting Goliath."

Beck finished eating, then stretched out on the sofa while Zane and Ron played cards on the small coffee table.

"What they got you working on so far, Beck?" Ron asked without taking his eyes off the card game.

"Let's see: I got a guy who shot his neighbor to death over a barbecue grill. That should probably plead out. Then, I have a double-homicide gang-related case that should be going to trial this summer. Beyond that, though nothing else."

"I take it none of those cases are on my docket?" Zane asked.

"No, Judge," Beck relied. "Those cases are before other judges."

Beck stopped for a second.

"Of course, they also got me baby-sitting the Rachman case. We don't have a suspect yet, but Homicide detectives are working on it. The assigned detectives are Lucas and Siscowicz."

"Really?" Zane said. "Those two are very good Detectives. What do you have so far?"

"Not much." Beck stretched before continuing. "Rachman's neck was broken by the killer, and then he was left to deep freeze in the empty lot they found him in. The M.E. said, considering the force that was used to snap Rachman's neck, the killer had to be either very big, or very strong."

"Or very angry," Zane added.

"Sounds like a professional hit," Ron said.

"We're not so sure. I mean lots of people wanted

Rachman dead, but who'd be able to get close enough to him to kill him with their bare hands?

Zane leaned back in his chair and looked at Beck.

"Don't discount some disgruntled people in the community. There are a lot of fed-up citizens out there angry enough to want him dead."

Ron nodded in agreement. "Like that guy Gaylen Turner, Toro, what's his name? Y'all looking at him or his group?"

"Gaylen Torres, you mean", Beck said. "Yeah, we have him and some members of ROC as persons of interest. Unofficially, that is."

Ron stood up and stretched. In doing so, his rolled-up shirtsleeve exposed the mongoose tattoo on the inside of his right forearm.

Beck had never seen the tattoo so clearly before. *'Serpent Killers.'* He wondered what it meant, but decided against asking him.

Ron looked at Zane, then at Beck.

"I'm going to get some water," he said. "Y'all want anything?"

"No, I'm good, Ron. Thanks," Zane answered.

"Nothing for me, thanks," Beck said.

"Beck, did Rachman have anything on him when they found him?" Zane asked after Ron went upstairs. "Like a weapon, ID, anything like that?"

"A bunch of stuff," Beck answered. "At least what you'd expect from a drug dealer: a bundle of heroin, $500 in cash, mostly in ones and twenties, some matches. They also found a cell phone, a nearly empty pack of cigarettes and a loaded semi-automatic pistol," Beck answered.

Zane shook his head and eased back into the chair, just as Ron came back down the stairs. Beck heard the ice clink against the glass as Ron hit the bottom step.

"Oh, yeah, we did find something else. A white card with a Bible verse on it. It was wrapped in a sandwich baggie inside Rachman's jacket pocket. That was kind of weird since it appears Rachman wasn't a Christian."

"Maybe he was converting to Christianity," Ron joked. "It was probably time for the little fool to repent."

"Yes, you just never know," Zane said. "God moves folks in strange ways sometimes."

Beck sat up to make room for Ron on the couch.

"I also found out that the same type of card was found in Richard Melnick's jeep, near his body. That's not my case, but Lucas and Siscowicz are working that case as well."

Zane stood up and went to the window, which overlooked the manicured back yard.

"I didn't hear anything on the news about the card in Melnick's jeep," Zane replied.

Zane and Ron glanced at each other quickly.

"We're not releasing all of the details until we can put all of this evidence together," Beck said.

Zane moved away from the window and faced Beck.

"I remember those days in Homicide," he said.

"Judge, I'll bet you had some crazy cases when you were up there, huh?"

"Beck, I took great pleasure in prosecuting some of the scumbags that I encountered as an Assistant D.A. Judges were almost as bad, though."

"Really?"

Zane nodded. "Old Judge Pete Tillery made Manigault look like the Pope. He was so blatantly anti-prosecution that he would literally get angry anytime he had to find a defendant guilty."

"Where's he now?" Beck asked.

"Who cares?" Ron shrugged.

Zane looked at Beck.

"He left the bench unexpectedly a few years ago." Zane said. "Rumor is the feds were looking to indict him."

"Why?"

"Apparently someone told them of some of Tillery's illegal activities," Zane replied.

Ron mumbled something to himself.

Walking over to Beck, Zane put his hand on his shoulder.

"Remember this Beck: evil won't thrive for long, because there's always someone watching, someone looking to do *whatever* it takes to stop it," Zane said. "And when that happens, the predators become the prey.

CHAPTER TWENTY-EIGHT

FEBRUARY 11TH, 9:00 A.M.

"Daddy, where are my new earrings?"

"They're on my dresser, that's where I left them when I wore them last night."

"Daddy!"

Sisco grinned as he shifted on the couch, stretched out in his bathrobe and enjoying a rare Sunday off. After rousting the family for 7 a.m. Mass, Sisco was prepared to spend the rest of the day in his robe watching the football games. Beast relaxed in his usual spot near the refrigerator.

"Honey, where are my car keys?" Helen asked, zipping up her jacket in the hallway. "I know you had them last. And I just know you remembered to put them back on the hook near the refrigerator."

"You know what? I think I left them in my jacket," Sisco said, walking to the front door. "They should be there."

Opening the door was no simple task, considering the cold air on the other side. Sisco wondered if braving the cold was worth a quick trip outside to get the newspaper.

"Got 'em," Helen called out from the hall closet. "Maybe someone could put them back where they belong next time."

"Someone gets the picture," Sisco responded, walking in with the paper. "*I'm sorry.*"

He quickly scanned the front page.

"Aw, hell," Sisco groaned.

"*WERE TWO OF PHILLY'S MOST WANTED MURDERED BY A SERIAL KILLER?*"

Sisco read the article to himself as he closed the front door behind him.

"*Police are investigating the recent brutal slayings of Raheem Motley aka, Rachman, and Richard Melnick, the alleged "Black Glove Rapist", as the work of a possible serial killer. Motley, one of the city's most notorious criminals, was found with his neck broken in a vacant lot in South Philadelphia over a week ago. Melnick, suspected of brutally raping at least four women, was also slain last week. He was found in a dumpster in the parking lot of the Philadelphia sport complex center. Police sources say there is evidence linking both murders.*"

The article also featured mug shots of both criminals.

"Helen, it never ceases to amaze me how quick the media gets these cases," Sisco said. "Sometimes they seem to know stuff before we even get it."

"Maybe you should go to the media to get your

clues, then," Helen joked as she walked past to the door with Marte'.

"Clearly, somebody's been talking to them. Anyway, we're leaving. There are pork loins in the fridge." She gave him a peck on the lips on her way out the door behind their daughter.

"Behave yourself," she said.

"Be careful, honey. Turn on your cell phone, and don't give Marte' the credit card," he said closing and locking the door behind them.

Rereading the headline, Sisco wondered why the paper didn't mention the card found in Manigault's house.

The phone rang breaking his concentration.

"Hello?"

"So, old people do get up this early." It was Luke. "Well, rest those old bones and enjoy your Sunday, pops. We got a busy week ahead of us starting tomorrow."

"I know. Don't remind me. What you got goin' on today?"

"Hopefully, a whole lot of nothing. However, that's probably just wishful thinking," Luke said. "You see the front page of the Local section today?"

"Unfortunately, yes. I'll bet the Captain is goin' bananas." Sisco said, tossing the paper on the couch.

"Hell, maybe goin' bananas is the only way to deal with this mess," Luke responded.

11:00 A.M.

The first two miles of Beck's runs were usually the toughest these days. Stretching helped loosen his legs, but nothing worked like actually getting out on the trail. It didn't take long, however, for Beck's body to cooperate. He figured that during his boxing career, he had run several hundred miles.

The years of roadwork and pounding had strengthened his legs. Since leaving the ring, however, some arthritis had crept in. Now, Beck's main activity was jogging.

"Legs are a bit tight today," Beck said as he and Serene rounded the winding dirt path deep into Valley Greene. "I am not sure I can do five miles today."

Barely winded, Serene looked sleek in her black compression tights and light blue fleece sweatshirt. A matching light blue ski cap covered her head. Black mittens covered her hands.

Always scenic, this section of the Chestnut Hill park took runners and sightseers through some of the city's most beautiful foliage. While there was no way Beck could live on "the Hill" at his current Assistant District Attorney's salary, he figured that at least they could enjoy the view sometimes.

It was an hour before Beck and Serene finished their run. Walking back to Beck's car, Serene spotted a couple holding hands sitting on an old bench.

"That's so sweet," Serene said. "I bet they're planning a romantic evening. Maybe they're even planning their wedding."

"Only you could get all that from two people holding hands," Beck said, chuckling. "What if she was actually his side chick or something?"

Both slowed after passing the old Valley Green Inn, then stopped to rest near the inn's porch. He sat on the bench, while Serene stood and stretched to cool down.

Beck took two apples from his backpack, gave one to Serene, then bit into the other.

"Beck, what's with the attitude change whenever the topic of weddings comes up?" Serene's face was set.

"First, *we* weren't talking about weddings. You were," Beck said between bites. "Second, why all the drama lately about relationships? Why are you so sensitive? You know I'm only joking."

Beck knew he'd hit a nerve when he saw Serene's face.

Serene Douglass was a fine woman by even a blind man's standards, and her demeanor was usually calm and cool.

However, when she got angry - which was not often - Beck knew it would be a while before her anger subsided.

Beck sensed the day's run was over, and began packing up.

"I'm ready to go," Serene said quietly without

looking at Beck. He didn't need to look at her face to see her tears. He heard it in her voice.

Once inside his car, Beck tried to find something to say to beak the glacier-thick ice.

Serene fastened her seat belt, removed her gloves and stared straight ahead. Realizing he had crossed a line, Beck knew there was little he could do to lighten the mood. If he was lucky, she might speak to him by the end of the week.

He shut his door.

"Serene," Beck said, "I didn't mean anything by what I said. I got a lot of stuff going on at work, and I just need you to understand."

With the car doors shut, Serene's stony silence spoke volumes. Both sat silently in the car; neither looked at the other.

"Just drive, okay," Serene said softly, looking down in her lap. "Just drive."

Beck knew that they had just broached a critical relationship issue. His chest felt heavy. He and Serene had a good relationship on the surface. After three years, Beck had come to trust Serene and care deeply about her.

However, the deeper their relationship became, the more Beck knew they had to discuss things like marriage and family. Beck loved her, but he was afraid to take the next steps.

Like an unopened bill, Beck pushed the marriage issue aside until he was ready to deal with it. He secretly feared that Serene may not love him as much as he loved her. Beck figured it likely stemmed from his trust issues with his father.

The short ride to Serene's house was quiet. The silence turned a twenty-minute trip into what seemed like an eternity.

Beck easily found a space in front of Serene's door. Before he could get around to her, however, she was out of the car and up the steps to her house.

"I have a teacher's convention in New Jersey later this week," Serene said. Once at her door, she turned to face Beck. "Then, I'm going to see my parents in Maryland. I'll call you."

"When?" Beck asked, but Serene had already closed the door.

CHAPTER TWENTY-NINE

FEBRUARY 13th, 5:30 A.M.

BEEP. BEEP. BEEP. BEEP.

Zane groaned as he was awakened by the steady drone of his alarm clock. He glanced at the time and groaned again.

Note to self, Zane thought as he slipped out of the warm bed. *Move that stupid clock to the basement*.

Even while he complained, Zane loved this time of the day. To him, the silence was warm and comforting.

Zane slipped on his exercise clothes and sneakers. These early morning workouts always set the tone for his day.

Soon, Zane began to feel his body tuning up to the new day. Years of pre-dawn missions in the military had trained his body to quickly adapt to the early hour.

He turned on the small lamp on the nightstand and reached for the clear plastic bottle of vitamins.

On the nightstand was Zane's worn Bible, which was opened to his favorite passage found in the Book of Romans 13: 3-5.

Glancing at the highlighted passage, Zane read silently. *Do you want to be free from fear of the one who is in authority? Then do what is right and he will commend you. For he is God's servant to do you good. But if you do wrong, be afraid for he does not bear the sword for nothing. He is God's servant, and agent of wrath to bring punishment on the wrongdoer.*

Working in the criminal justice system was intense, both physically and emotionally. Zane felt energized every time he meditated on this passage of Scripture.

Zane was in great shape for a man his age. However, lately he noticed he had been having a hard time getting out of bed each morning. His extracurricular physical activities took more out of him than he was willing to admit.

Zane walked downstairs to the basement. He opened the door to the recreation room and flicked on the light. The exercise equipment set to one side of the rec room was small, but effective. An elliptical cardio machine filled the far corner of the room, along with a modern weight bench and free weight rack.

Rounding out the equipment was a chin-up bar, dip machine, rowing apparatus and a heavy bag for boxing.

The other side of the room contained an entertainment area complete with sofas and a wide-screen television.

The cordless phone on the wall rang. Zane pushed a small button on the console next to it.

"Good morning Ron," Zane said.

"I see you up," Ron responded. "I'll be there by 8:30."

"I will be ready. I am about to start my workout, so we can get an early start today. It looks like a busy day on the bench."

Other than the weight equipment, the floor of the room was bare, except for a fairly sizeable karate mat.

The walls, however, were a tribute to Zane's martial arts and combat prowess. Various medals and awards were hung in no particular order.

As he worked up a sweat, Zane went over the day's itinerary. No matter what else was going on, he had the ability to shut out everything else and focus on the task at hand. Experts labeled this ability compartmentalizing, and Zane believed it helped him to become successful in such a stressful career.

Working out also helped him forget the pain in his life: a failed marriage after twelve years, and an estranged relationship with his son, Troy. Zane was in denial about these failures. He blamed them on weaknesses in his ex-wife and son, rather than on his own character flaws.

In truth, Zane could be rigid and difficult toward people not in his inner circle. To some, he was aloof. Many of his principles, like his tough stance on crime, could almost be called fanatical. Considering that, it was only a matter of time before his marriage, and other personal relationships, would crumble under the weight.

By the time Zane was finished on the Stair machine twenty-five minutes later, he had built up a considerable sweat. Towelling off, he moved to the weight bench.

To warm up, Zane placed a forty-five pound plate on each side of the barbell. Despite his age, Zane still made weight training part of his daily routine. In addition, Zane usually watched his diet carefully, only occasionally allowing for a cheat day.

For the next half hour, the clanking of iron weights and Zane's controlled breaths were the only sounds heard in the exercise room. By the time he was done with his weight-lifting session, Zane felt nearly invincible. He completed his morning workout with several martial arts katas and stetches.

Once back upstairs, Zane headed for the guest room. Since he had so few guests, Zane usually used the room for his morning stretches. It was also perfect because it faced the front of the home and received the most direct sunlight. An added bonus was the room had its own bathroom and shower.

Zane stripped off his workout gear and stepped into the glass-enclosed shower. The first rays of the sun shined down into the bathroom through a skylight.

An hour later, Zane was putting the finishing touches on his work attire. Dressed smartly in a custom-tailored three-button, brown pinstripe suit, and print tie, Zane slipped on his footwear. His black cap-toe shoes were so highly-polished they gleamed like glass. The judge was now ready to mete out justice in the courtroom.

When Zane turned on the CD/DVD system, gospel music filled the room. He hummed to himself as he went into the kitchen to make breakfast. He grabbed a plastic Tupperware bowl of fruit from the refrigerator. He took the fruit to the counter, and with surgeon-like precision, began cutting the strawberries, bananas, and apples into small chunks. He then tossed the sliced fruit into the blender with a handful of baby spinach, a heaping scoop of whey protein powder and a few drops of honey. A cup of water rounded out the recipe.

The blender roared to life when Zane hit the whip button on the front of the machine, and the fruit and spinach medley instantly morphed into a frothy pink liquid.

After emptying the shake into a large glass, Zane settled down on the living room couch to wait for Ron. While waiting, he lost himself in the gospel music filling the room. Zane didn't know why people listened to anything other than gospel – except for jazz, that is. He loved the uplifting music, the massive choirs and heart-felt singing. Like athletes who listened to rock or hip-hop music before big games, Zane looked to gospel to energize him before taking the bench each day. To him, gospel was his battle music, as Zane felt he was at war each day in the criminal justice system.

A few minutes later, Zane heard a car pull up to the front porch. He then heard two sharp honks of a car horn.

Right on time, Zane thought, gulping down the last bit of his protein shake. He switched the CD player off, then put the glass in the kitchen sink. He threw on his overcoat and grabbed his briefcase on his way to the front door.

Time to go to work.

9:15 A.M.

Driving down Broad Street, Sisco admitted that the construction taking place in downtown Philadelphia made a positive difference in the city's aesthetics.

"The mayor is really serious about giving the city a facelift," he said to Luke.

"It's about time, don't you think?" Luke replied.

"Seems like the streets down here have been torn up for years."

The detectives knew they needed to make up some lost ground this week. They now had several seemingly identical Scripture cards found near crime scenes and three murders.

They needed a breakthrough before more bodies piled up.

"With these cards turning up, we need to get something new on the Rachman murder. It's probably safe to say that if we find Rachman's killer, we'll s also aolve the other murders and discover who visited Mangiault," Luke said.

"It's almost two weeks now, and we still don't have any real solid leads, except for that info we got on Torres," Sisco said. We gotta talk to him."

Luke munched on a cinnamon bun while Sisco drove.

"The guys from the Cold Case Unit keep circling my desk," he replied.

"I know. We need to be careful about implicating Torres, though," Sisco acknowledged. "He's getting to be real popular for all of his anti-crime, take-back-your-neighborhoods talk. We might need to get permission from upstairs to talk to him."

* * *

Light snow fell as the detectives reached their

destination. Dark clouds moved in from the west and threatened heavier snow later in the day.

There was surprising little activity on Federal Street for an early Monday morning. That bode well for Sisco and Luke who sat in their car. They watched the street for any unwanted neighborhood attention.

Today, they were headed to Lurline Pendleton's home.

One of Sisco and Luke's confidential informants named her as someone who might be able to provide more insight into Rachman's activities. In addition, she was one of the neighborhood block captains. By all accounts, she knew many of the local players.

The detectives approached her front door. Luke rang the bell of the tidy row-home sandwiched between two run-down properties.

"I'm coming," said a small voice from behind the door, as Sisco and Luke stamped their feet and huddled under their coats to ward off the cold.

A small brown face peered through the diamond-shaped window in the faded wooden door.

Who is it?" she said from behind the door.

"It's Detective Siscowicz and Detective Lucas from the Philadelphia Police Department's Homicide Unit, ma'am," Sisco answered. He tried to keep his voice down, not wanting to inform neighbors of their presence. He held his badge up to the small window in the center of the door.

Luke watched Sisco's back and the street.

"What y'all want with me?" the woman asked without opening the door.

"Mrs. Pendleton, we just want to ask you some questions about Rachman." Sisco tried to be as non-threatening as possible.

"I ain't kill him," she said. "But, I could have. So could everyone else in this neighborhood, if you want the truth."

Luke grinned, but tried to keep a straight face.

"Mrs. Pendleton, we'll only take a few minutes of your time," Luke said, wanting to get out of the cold.

"Alright, alright, hold on," she said, disappearing from the window. After a few moments there was the sound of several locks being opened.

A small, cocoa-colored woman with thick glasses, Lurline Pendleton eyed the detectives warily. Satisfied that no one was watching, she opened the screen door and quickly ushered them in.

Once inside, a cozy warmth greeted the detectives, along with the aroma of roast beef, collard greens and freshly-brewed coffee. Gospel music played softly in the background. Faded pictures of family members took up one of the living room walls, and a tattered Bible lay open on the small coffee table in front of the couch.

"Sit down," the old woman commanded. "Coffee? All I got is decaf. That's cause of my high blood pressure." Without warning, she disappeared into the kitchen.

"No thanks, ma'am," Luke replied. "We're fine."

"Suit yourself," the old woman called out from the kitchen. "Now, what about Rachman?"

Sisco sat at the end of the old couch, while Luke remained standing.

"We understand you were at the anti-drug rally held at Stella Lane Rec Center about two weeks ago." Sisco removed a pad from his jacket pocket.

"I was," she yelled from the kitchen.

"And, Gaylen Torres was there speaking, right?" Sisco asked.

"Uh, huh. Talked about getting rid of the drug dealers in the neighborhood."

Lurline reappeared with a small white mug in one hand and a cracked white porcelain dish in the other. She sat the dish on the coffee table down in front of the detective, she fished a small spoon from her sweater pocket, and sat that next to the dish. She scooped a small amount of the sugar from the dish, then dumped it into her coffee. She then sat in the chair across from the sofa.

Sisco continued.

"Mrs. Pendleton, we understand Rachman and Gaylen Torres had some sort of altercation sometime after the rally at the rec center."

"Yeah, that was about a week after that demon got let loose after he killed them people."

"Could you see who started the fight?" Luke asked.

"Hell, there wasn't no fight," she replied, waving

her hand dismissively. "After the meeting, they just had an argument outside. Rachman and some of his thugs threatened Torres and his boys as they left the meeting. I ain't see no fight, though."

"What exactly did Rachman say to Torres?" Luke asked, scribbling furiously.

"You know, just the usual foolishness: 'I'll do so and so if I see you around here. Mind your own business,' Stuff like that."

"What'd Torres say?" Sisco asked.

"Same stuff," she said. "You the kind of people this neighborhood don't need,' and 'We gonna run you outta business.' Basically it was just men bein' men."

"Anything happened after that?" Luke asked.

"Not that I know of," she replied. "People went they separate ways after that."

"Do you know if there was any fallout after that?" Sisco asked.

"I heard Rachman's boys paid Torres a visit," Lurline lowered her voice, "if you know what I mean?"

"How do you know that?" Sisco asked.

"Don't matter how I know," Lurline snapped back. "I just know."

"What else do you *know*, ma'am?" Luke asked.

"Word is that Torres told Rachman he'd pay him back. That the situation wasn't finished, and that Torres would definitely finish it."

"Did he?" Sisco asked, leaning closer to Lurline.

"Ain't it obvious?" she chuckled. "You the detectives, and I got to put it together for you?"

"Anything else you can think of about that night?" Luke asked.

"No, that's about it. That's all I know."

Luke stopped scribbling and put his pad and pen in his coat pocket. Sisco tapped him on the arm and nodded toward the door.

"Let me ask y'all something," she said with a frown on her face. "Don't y'all got nothin' better to do than waste your time investigating who took out Rachman? Why ain't y'all trying to find who killed Miss Rosen's boy last month? He was a good boy, but he was shot dead in the street in broad daylight right around the corner here!"

Lurline gestured with her left hand toward the back of the house.

She picked up her cup of coffee with her right hand.

"Ask anybody in this neighborhood: Around here we could care less about who killed Rachman, just as long as *he's gone*." Lurline shook her head. "Why the hell was he walking around the street anyway? Shoulda been in jail for killing those people. He was bad, and everybody knew it. Just let it rest."

Sisco rose and thanked Lurline, then they headed for the door with her behind them. Outside the door, Luke stopped and scanned the block again.

"Think she's right?" Sisco asked him. "Do you

think we're wasting too much of our time on Rachman's case? Same with Melnick. Hell, even Baby Mike. These guys were scum."

Luke sighed and pulled up the collar of his coat.

"Bruh, I don't get into all that stuff anymore," Luke said stopping at the car. "I stopped asking myself 'why' a long time ago. I have a job to do, so I just do it. Period."

"You sound like this stuff is getting to you, partner," Sisco said. He opened the driver's side and got in.

Luke slid into the passenger's side.

"Maybe it is, my brother," Luke said buckling his seat belt. "But, after all the innocent people we see slaughtered in these streets, I can't honestly say I have a problem with whoever it is that's taking out Rachman and other fools like him."

10:00 A.M.

"What time is that sentencing this morning, Felice?" Zane asked.

It had been a week since his heated meeting with Judge Friedmann, and Zane still simmered every time he thought about it. He tried to suppress the agitation in his voice.

Felice entered the chambers and handed Zane a pile of folders.

"The Manning sentencing is set for 10:00 this

morning. Then, you start the John McDougall robbery case. Lester is down in the jury room now."

"Defense counsel call yet?"

"Not that I know of, Judge. Anyway, the A.D.A. handling that case is in another courtroom right now. He already checked in. Oh, and Beck called to see if you were still on for dinner Sunday night."

"Good. I want to get that jury going. I expect the press to be here in droves for that one. Please call Beck and tell him Sunday's good for me. Thanks, Felice."

Slipping on his black robe, Zane gathered up the files. Flipping open the top folder, he began reading the pre-sentence investigation report on the defendant, Calvin Manning.

Even before police arrested him for his latest case, Manning was a menace to society. By age sixteen, he'd already rung up a string of convictions that got worse as he got older. According to the report, Manning's third strike conviction was the one for which he was to be sentenced today: the brutal rape and torture of Victoria Long, a fifteen-year old girl he abducted on her way to school.

For three days, Manning kept her tied up in the filthy basement of an abandoned home, raping her repeatedly. In addition, he beat her so bad, she was unrecognizable when she was found. Had it not been for a sanitation worker who heard whimpers coming from the home and went to investigate, Victoria Long would be dead. As it was, she was so badly injured and emotionally traumatized, psychologists testified at trial that Victoria would never live a normal life.

"Fourteen arrests, five convictions – three of them for armed robbery, eight bench warrants."

Zane read his criminal record, carefully noting the details of each offense.

"How in the world did this animal get loose?" Zane asked.

"Zane, you know the press is gonna be all over this case," Ron said from the doorway behind Zane. "The people want to see you hang this monster."

"I know," said Zane, without looking up from the folder. "Freidmann will probably have a stroke when I do. Hope he does. Fat bastard."

Zane turned to face the huge bay window.

"Ron, you should've seen Friedmann's expression when I got in his face," Zane smiled broadly. "He looked like he was about to wet himself!"

"Let him," Ron added. "He needs to know you ain't afraid of him."

Zane nodded in agreement.

"Well, if he didn't know before, he knows it now: I answer to the people, not him," Zane said.

Ron stood next to Zane by the large window overlooking the city. He looked down at the street below.

"Want me to seat the press up front?" Ron asked.

"No," Zane replied. "The victims and their

families get those seats. Seat the press in the back."

"You got it."

Ron headed toward the door but turned back as he got there.

"I heard some folks talking about you in the coffee shop across the street this morning. Word's getting around that you mean business. A couple people even talked about you running for Mayor."

Zane lingered for a minute, smiled, then turned away from the window and walked toward the hallway door.

10:40 A.M.

"What I'd like to do," Zane said, staring down at the defendant from behind the judge's bench, "is to turn you over to Victoria Lowe's father and her uncles and grant them immunity for whatever they might decide to do to you. Calvin Manning, you are an animal, and …"

"I object, Your Honor!" Marvin Simkins, Manning's attorney, yelled, springing from his chair. "Your Honor, that statement is highly –,"

"Sit down and be quiet, Counselor!" Zane said, as he stared at the defendant. This is MY courtroom and MY sentencing. I have the authority to say what I want before I impose punishment."

Zane's jury trial had settled earlier that day,

so the only matter left on his docket was the Manning sentencing.

He continued.

"Your client has now been tried and found guilty by a jury of some very serious crimes. Now, it's my turn to do my duty and make your client pay for his heinous crimes."

Zane then stood up. "Now, it's *my* turn to do the people's business."

The crowd in the packed courtroom murmured almost collectively at the drama being played out before them. The reporters present in the gallery couldn't write in their pads fast enough.

Zane's statement highlighted a morning where Simkins did his best to try to point out to the court his client's few positive attributes, despite having committed two prior "strike" crimes.

For his part, the Assistant D.A. on the case reminded the Court why Calvin Manning, aka "Caveman", should basically die in jail as a "three strike" felon. Since Pennsylvania law didn't allow the death penalty for rapes, the only thing Zane could do was impose a lengthy prison sentence.

"As I was saying, Mr. Manning, you are done. You will never walk the streets again. You WILL die in prison like the dungeon rat you are. Stand up, sir."

Manning rose from his chair behind the defense table. Simkins did the same.

The courtroom became eerily quiet.

"For your crimes in this case, under bill# 58524,

I am sentencing you to the maximum under law, as I find this conviction to be your third strike under Pennsylvania Statue 42 P.A.C.S, Section 9714. On the count of rape, graded as an F1, I sentence you to twenty-five years to life."

Manning slumped back down in his seat, his eyes stared blankly in front of him.

Zane continued.

"On the count of aggravated assault, graded as an F1, I sentence you to 25 years to life. On the count of aggravated indecent assault, graded as an F1, I sentence you to …"

By the time Zane had finished reading all the counts, Manning had been convicted of six different crimes.

In addition, Zane ordered that all the sentences run consecutively. This meant that each sentence would run one after the other. Altogether, Zane sentenced Calvin Manning to 125 years in jail.

If he were lucky, Manning might get out at the Rapture.

CHAPTER THIRTY

FEBRUARY 15th, 9:00 A.M.

Each of the Scripture cards found at the crime scenes bore the name of a company called Hastings Religious Specialties, in Reddington, Mississippi.

After a diligent internet search yielded nothing about the company, Sisco decided to go straight to the source.

Working the phones, he contacted the Reddington city, police department, and asked for their help. From them, he learned Hastings Religious Specialties had gone out of business some time ago. They directed him to the local Chamber of Commerce to see if anyone knew about the defunct business.

Sisco dialed the phone number and fingered one of the small white cards. He focused on the small series of numbers and letters on the bottom right hand corner of the card.

"Reddington Chamber of Commerce," said a female voice with a cordial southern twang. Sisco guessed her to be about early to mid-seventies, Caucasian.

He also thought he noted a twinge of southern pride.

"Good afternoon, ma'am. I'm Detective Gary Siscowicz of the Philadelphia Police Department's Homicide Unit. I'm looking for information about a business I believe is located there in Reddington, Mississippi."

"Well, let's see if I can help you out. What's the name of the business?" she said.

"Hastings Religious Specialties," Sisco said. "It's spelled H-A-S…"

"Oh, no need to spell it," the woman replied in a chipper tone. "I know that business well."

Sisco tensed in his seat.

"Well, maybe I should say *knew* that business. It shut down nearly 20 years ago. By the time it closed its doors, it had been in business since the early 1900s."

Sisco was disappointed. Even though it had been a long shot, he'd hoped for some kind of lead. This looked like another dead end.

"Fine company," she said. "Sold the nicest little religious items, Bibles, crosses, you know. Things like that. You name it, they had it."

"What about Scripture cards?" Sisco asked.

"Oh my, yes," she said. "Old Testament, New Testament. You could even get a set with only the Psalms on them."

"Why'd they go out of business?" Sisco asked, hoping to keep her talking.

"The owner, Solomon Doyle, just got too old to run the company," she replied. "Even though they had quite a few employees, it was still just a mom and pop shop at heart. I mean, everyone in the family worked there. The company was originally founded by Wainwright Doyle back in 1902, and he just passed the company down. It was very organized, and they kept really good records. They could tell you the name of each and every customer they had right down to their last order. By the time Wainwright's son, Solomon, took over, however, the company had gotten real big. Besides, that, a lot of the family members had either quit or died. By the time it closed, it was just old man Solomon Doyle and his wife Greta running the place."

Sisco couldn't believe his good fortune. If he just kept her talking, she might be able to give him the information he was looking for.

"Did Doyle and his wife have any kids to pass it on to?" he asked.

Sisco heard the woman suck her teeth.

"You mean them two no-good boys of theirs?" she responded. "Solomon and Greta couldn't get those boys to make anything of themselves. I heard they turned to gambling and running moonshine. Darn near broke their folks' hearts."

"Well, what happened to the shop?" he asked.

"Oh, it's still there, *physically*," she said. "But now it's a made-to-order greeting card company, Glad-Time Greetings, or something like that.

Solomon sold the business right before he died. Made a nice little profit off it, too. The new shop kept the building and moved in. It does pretty well I must say."

Sisco scribbled furiously on the yellow legal pad on his desk. He took copious notes.

"Ma'am, what happened to the records from the store? Did they get rid of them?" Sisco asked. He wanted to bring the conversation back to the Scripture cards.

After a long pause, she said, "Detective, I honestly don't know. A lot of businesses here in the Chamber keep their old records on file, usually on disk. Some very old ones might even keep theirs on microfiche. You might try calling down to the local library here in Reddington to see if they have anything."

The hits just kept on coming. Sisco couldn't believe his good luck.

"I have that number for you. Hold on, I'll get it," she said.

Sisco heard fumbling and rustling on the other end. *Microfiche?* Siscowicz thought. *Like a modern-day Mayberry.*

"The library's number is 769-555-5532. Ask for Geraldine. She's really nice, and she'll help you out with whatever you need. Tell her Doris sent you."

"Ma'am, thank you so much. You're very nice. It's been a pleasure talking with you."

"Oh, you're welcome Detective," she said. "Always

glad to help out law enforcement. You take care of yourself up there in Philadelphia, okay?"

11:00 A.M.

Zane was right. Today turned out to be one of his busiest weeks so far.

After Manning's sentencing two days ago, Zane heard several bench trials: two gunpoint robberies, a complex forgery case, and a three co-defendant drug case.

In one of the robbery cases before him today, the defendant requested a jury trial, but ultimately pleaded guilty. In all the cases but the forgery, Zane had found all the defendants guilty.

"This court now stands adjourned to the call of the crier," said Stewart as he stood up to announce lunch recess. "This Court will resume again at 2:00 P.M."

Attorneys packed their briefcases and conferred with clients, while family members of the victims and defendants bundled up their clothing to ward off the fierce chill awaiting them outside.

"Where to Zane?" Ron asked.

"I'm not going out for lunch, Ron," Zane answered, stepping down from the bench. "I'm just going to order a salad from the deli down the street. I have some things to take care of upstairs."

"Alright, then. I'll be back around two."

Zane nodded as Ron opened the door for him, then followed him into the robing room in the back.

"Judge, do you need me to help you during lunch?" Felice asked.

"No, I'll be fine, Felice," Zane answered. "Go and enjoy your lunch. We're adjourned until 2:00."

"No problem, Judge. I'll probably be back early, in fact." Felice then hurried off to meet one of her girlfriends who was sitting in the back of the courtroom. She had asked Felice if she could sit in on some of the judge's court cases that day.

Back in his office, Zane removed his judicial robe and sat down. He picked up the black phone from the desk in front of him and quickly punched in some numbers.

A woman picked up on the other end.

"Mitchell's Deli, can you hold?" The line then went silent.

"Geez, I didn't even get a chance to answer yes or no," Zane muttered to himself.

While he waited, Zane thumbed through the local newspaper, scanning the day's news stories.

One story on the front page in particular caught his attention: "*Police Still Seeking Clues in Brutal Slayings of South Philly Drug Kingpin and Alleged Black Glove Rapist.*"

"Mitchell's Deli, can I help you?"

Zane was so busy reading the story he didn't even hear her.

"Mitchell's Deli, can I help you?" the woman repeated.

"A large Caesar's Salad with fat-free Vinaigrette to go," Zane said, still reading the news story.

"Anything else?"

"No, that's all. I'll pick it up in about fifteen minutes. The last name is Russell."

"That'll be five-twenty plus tax. Your number is 212."

She hung up.

Zane read and reread the article.

According to the story, while police had few clues in the murders, they were looking at several "persons of interest" to interview about the drug dealer's murder in particular.

Which 'persons of interest do the cops have in this case? Zane wondered. He remembered his conversation with Beck, but he knew the D.A.'s Office and the Police Department didn't always tell the other what they were doing.

Everyone knows Rachman was scum. What's the big deal? Zane thought as he closed the newspaper. Putting on his heavy coat, he folded the paper under his arm and headed out the door.

Try as he might, Zane could not stop thinking about the phrase "persons of interest."

CHAPTER THIRTY-ONE

February 16ᵀᴴ, 12:00 P.M.

Homicides, like most crimes, are solved through solid investigative work.

Getting choice information from people on the street is the hardest part, because most witnesses avoid cops and law enforcement. Having someone on the street who can get good intel, and who is willing to pass that information on to police is invaluable.

Which is why Detectives Lucas and Sisco were looking for Antoine Wilson, one of their best sources of good street information.

"Let's check his job," Luke said

Antoine, or Twan, as he was known on the street, was a small-time hustler and full-time wannabe thug, who always knew what was going on in Philly's streets.

Sisco met him nearly a decade earlier when the Detective was a uniform cop assigned to the 12ᵗʰ Police District, and Antoine was just 17 years old.

Twan drove a beat-up Chevy that ran a stop sign in front of Sisco. After pulling the car over, Sisco discovered a bag of marijuana on the seat next to Twan in what turned out to be a stolen car.

Since Antoine was a juvenile, with no prior criminal record, and Sisco was in a good mood that day, he let Twan go. He also discarded the weed and returned the car to its rightful owner. To show his gratitude, Antoine gave Sisco more than a few choice leads. These ultimately resulted in several key arrests and major busts for Sisco while he was a uniformed officer.

Since then, Twan became one of Sisco's best go-to confidential informants. For his part, Sisco, and now Luke, tried to keep Twan on the straight and narrow.

Lately, though, the petty thug had been scarce. The detectives figured he had either picked up a new criminal case or had gotten himself killed. Sisco had heard he was working part-time at the new mega home improvement store at the shopping mall near Columbus Avenue.

Luke spotted him around the store's entrance as they pulled into the parking lot. He nudged Sisco, who slowed the car to a crawl. Despite the early February date, the weather on this day was more balmy than crisp, and a few people even dotted the streets.

"W'sup Twan?" Luke greeted him the from passenger

side. The young man in the orange apron nodded at the detectives, then walked up to the car.

"W'sup oldheads?" Twan said, scanning the parking lot. "I'm on my break, so I got some time to talk."

"Where you been, bruh?" Luke asked. "We thought you picked up a new case."

"Naw, Detective. I been straight ever since I walked off my last probation."

"So, what are you doing now?" Sisco asked.

"My uncle Tony said he'd hook me up with a job doing construction when it gets warmer."

"That's not the same uncle selling bootleg CD's down on Temple University's campus is it?" Luke inquired.

"No. This a different uncle," he said.

"That's good," Luke said. "You know there's nothing out here for you but trouble."

"So, why y'all stalking me? What I do now?"

"Relax," Sisco said, turning down the car's radio. The police chatter over the radio had gotten too loud. "We just wanted to see if you knew anything about Rachman."

Twan checked the parking lot again.

"Well, I can't be talking about it right out here. I'll be right back. Meet me in the back lot."

Sisco drove around to the back lot.

Twan walked into the building and returned a few seconds later without his apron. He walked around the side of the building to the back parking lot of the store.

Sisco unlocked the door, and Twan slid into the backseat. Luke scanned the vast parking lot, satisfied that they hadn't gotten any unwanted attention. Luke gave Sisco the okay to move.

Easing the car into gear, Sisco pulled out of the space, then around to the traveling lane of the busy parking lot.

"What do I know 'bout Rachman?" Twan resumed the conversation. "That fool is dead. What else you want to know?"

Sisco grinned at Luke.

"Oh, so now we playing games, huh?" Luke turned to look back at Twan.

"Naw dog, I'm just kidding. From what I'm hearing on the street, a whole lot of wanna-be kingpins is trying to take over Rachman's operations."

"Any idea who took him out?" Sisco asked, turning a corner.

"The word is Malik Townshend did it. They call him "M Town", but I don't really believe it."

"Why not?" Luke pressed.

"Cause Malik don't have the brains to take over an operation like Rachman's," Twan replied. "Malik is really a soldier -- not a boss. Even though he's definitely big enough to snap that little fool's neck."

"Got anything on the Black Glove Rapist killing?" Luke asked, switching topics. He jotted down notes on a small pad.

"I don't have too much on that one," Twan

answered, shrugging his shoulders. He looked out his back window. "Probably the dad of one of them girls he did. Man, I read in the paper that the killer like stomped his nuts in, or somethin'."

"Ever hear of Gaylen Torres?" Luke asked.

Twan didn't answer right away.

"Why you askin'?" Twan asked.

Luke noticed the slight apprehension in Twan's voice. He knew Sisco caught it, too.

"Because I want to know, okay?" he responded. "I want to know what you know."

Twan's pause spoke volumes.

"Look, Detectives, we cool and all. But, y'all asking me to put myself in a tough spot. Torres and his people are crazy. Word has it he may be down with the Scarlet Cord and all that. And, them people are scary. Loco. Know what I mean? That's all I gotta say."

"Is that a yes or a no?" Luke asked, not willing to back off the line of questioning.

"That's an I-don't-have-no-further-comment-on-that-subject."

"I heard someone mention the Scarlet Cord a few years ago," Sisco responded. "Thought it was some urban legend, or something."

Twan looked out the back windows, then lowered his voice.

"The Scarlet Cord ain't no damn urban legend, that's for sure, man," Twan said. "A few years ago,

I knew a lady who needed some drug dealers taken out. Remember Miss Loretta Florence?"

Luke pondered for a few seconds.

"The nice lady up in Germantown who was being threatened by those crack dealers from the G Street Mob?"

"Yeah. That's her. Anyway, word is she told the network where they could find them, and bam! Two weeks later, two of them drug dealers was found dead in a small swamp in Fairmount park, and the other two got beat so bad they now have brain damage. Them niggas now just be walkin' around the 'hood with pajamas on babbling to themselves."

"So you think this Scarlet Cord is real?" Sisco asked.

"Did you hear what I just said?" Twan replied emphatically. "They on the streets, and they tired of the crime and thugs getting off easy."

"What exactly does this network do?" Luke prodded further.

"Depends on what needs doing," Twan said, looking over at Luke. "From what I know, they got a whole underground army of people out here, ordinary everyday people who are just tired of crime, and the do-nothing cops - hey, no offense - and get together to try and get rid of the criminals."

Luke nodded. "Go on."

"These people apparently take a secret oath to spread the word about where the bad guys are, and then, you know."

"No, what?"

"Take them fools out. Kill em', torture em', whatever needs to be done. Clean up crime scenes so the cops find no evidence. Even hide the bodies if necessary. Word has it that a few mothers got together after their sons were killed and formed a secret group to fight crime. Like an urban CIA."

Sisco returned to the hardware store parking lot. This new mall was in an upscale neighborhood, so it was unlikely their arrival drew any attention.

Luke and Sisco glanced at each other. Luke turned back to Twan.

"Y'all good detectives, but y'all obviously don't have a clue about how deep these people are," Twan continued. "These people are fanatical."

"I'm curious," Luke replied, "how do they communicate with each other?"

"I don't know. Sign language, secret handshake, homing pigeons, whatever. They find a way to get their message to each other without nobody else knowing. I even heard they all wear purple bracelets on their wrists. Ordinary-looking things that, unless you know about their group, you won't even know what they mean."

Twan looked around again, then paused.

"Look Luke," he whispered, "I done talked too much already. These mofos mean business. They operate in the shadows, and they'll take out whoever they need to. My people tell me they not only kill the bad guys, but even snitches in their own organization. *Even people who ain't in their organization."*

Twan paused.

"Y'all need to let that sink in," he said.

"Do you know who the actual killers are in the Scarlet Cord?" Luke asked.

Twan sighed. He was worried he'd said too much already.

"Don't know," Twan admitted. "I don't think nobody knows. And, they want to keep it like that. I done told you the Scarlet Cord operates in secret. And they real organized. Not even the folks on the street know who the enforcer is. They just put the request out there on the network, the intel locates him, and the enforcer eliminates him."

"Damn," Luke said. "It's like they put contracts out on the bad guys."

"Now you getting the picture," Twan said, nodding his head.

Sisco eased the car back into an empty parking space near where they had initially saw Twan.

"Y'all know where to find me," Twan said, quickly exiting the backseat. "Peace," flashing the first two fingers of his right hand.

Sisco waited for a car to pass before pulling back into the main parking lot.

"What the hell are we dealing with here, Luke?" Sisco said. "This is getting more bizarre all the time."

Luke nodded, staring straight ahead. "No kidding. And, something tells me it's only gonna get worse."

Sisco massaged his right temple with his right hand, driving the car with his left. He then turned down Delaware Avenue and melted into the steady flow of early afternoon traffic.

CHAPTER THIRTY-TWO

February 18th, 2:00 P.M.

Bill couldn't remember exactly when he noticed the change.

Maybe it was about a week ago, after Judge Manigault took the bench following what he called a "crazy weekend." He also noticed that the usually gregarious judge was much quieter, but his temper was worse.

That was the Monday Judge Manigault tore into Walt Renfro, one of the city's oldest and most respected Public Defenders, over a simple matter.

Renfro's client, Roger Newsome, had asked to postpone his robbery trial to attend an aunt's funeral out of town. Bill, who had been Manigault's court crier for the past five years, had never seen the judge so hostile toward defense counsel. Usually, it was the prosecutors who bore the brunt of his anger.

"What the hell's gotten into him," Walt asked

another court clerk when Manigault left the bench that morning for a brief recess.

"Don't know Walt," the clerk replied. "Maybe he and his old lady are having marital issues."

"I doubt it. He and Miriam have been together over twenty years. She's probably the only one who can put up with him."

Things got even more bizarre after court resumed.

The day's first trial involved Leon Leskowitz, charged with selling meth from his home. All the Commonwealth's witnesses were cops – which was good news to Leskowitz – knowing Manigault's hatred of cops. To take further advantage of this good fortune, the defendant chose to waive his right to a jury and have Judge Manigault hear the case. On any other day, this would be a slam dunk "not guilty" for even the most inept defense attorney.

Bill had to pinch himself twice when Manigault ultimately found the defendant guilty quicker than the court clerk could write down the verdict in the court file.

The next case involved Maceo Dominguez, who had been convicted of aggravated assault a few months earlier, and who was scheduled to be sentenced today. It took a jury nearly a week to find the career criminal guilty of robbing and pistol-whipping a man on his way home from work. While the victim suffered some injury, it wasn't serious.

Normally, the judge would sentence the defendant below the state sentencing guidelines, unless the victim was seriously injured. Then he'd give his standard line, "Pal, I'm gonna do something for you that you didn't do for your victim -- show you some mercy."

Manigault typically would then attach some serious-sounding, but meaningless conditions to his weak sentence.

Bill and everyone in Courtroom 819 soon found out just how wrong they were.

That was the *old* Judge Manigault.

"Stand up," the Judge said to Dominguez before sentencing him.

"Your prior record is horrible," Manigault said. "Your presentence investigation report states that you really don't want to work, and that you are unlikely to stay out of trouble if given probation."

The defendant and his attorney shifted back and forth and looked at each other nervously.

"You think this a joke?" Manigault asked "Well, then here's the punchline, pal. On the robbery bill, I sentence you to five to ten years in state custody."

Bill saw the air leave Dominguez's body as he grabbed the table for support.

But Manigault wasn't finished.

"On the aggravated assault bill, I sentence you to five to ten years in state custody.

When he was done, Manigault ordered all the sentences to run consecutively. All together, Manigault sentenced Maceo Dominguez to an unbelievable total of fifteen to thirty years. Family members were stunned as the sheriffs led Dominguez out of the courtroom.

"I must be goin' nuts," Bill mumbled to Irene, the quarter sessions clerk seated next to him. "I can't believe what I just saw."

"It's about time," Irene nodded approvingly. "Something must've happened to him. Jesus himself must have visited that man."

CHAPTER THIRTY-THREE

FEBRUARY 19th, 6:30 A.M.

Between her husband's flu, and their dog's new litter of pups, Homicide Captain Gail Kwan had gotten a total of four hours of sleep the previous night.

As she dragged herself out of bed extra early this morning, she knew he had an important meeting with two of her detectives. She came in well before her shift started.

Two hours later, Detectives Gary Siscowicz and Isaiah Lucas were sitting in the outer lobby of the captain's office. Captain Kwan walked into the office a little after 8:30 a.m.

"Gentlemen," she nodded to Sisco and Luke, motioning them to into her office.

Once inside, the captain took her place behind the large desk.

"Please close the door, Detective Siscowicz," she said, motioning for the Detectives to sit.

A short woman in her early fifties, Kwan had sharp

facial features and wore rimless glasses. Looking younger than her age, she had risen through the ranks of the Philadelphia police department. Many believed she was next in line for the Commissioner's spot. If appointed by the next Mayor, she would become the city's first Asian-American police commissioner.

While she was personable, Captain Kwan could also be intimidating. When she on the street as a uniform police officer, her nickname was "Ghenghis Kwan" because of her toughness. She worked her way up the ranks for twenty years the hard way, assigned to some of the department's toughest units. Besides the bad guys, she fought with more than her share of chauvinism and racism.

This morning, however, the Captain fought sleeplessness.

"It's your show, Detectives," she said without preamble.

Sisco removed four plastic baggies from a manilla envelope and laid them on the desk in front of her. Contained in the smaller baggies was a small piece of laminated cardstock, the size of a business card. Bordering each card was a gold band. Inscribed on the front of each card was a Bible verse.

The captain studied the cards, then looked up and nodded at the detectives.

Sisco took the cue and started talking.

"Two murders, so far, one dead fat thug and one intimidated judge," He said. "One card was found in

Rachman's pocket. One found in Baby Mike's car. And another was found in Melnick's truck. Manigault's card was found taped to his bathroom mirror."

"Along with a lock of Manigault's hair," Luke added.

"Melnick was the 'Black Glove Rapist', and I understand Mike was found dead in his car," Kwan stated.

Sisco and Luke nodded.

"Could you lift any prints from the cards?" the captain asked.

"No," Luke answered. "Even though each card is laminated, the killer must have used gloves to handle them. Crime Scene couldn't lift a print off either the cards, or the bags."

The detectives were interrupted when the captain's phone rang.

Kwan picked up the phone. "Sargeant, I asked you to hold all my calls until noon. I don't care if it's Commissioner Brockett. Please take a message."

She hung up the phone.

"Sorry about that, Detective Siscowicz," she said. "Please, continue."

Captain Kwan had taken her share of beatings in the press about the city's soaring crime rate and the department's low homicide clearance rate. Despite that, her popularity among the rank and file officers, especially those in the Homicide Division and the Fraternal Order of Police, remained high. Captain Kwan had earned a reputation as a woman of integrity who made time for her officers and who supported them. Luke and Sisco now saw why.

"The cards appear to be from the same set," Sisco said.

"Why do you figure that?" the Captain asked.

"Hastings Religious Specialties, Inc. is printed on the back of each card, along with a series of numbers. Each of those numbers begins with the letter J. We are pretty certain Hastings Religious Specialties made these cards. I've been talking to a lady from the Chamber of Commerce down in Reddington, Mississippi, where the company was located. It went out of business years ago, but she referred me to the library to see if the company's records may be on microfiche."

"Microfiche?" the Captain asked. "Do libraries still use that stuff? I thought everyone switched to computers years ago."

"It's a small town, Captain. Population of about 7,500," Sisco explained. "I'm expecting a call from someone who worked for the company years ago."

The captain picked up one of the baggies and leaned back in her chair. "Any possible suspects?"

Luke took over.

"Well, we developed a list of possible persons of interest since we have not received any confidential tips or leads," he said.

"No hotline calls?" the Captain asked.

"None, Captain," Luke said. "The anonymous tip

hotline has been silent when it comes to these cases."

"Who's on your list?" she asked.

"Baby Mike was Rachman's second-in-command and lieutenant, so Rachman's enemies were probably Mike's as well," Sisco added.

"But, these cards put things into a whole different category," he said. "It is quite possible that the same person who did Rachman also took out Mike and Melnick. Not to mention scared Mangault."

Kwan eyed both detectives. They all knew what Sisco meant.

A serial killer, even one who targeted bad guys, was the last thing Philadelphia needed right now.

While it may seem a noble cause, street justice was not *real* justice. Innocent people could get hurt. More important – and more ominous – was the idea that someone was deciding who should live and die.

"From our profile, we're looking at people who view themselves as crusaders," Luke said. "People and groups who want to get rid of crime by getting rid of bad guys, and who generally distrust the court system."

Luke paused and adjusted his suit jacket before continuing.

"Gaylen Torres' name keeps popping up as a person of interest," Sisco said.

"Torres heads Reclaim Our Communities," Kwan responded, leaning back in her chair. "Rumor has it he's gotten so popular with his grassroots movement that he could be a serious candidate for Mayor in next year's election."

Kwan pinned Luke with a look. "What have you got on him?"

"Word on the street is that Torres and ROC may be behind a lot of vigilante activity. So far no murders, but assaulting drug dealers, paybacks for robberies, stuff like that. It's also no secret that Torres blames Judge Manigault for letting thugs back on the streets," Luke finished.

Kwan leaned forward, shaking her head.

"ROC's not that big. How can they be responsible for all of this?" she asked.

"Captain, it may be bigger than just Torres and his group. They may have a network of hundreds of sympathizers throughout the city, including many disgruntled citizens."

"None of this explains how Torres could go from intimidating some drug dealers to murder," Captain Kwan said, regretting her lost sleep. The more information she got on these cases, the less sleep she knew she'd be getting as long as these cases remained unsolved.

"Not only that, but how do you explain the Bible verses?" Kwan asked.

"Torres claims he's saved," Luke answered. "Ever since he got out of prison, he claims he's turned his life around. Given his heart to the Lord, confessed his sins. Leaving Scripture cards, or some kind of religious symbol at each crime scene, definitely seems like some kind of a divine crusade."

Kwan stood up and studied the large city map covering the back wall of her office.

"Have you talked with Torres or any of his people?" she asked.

"Not yet, Captain," Sisco responded. "Sgt. Marinovitch wanted us to talk with you first." Luke said.

Turning to the Detectives, Captain Kwan took off her glasses. She ran her hand down her smooth cheek.

"Alright. Talk to him. Just *talk*. See if you can come up with anything. If you think you have something, by all means get a warrant. I will back you up. However, let's take a minute with Torres," she said to the Detectives.

"Right now just keep any eye on him and his people. If he's willing to talk, fine. But, if he's not willing to talk, let it be -- for now. Torres is a media hound. If he feels any pressure, he'll run right to the news, and that's not what we need right now."

When Sisco and Luke nodded, Kwan continued.

"Torres did some time. Does he have any open cases, or any probation violations we could bring him in on?"

"We checked, Captain", Luke answered. "His record since coming out of prison is clean. According to his Probation Officer, Torres was a model client, always reported, never missed an appointment, no hot urines. Nothing. Torres finished his probation two years ago."

"Okay. Keep me posted," Kwan said. "If Torres and ROC are involved with these killings, things may get hot."

"And, if we ultimately need to get a warrant, Captain?" Sisco asked.

"I'll talk to the D.A.'s Office about approving one. But, don't worry about that right now. At this point, we don't have enough probable cause to get a search warrant on anyone, let alone a body warrant."

"As I understand it," Luke said, "Torres isn't the mayor's favorite person," Luke said. "Wouldn't he and the commissioner be on our side?"

She put her glasses back on.

"Sure, the mayor will give us a lot of latitude," said Captain Kwan. "And Commissioner Klein, well, he's got no spine. He'll go along with whatever Mayor Pratt says. But that won't really help us. Pratt's approval numbers have dropped. City Council is on his back about stopping crime, and nationally he's become a joke."

"That bad?" Luke asked.

"That bad. We may be better off without the mayor's blessing. Hell, we'd probably get more support if we arrested Mayor Pratt and *locked him up*."

9:30 P.M.

The last thing Luke remembered was kickoff. Monday Night Football at its best, with the cheerleaders and flashy music videos. Too bad he missed most of the game because he was asleep by 8:00 that evening.

The insistent ring of his cell phone on the coffee table woke him up.

He gathered himself up off the couch and picked up the phone. He glanced at the clock.

It was 9:30 p.m.

"Hello?" Luke mumbled, still trying to wake up.

"You sound sleepy, Detective. You got company?" Luke recognized Jada's sassy voice.

"Jada, I just know you have some great news for me, right?" Luke replied. "I mean, Rachman's killer's address, the Lindbergh baby murder caught on tape, something. Do you know what time it is? I was deep in a nap."

"You getting old Detective," Jada said. "Nothing starts happening until *after* midnight. Anyway, my sources just told me that Rachman and Melnick's case files are missing from the records room at the CJC, and from the D.A.'s Office."

Luke was silent as he absorbed this new information.

"Yes, be stunned honey. Be real stunned. You can thank me later."

"And who would want to take these files, Jada?"

"Ain't my job to figure all that out. All I know is they're gone. Now, you need to do some of that detective stuff you do," Jada said.

"I will definitely look into it," Luke replied.

"I knew you would," Jada purred into the phone.

"Let's meet tomorrow," Luke said. "I'll call you at noon with the time and place. Be available."

Luke grabbed his small black book that served as his daily calendar. He scribbled "Call Jay" in one of the pages in the spot marked with the next day's date.

"I'll be available," she replied. "You know I wouldn't miss seeing you for the world."

Luke began to shut off the phone, but stopped abruptly.

"Jada, hold on a minute. Do you know anything about the Scarlet Cord?"

It was Jada's turn to be silent.

"Jada?" he repeated.

"I'm here," she said. "Baby, you don't need to be digging around about no Scarlet Cord," Jada said, her playful tone gone. "Just leave that alone."

"So, you know about it?" Luke was now really interested.

"I don't get involved with them, and I like to keep it that way," she said.

"I just want to know who or what they are."

Luke heard Jada shifting around on the other end.

"Listen, Detective, when I tell you stay away from the Scarlet Cord, you should just stay away."

Then she hung up leaving Luke staring at his phone.

CHAPTER THIRTY-FOUR

FEBRUARY 20th, 12:00 NOON

It was noon when Sisco and Luke pulled into the small parking lot next to the Damascus Road Baptist Church.

It was the old church that now housed the Reclaim Our Communities organization. The rounded archway of the door was evidence of the stone and mortar building's historical architecture. The sign hanging from the second floor window ledge displayed the ROC banner with the familiar red lion. The detectives noticed the small surveillance camera tucked away in the corner of the archway.

Luke pushed the small black button to the right of the door.

"Can I help you," asked a female voice from the intercom a few seconds later.

"Detectives Lucas and Siscowicz to see Mr. Gaylen Torres," Luke said into the intercom.

After a short pause, there was a buzzing sound followed by a muted click.

"Please come in. The main office is in the rear," instructed the voice.

Entering into a large foyer, Luke noticed a small staircase on the left. Once up the stairs, the detectives found themselves at the rear of the church sanctuary. Far down the aisle stood the antique podium and altar. The stained-glass windows, though dusty, still held their magnificence. The carpet was a dingy red velvet, which also lined the rows of pews.

Another ROC banner hung across the top of the altar.

A small white woman in black-rimmed glasses stood next to the podium.

"This way, detectives," she said motioning them down the aisle.

As they walked toward her, Luke remembered how long it had been since he had last attended any church service.

The woman led the detectives down a small hallway that contained several offices, stopping outside a large office at the end of the hallway.

"Please go in." She motioned them through the door.

"Good morning Detectives," Torres said, rising from behind a large wooden desk. He offered his meaty right hand to Sisco and Luke, who shook it.

Not a small man himself, Luke felt average compared to Torres. Torres had to be at least

6-foot-3 or taller. Furthermore, Torres' shoulders were nearly as wide as the doorway.

"Please." Torres motioned for them to sit down.

Although the room was sparsely-furnished, it was neat and orderly. Numerous photos of Torres grinning and shaking hands with who's-who of Philadelphia hung on the walls. There was even a photo of Torres with a popular Democratic presidential candidate a few years back when the candidate was stumping in the city for votes. The sounds of jazz played softly in the background. An open Bible lay on his desk next a Koran and a few other books.

"I see you know your jazz, Mr. Torres," Luke said. "Coltrane?"

"Sonny Rollins." Torres replied. "And thank you, it helps me unwind."

"Sinatra does it for me," Sisco said.

After a few moments of silence, Sisco got down to business.

"Mr. Torres, thanks for seeing us. We have just a few things we want to ask you."

"What 'things' detective?" Torres asked. "Should my lawyer be present?" Torres was calm, but they all knew they were getting close to the line between voluntary police encounter and custodial interrogation.

"Not at all," Luke said. "We're investigating the Rachman killing and hoped that maybe you could direct us to anyone who might be willing to talk to us."

"You mean snitch on whoever it was that took out that scumbag Rachman?" Torres' tone turned serious. Luke wondered what happened to the calming effect of the jazz.

Torres continued.

"Even if I knew who did Rachman, I'd take it to my grave," he said. "Y'all should give whoever did it a damn medal. That's how you take back a community."

"Citizens helping law enforcement keep their streets safe isn't snitching," Luke added. "And, murder isn't how you take back a community."

Torres leaned back in his chair, clearly enjoying the fact that the detectives needed his help.

"Why would the Philly PD think that a simple ex-con like me would know anything about what happened to Rachman?" Torres said.

"You're a popular man, Mr. Torres," Sisco said, taking a different tact. "Popular people know a lot of things and a lot of people. And since you claim you're interested in empowering the people, we just hoped you might give us a name, a place, something to help us out."

Luke decided to push the envelope.

"And, we also know that at some point you and Rachman had an altercation prior to his death."

Luke's hand involuntarily went to his weapon when Torres rose from his chair.

"It's no secret, Detectives, that I'm not the most popular guy among the thieves and thugs in this city," Torres said, walking to the CD player on the far shelf.

Sisco and Luke shifted toward him.

"Rachman was no different," Torres continued. "If you're talking about our incident at the Stella Lane Rec Center a while back, it was nothing more than us letting him and his demons know we weren't going to stand for his criminal behavior."

"I take it he didn't like what you were saying?" Sisco asked.

"Of course he didn't like it. He and his thugs got mad at us, but that's how it ended. We squashed it right there."

"We understand there were threats made -- on both sides," Luke asked, looking at Sisco.

Torres turned back to the detectives.

"So?" Tores responded. "Yeah, we said some unpleasant things, and they said some unpleasant things. Ever been to any of my stop the violence rallies, Detectives?" Torres walked back to his desk and stood behind it.

"The bad guys in the neighborhoods always threaten us because they don't want to be exposed. They have been dug into the community for so long that they aren't used to being told to leave. You think the roaches welcome the exterminators?"

Sisco and Luke knew any further questioning would be interrogation, and at this point, they really had nothing linking Torres to any of the murders. Besides, Torres was too savvy to give them anything more -- even if he was involved.

Torres, however, seemed to read their minds and threw them a bone.

"If you're wondering where I was on the night the news claims Rachman was exterminated, talk to state senator Lloyd Bishop," Torres offered. "I was in Harrisburg that night for a meeting I was having with him the next day. I stayed at the William Penn Hotel up there, room 21. Senator Bishop and I met for lunch the next day for about three hours. You can check it out with his staff."

Luke scribbled the information in his ever-present notepad.

"Mr. Torres," Luke asked, "We're also investigating Richard Melnick's killing. Are you familiar with him?"

"You mean the demon called the "Black Glove Rapist? Yeah, I definitely heard of him."

"Any thoughts on who may have done him?" Luke asked.

Torres chuckled. "I'm sure a whole lot of folks would've liked to exterminate him. Angry mothers, fathers, abused women, take your pick."

Luke figured Torres wouldn't have much info on Melnick, but he felt he had to ask anyway.

"Mr. Torres, ever heard of the Scarlet Cord?" Sisco asked casually.

Torres' casual tone instantly turned serious - again.

"This meeting is over, detectives." Torres said abruptly, moving toward the door and opening it. "I'm a patient man, Detectives, and you'll agree that I've been more than cooperative with you today. Way more than I have to be, especially since I haven't been charged with a crime."

The detectives rose and walked slowly to the door.

"Now, if you'll excuse me, I have more important work to do today than waste my time talking with you about urban myths and ghetto legends. My secretary will show you out."

When they left the church, the detectives were silent until they reached their car. Sisco got in and turned on the ignition. The car hummed to life.

"What do you think?" Luke asked after a few minutes.

"Torres is slick," Sisco answered, pulling out of the parking spot. "Even if his alibi checks out, that doesn't mean he wasn't involved in Rachman's death, or Melnick's for that matter. If he is part of the Scarlet Cord, and if their reach is as big as people say, anyone in that network could've killed them."

"And, even Torres' alibi didn't help us," Luke said. "Because he knows that if we talk to Senator Bishop's office to confirm the alibi, they'll know Torres is a possible suspect in the killings. Which is exactly what Captain Kwan doesn't want."

CHAPTER THIRTY-FIVE

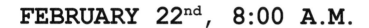

FEBRUARY 22nd, 8:00 A.M.

Beck glistened with the sweat of a vigorous speed bag session. The Slaughterhouse was especially crowded on this Saturday morning as a number of local pro and amateur fighters were training for upcoming bouts.

Between the Rachman and Melnick murders, as well as the rest of his caseload, Beck had been neglecting his fitness.

He figured some gym time would fix that.

Skipping rope in front of one of the full-length mirrors was Teddy "The Hangman" Holmes. He was a solid middleweight whose last bout was televised from Atlantic City. While a nice enough guy, Teddy's hands were too slow and his jaw too fragile to really do any serious damage in such a hard-hitting division. If you can't bring the power, stay in the lower divisions, Beck had been taught.

Sparring in the center ring were Tremain "Diesel Train" Nixon and another fighter whom Beck did not know. Leather and trash talk flew like flies inside the ring, and some of the fighters at ringside had paused their workouts to catch a glimpse. Once his talent caught up with his mouth, Beck thought, 'Diesel Train' might have a future in the welterweights.

Beck's wrapped hands beat a steady rhythm on the speed bag. To the casual observer, Beck's hand speed was quite impressive.

To the trained fighter, however, it was mediocre at best. It was just another example of a former-boxer-turned-weekend-warrior. Beck had become what he had once ostracized: a regular joe who came to the gym, pounded on the heavy bag and skipped some rope to relieve the stress of his *real* job.

As he bobbed and weaved, Beck used an impressive array of punches, left hooks, jabs and combinations into his workout. He felt the heaviness and dull ache in both his shoulders and arms, but he kept on punching.

As he worked the bag, Beck thought about his cases at work, specifically the Rachman and Melnick cases. *What was the killer trying to say with the cards? Was it more than one killer? Did he/she have some kind of a hit list, and if so, who was next?*

Beck's bag workout lasted nearly 30 minutes, and by the time he was done, he was exhausted. Had he still been boxing however, this would have been only a part of his training regimen. Sparring and roadwork, running at least 10 miles a day, would make up the bulk of his pre-fight workouts.

"Lead legs make fighters easy targets, son," Mojo would drum into his head. "Train them legs. Punches don't hurt nothin' if you got no legs behind them."

While the gym had a few showers, Beck preferred to shower at home. After his workout, Beck toweled off and packed his gym bag. He walked toward the door. He also made a mental note to himself to stop by the market and pick up some more milk and dog food for Hannibal on his way home.

Becks' cell phone vibrated as he walked to his car.

"Hello?"

"Counselor, this is Detective Siscowicz. Sorry to bother you this weekend, but I wanted to update you on the Rachman and Black Glove Rapist cases."

Once inside his car, Beck put his cell on speakerphone.

"No problem, Detective," Beck said. "I was just finishing up at the gym. What's up?"

"A couple of things," Sisco said. "One, someone broke into Judge Manigault's house last week and left what appears to be one of our Scripture cards taped to his bathroom mirror."

Beck immediately took the key out of the ignition.

"Also, Rachman's Second-in-command, Baby Mike, was found dead about a week ago in his car," Sisco continued. "The coroner said he was killed by a poison dart. They also found a Scripture card in his car."

"None of that ever made the news!" Beck replied, trying to keep his voice down. "So, now that's three Scripture cards. What the hell is going on?"

Sisco continued.

"We are trying to keep this situation contained as best as we can, Counselor, because we don't want a serial killer panic in the city," Sisco countered. "We already had some leaks to the press about the Melnick card."

"Anything else?" Beck asked.

"We are looking at Gaylen Torres as a possible suspect in the murders," Sisco said. "Our sources tell us Torres and his group ROC may somehow be involved."

Beck absorbed the information as best he could. He knew a possible serial killer had serious implications.

"You know this guy Torres is pretty popular because of his anti-crime stance," Beck asked. "Does he have a prior record?"

"He has a prior armed robbery conviction," Sisco said. "He got out a few years ago after doing almost six years in state prison for that. Beyond that, though, he's clean."

"Got a body warrant for him?" Beck asked.

"Not yet, but we're still investigating. We'll definitely let you know if we pick him up," Sisco said.

"Thanks for the update, Detective," Beck replied.

Beck always worked hard. But, since being promoted to the Homicide Unit, his workload tripled almost overnight. These cases were some of the most serious and most tragic, and as such, there was little room for error.

To prepare, late nights and even weekends at the office were common for Beck. However, the hard work he was putting in was beginning to pay off as he was becoming more comfortable with his cases.

Beck likened it to his early boxing training. He remembered how his legs burned so much during his morning runs that he felt they would spontaneously combust. As his legs got used to the training, though, he almost welcomed the lactic acid burn.

It was one of those fights nearly 13 years ago which now haunted Beck. It was also the last time he stepped into the ring as a professional fighter.

12:00 NOON, same afternoon

Luke and Sisco hated paperwork, as did most cops. They looked at it as a necessary evil, something to endure.

Much like going to the dentist.

Prosecutors, on the other hand, agonized over police paperwork. They knew just how crucial these documents were and just how important they were to build solid cases. With every undotted "i" and uncrossed "t", prosecutors were well aware of just how quickly a good case could fall apart at trial

Similarly, good intelligence also helped to build solid cases.

Luke's cell phone rang. He immediately recognized the number as Jada's.

"What's up," he answered.

"You home alone?," the sultry voice on the other end asked.

"Yeah," replied Luke. "Just catching up on my laying down."

She chuckled.

"Anyway, I got some more info for you." she said.

"I'm listening," Luke said.

"The people you asked me about, well, they may be behind some of the drama that's been going on lately."

Jada took great pains to be as vague as possible. Even though she was pretty sure her cell was safe, she didn't want to take any chances.

Luke sat up in his chair.

"Okay, you got my attention."

"I ain't talking about this on the phone," she said. "I want to talk face-to-face. I should be done at the hairdresser's by four tomorrow afternoon. Pick me up in the parking lot."

* * *

3:30 P.M.

Luke drove his own truck to meet Jada. Traffic was heavy as he picked up Interstate 76 from the Vine Street Expressway in downtown Philadelphia. From there he would hopefully have a smooth ride up the Schuyllkill Expressay past Conshohocken to the King of Prussia Mall. Jada was getting her hair done at Soliloquy, one of the premier upscale hair salons in the area.

As he pulled into the parking lot, Luke checked out the auto show near the hair salon. Mercedes, Jaguars and BMW's. Soliloquy's clientele was largely female, white and wealthy.

All it needed was a red carpet, and this could be the Grammys.

As soon as he pulled up, Luke saw a pretty young African-American woman in sunglasses wrapped in an expensive coat and leather boots step out of the doorway of the salon. He timed his stop to meet her at the passenger side.

Jada hurried to the car, slid in, shut the door and buckled her seat belt before greeting Luke with a big smile.

Luke nodded, then pulled off slowly, partly because the parking lot was crowded, and partly to see if they were being watched or followed.

"What's going on Jada," Luke greeted her.

"You know, baby, we've gotta stop meeting like this," Jada said, settling in for the ride. "I

don't know, Detective, you could get used to this…
if you let yourself." Jada eased back one side of
her coat so Luke could see her shapely legs through
her tight jeans.

For all of her sass and all of his seriousness,
however, she knew that the big detective truly
cared for her.

The feeling was definitely mutual. While she had
the prime street intel, and the detective paid well
for it (despite department policy), the two had an
unspoken bond: You watch my back, and I'll watch
yours.

Besides their age difference, Luke kept in mind
that he was still a veteran cop, and she was his
informant. Because of this, Luke was very careful
not to cross the line where business turns to
pleasure.

Jada felt differently.

"Jada, why are you playin' me? Don't make me have
to pull teeth to get intel. I pay you good money,
and I want good info – the first time I ask," Luke
said, never taking his eyes off the road.

Jada became serious.

"I'm scared, okay?" she said. "I'm scared of what
these people might do to me if they knew I knew
what they was about."

She wiped her eyes with the back of her left
hand.

Luke saw she was crying.

It was Luke's turn to be silent. Jada was

definitely beautiful, and she was as gutsy as any cop he knew. It was these qualities that allowed her to get into some of the tightest spots to get some of the best information.

However, he just realzed that for all her style, sensuality and snarl, she was still just a young woman trying to keep her head above water in an ocean of sharks. At some point, Luke realized that Jada would want – *would need* – to get a legitimate profession if she wanted to have a future.

Luke drove out of the parking lot and into the steady traffic on Mall Boulevard.

"Look, you know I got your back, right Jada?" Luke asked while merging lanes. "I've never let anything happen to you, have I?"

Jada looked at Luke.

"No, baby, you haven't," Jada conceded. "I gotta admit, you always there for me. But, this is different. Totally different. These Scarlet Cord people is different. They're dangerous. Baby you good, but you can't be everywhere at once."

"How different, Jada?" Luke said. "Tell me what they're about."

Jada sighed. She stared out the window at the passing traffic on the interstate.

"Fifteen years ago, when my brother Reno was killed, I almost lost my mind. I was a senior in high school. My mom and grandma couldn't take it either. My grandfather was in the streets, so I never really met him. We was so upset because Reno was a good guy, straight-A student, star athlete, the whole nine yards."

"Gunned down one Christmas Eve by that kid Donovan Bigler, right?" Luke responded. "Gang member and convicted felon."

"Yep, that's him," Jada said. "They called him 'Big Time' on the streets. Anyway, when the cops finally arrested him, we all thought justice would be done, you know."

"I know," Luke agreed.

"Well, when Donovan had the eyewitness to Reno's murder killed before trial, the judge had no choice but to throw out the case. And, that damn killer just walked out the courtroom smiling." Jada dabbed at her eyes.

Luke fished out a tissue from the console and handed it to Jada.

She continued.

"Grandma and mommy really lost it then. They got mad, then they started organizing people on the block, since Grandma was a block captain. They also started meeting with some other moms whose sons had been killed by street violence."

"What happened then?" Luke asked.

"Well, I used to overhear some of their meetings at our house, even though Mommy used to make me go up to my room whenever they came over. One meeting, I heard them talk about getting someone to 'get to' Donovan, if you know what I mean." Jada said.

"Yeah, they wanted someone to kill him," Luke replied.

She nodded.

"During their meetings, I started hearing them call their group the 'Network'. Then, I heard they had put a hit out on Donovan."

"Your grandmother's group?" Luke asked quickly glancing at Jada.

"Yep. I don't know how they did it, but the word on the street was that Donovan was one of the network's targets," Jada replied.

She paused then continued.

"Did they ever get him?" Luke asked.

Jada paused before continuing.

"About a week later, a homeless man found him dead in some abandoned warehouse near the airport with his throat slashed. I don't know who actually killed Donovan, but about a week before that my grandma took me with her to meet with some man at the bus station.

He looked real familiar. She said he was an old friend and that he had connections in the court system. I heard her talking with him about the 'Donovan thing'."

"Did she give him any money, or any kind of payment?" Luke asked.

"I don't think so. She took some money to pay him, but he refused. I overheard him tell her something like he didn't take money for doing 'the people's business.'" Jada said.

Luke's head was spinning with Jada's revelations.

"What about your mom? Was she involved with that deal?" Luke asked.

"At first, Mommy wanted Donovan dead. But, after she thought about it, she got scared and said she didn't want to get mixed up with no hit man or nothing like that."

"What did the man your grandmother meet with look like?"

"Short, dark-skinned muscular man," Jada said. "Bald-headed with real scary eyes. I won't ever forget those eyes. However, like I said, there was something real familiar about him. It was weird."

Luke maneuvered onto I-76 West back to Philadelphia.

"Did you and your grandmother ever talk about it afterward?" Luke asked.

"All she said was that I should never talk about what happened. She said I needed to always keep it a secret, even from mommy. After Donovan was found dead, I really got scared. All I knew was that grandma met with some man, then Donovan was killed."

Jada paused.

"Plus, the man knew who we was. Hell, I was prepared to take that to my grave." she said.

"So, when your grandma kept working with the Scarlet Cord, you knew she was just getting in deeper and deeper, right?"

Jada shook her head.

"She told me that everyone in the network was sworn to secrecy, and that they were even prepared to kill other members to protect the group," Jada continued.

"That's why you think the Scarlet Cord may be involved with the Rachman and Melnick murders because of the missing Court files," Luke said. "Donovan's killer may have had ties to the Court system, right?"

Jada nodded in agreement.

"Is your mother still involved?" Luke asked.

"I don't know," Jada answered. "After my grandmom died a few years ago, mommy held some meetings, but not as much. Mommy did tell me that more and more people had joined the network. A lot of people."

Luke turned onto City Line Avenue and drove toward Jada's apartment in an upscale section of Roxborough.

"Jada, I know this was tough for you to tell me," Luke said. "I really appreciate this info. I know you're scared, but you did good giving me what you did."

Luke gently patted her leg, then passed her a small white business envelope.

She took it without looking at it, but she could feel the weight of the paper bills inside.

"Thanks, Detective. You know I'm going out on a limb for you. You better not let me fall."

Luke nodded, but said nothing. Knowing he

couldn't make any guarantees, Luke silently steered into the parking lot of the apartment complex.

5:45 PM

Mike's Monster Meals was but one of many of Philadelphia's little eateries that didn't look like much on the outside.

Inside, however, they served some of the best and cheapest comfort food in the region. Most cops knew these eateries, preferring these "greasy spoons" as some called them to the more well-known establishments. In addition to the good food and great prices, they provided a safe atmosphere to discuss police matters.

This is why Sisco and Luke decided to have dinner at "Mike's" today to discuss Luke's earlier meeting with Jada.

"What'll you guys have today?" asked Jen, one of Mike's two pretty waitresses. Jen and Caroline, the other waitress, were flirty, but never offensive and well-known to all the patrons.

"Let me get the hot roast beef sandwich with a side of fries," Luke said. "And, I'll have an iced tea please."

She looked at Sisco.

"I'll take the chicken parmesan, a Diet Coke and some apple pie," Sisco said.

"You got it. I'll be back with your orders in a bit," Jen said then left.

"Thanks Jen," Luke responded. Sisco nodded at Jen.

"Sisco, you gonna need all week to walk all that food off," Luke joked.

"I know, I know," Sisco said, unfolding his napkin.

Despite the cold weather, the atmosphere inside Mike's was warm and friendly.

"So, what did Jada have to say?" Sisco asked.

"According to Jada, the Scarlet Cord is an organization, like a citizen's group. It's a network of citizens who anonymously give information to each other on the whereabouts of criminals and defendants. Some of the information on the Citizen's Crime Hotline probably comes from these people."

"So, why do they share info with each other?" Sisco asked, looking around to see who else was in the restaurant.

"From what I got from Jada, to track down some of these fools," Luke responded.

"Track them down? For what?"

"Well, when the organization first started, they apparently were just supposed to share info on the bad guy's whereabouts, then anonymously alert the cops," Luke said.

"I guess they don't believe in the whole 'stop snitching' foolishness," Sisco said.

"Not at all," Luke said. "Somehere along the

line, however, sharing info wasn't enough for them. Some in the group wanted these bad guys taken out. Eliminated."

"So, they went from intel network to urban guerrillas?" Sisco asked.

"Yeah, Bro," Luke said, lowering his voice. "That's what it seems like. Sisco, from what Jada says, these people are *all over the place*. Some of these people may even work in the court system. Once they get the information, they pass it on to someone who then takes out the criminal."

"Like vigilantes?" Sisco asked leaning in toward Luke. "You mean the Scarlet Cord gathers info, locates the perps, then hunts them down?"

The conversation ended abruptly as Jen came by and gave Luke his iced tea. He nodded his thanks.

"You got it, bro," Luke continued when Jen left. "The network came about because the word in the community is that we ain't doing our jobs, and the court system can't be trusted. So, the people got together and handled their own business," Luke said, sipping the tea Jen just set before him.

"This is some serious stuff, Luke," Sisco replied.

"I know. I'm telling you, Sisco, Jada was shaking just telling me about the Scarlet Cord," Luke finished. "Bruh, she was terrified they were going to find out she was telling me about the organization."

"I know Jada to be tough, but she's still a young woman on her own," Sisco said. "That alone would scare anyone."

Luke shook his head.

"I've never seen Jada so scared. According to her, these people have no problem crossing the line to accomplish their mission."

"So, what are you saying, Luke? That they're not above murder?" Sisco asked.

Luke shrugged. "I'll bet a lot of our unsolved Homicides are a result of this Scarlet Cord. According to Jada, there's a whole network of people who not only track thugs down and take them out, but who also even dispose of the bodies and hide evidence."

Sisco sighed and sat back in the booth, spreading his arms out on the back of the booth. He looked out the window at the emptying parking lot and gray sky.

"Where'd they get the name the Scarlet Cord?" he asked.

"I did some research online," Luke said. "From what I got, the name likely comes from the Bible in the book of Joshua," Luke replied. "Apparently, there was a woman named Rahab who promised to hide Joshua and Caleb from the Canaanites because Joshua and Caleb were told by God to take her city. Things were so bad there, so God promised to give the Israelites the land. Caleb and Joshua were sent to Canaan as spies. They were invited by Rahab, a Canaanite woman, to stay with her. In return for hiding and protecting them, Joshua and Caleb promised to spare Rahab and her family when the

Israelites took over the city. All she had to do was have her family hang a scarlet cord in their window so Joshua and Caleb would know they were Rahab's family members and then would not destroy them."

"So, that was a sign to leave that house alone," Sisco replied.

"You got it," Luke said. A secret sign for a secret group of people who plan on taking back their city from criminals."

CHAPTER THIRTY-SIX

FEBRUARY 23rd, 11:00 P.M.

Beck woke up from another nightmare.

He wasn't sure how long he'd slept. Serene lay nestled between him and the cushions of his couch.

After he decided time off from their relationship wasn't the answer, Beck managed to patch things up with Serene. While not solid, their relationship had at least healed sufficiently over the past week or so. Things were going so well, in fact, that Beck managed to convince Serene to come over for a peace-offering dinner.

He gently peeled Serene's arms from around his waist as he sat up.

"Beck, what's wrong baby?" Serene asked. "Why are you so restless?" Serene propped herself up on an elbow.

"I'm having those nightmares again," Beck answered. He was still groggy.

"About June Bug? I thought they'd stopped?"

"They had," Beck said, rubbing his temples.

"Did you call Dr. Massingale?" Serene asked, sitting up.

"No."

"Why not?" she asked.

"I got this right now," Beck said. "Besides, I don't need to talk to a therapist."

"There's that old Beck Stephens ego, again," she said, standing up.

Beck was tired and scared. He knew Serene meant well.

"I don't need this right now," Beck said. "What I just need you to do is to understand, to be there for me. I didn't want or need a lecture." Beck stood up in front of Serene. "I don't feel like getting into another stupid argument like some old married couple."

Serene silenced him by holding up her hands. Beck knew he'd crossed the line, but he couldn't call the words back.

"You're right, Beck," Serene said softly. "You're absolutely right. You don't have to worry about me lecturing or nagging you anymore."

As Serene started gathering her things together, Beck knew he'd hurt her. As he watched her put on her coat, Beck realized that even the fear of his nightmares was nothing compared to losing Serene.

"Serene, I'm scared," Beck said suddenly.

Serene turned to look at him.

"It was never about you, or us. It was always me."

"Scared of what?" asked Serene, coming back into the room.

"Scared of losing you," Beck said, walking toward her. "You know my family life wasn't the most stable. My father was a con man who never had a stable job. My mother worked her tail off to give me and my sister the best life she could."

"Honey, I know all that. But what's that got to do with …"

"I'm scared that with all my commitment issues, and my issues with my father, that one day you'll decide that you don't want to be bothered with me anymore."

Beck now stood in front of her.

"I couldn't take it if you just walked away," he said. "Besides the judge and my sister, you are all I have."

It was Serene's turn to be silent as she tried to regain her composure.

"Baby, why are you just telling me this now? We've been seeing each other for over three years?"

Beck struggled to get a better handle on his feelings. He took his time answering.

"When we first started, I didn't think we'd get this far. I wasn't looking to get caught up in a relationship, know what I'm saying? The only relationships I know of that worked out were my grandparents."

"Yes, honey, but that doesn't mean --"

"I figured if I kept myself from falling in love, I wouldn't get hurt or abandoned," Beck said.

Serene stepped closer to Beck.

"So you thought if I left you while we were just in a relationship, the pain wouldn't be as bad if that happened while were married," Serene said.

"Yes," Beck said, turning away. He sat down on the couch.

"Now you know. So, what now?" He asked.

Serene went over to Beck, sat in his lap, then cradled his head to her chest.

"What we do now," she said, "is work on changing your mind."

CHAPTER THIRTY-SEVEN

FEBRUARY 25th, 10:00 A.M...

Sisco took his stance behind the safety line, raised his gun and took aim at the paper figure some fifty feet away. Gently squeezing the trigger, he put six quick rounds into the target's kill zone, the area around the upper chest. His standard issue earphones muffled the Glock's report.

"Not bad," shouted Sergeant John Truitt, standing nearby. "Not bad at all."

Sisco heard him desite his large ear phones.

John worked in the 5th Police District up in Roxborough. "It's amazing your gun still works, Sisco, considering the fact that you got that cushy homicide gig."

Sisco smiled as he placed his gun on the counter in front of him. He was separated by the other shooters by his own stall.

"John, I could wake up from a coma, come up here to the range in my pajamas and still qualify each month," Sisco quipped. "Between the military and the Police Department, firing a weapon is like breathing to me."

The Philadelphia Police Department required every officer, no matter the rank, to qualify at the firing range at least once a year. While Sisco rarely drew his weapon as a homicide detective, he didn't want to discover that his marksmanship skills had eroded should he need them in an emergency.

Sisco's cell phone rang just as he was aiming his weapon. Glancing down at the phone, he saw a number with an unfamiliar area code.

He holstered his weapon, stepped away from the range and left the large room. He then grabbed the phone from his belt holder and put it to his left ear.

"Hello?"

"Is this Detective Siscowicz?" The voice was that of an elderly female, maybe late 70s – or older. Most definitely southern.

"This is Detective Siscowicz, ma'am. How can I help you?"

"I'm Geneva Pickett. Dezzi, uh, I'm sorry, Miss Desiree Lake from the Reddington Public Library here in Mississippi gave me your number. She said you wanted some information on Gloria Stewart. The lady with the Scripture cards."

Sisco felt a rush of excitement, but the firing range wasn't the optimal place for an interview.

"Mrs. Pickett, I'm not in my office. Can I call you back in about a half an hour? Does that work with your schedule?"

"Honey, I'll be here," she replied. "I'm 76 years old. Where am I going? Well, except to meet my Lord one of these old days," she chuckled. "Take your time Detective. Today's my quiet day, so I'll be home. You can call me back."

He jotted down her number, then signed out and headed for his car.

11:25 A.M.

"Court will adjourn as the jury deliberates," Lester, Zane's Court Crier, said as he dismissed the jury in the case of *Commonwealth v. Demetrius Combs*. The audience stood silently as the twelve jurors and two alternates filed out of the Courtroom.

Demetrius "Boota" Combs was on trial for his life. Charged with several offenses, including Murder and Carjacking, Combs was looking directly at lethal injection if convicted. To his credit, Combs had hired Daria Troy, one of the city's finest defense attorneys as his counsel.

A one-time Assistant D.A., Troy had left the prosecutor's office a few years ago and opened up her own law practice. Since that time, she had represented some of the city's worst defendants.

Today, many of those defendants walked the streets as free men due to her legal expertise. Her new Rolls Royce Bentley was reportedly a gift from one of her satisfied clients.

Boota's case was Zane's third murder trial since the beginning of the year. To prepare for it, he'd cleared his docket for at least three weeks. Picking the jury took almost a week due to the horrific facts of the case, and the ensuing media attention.

Since the trial started, Zane had to force himself to sit through heart-wrenching testimony and evidence without losing his judicial professionalism. The latest recess was a chance for not only the jury to refresh themselves, but to allow Zane time to take a breather from the case and cool down.

Combs was a scary character.

A career criminal by trade, Demetrius Combs had an extensive criminal record. After stealing a bike at 12 years old, Combs had graduated to armed robberies by age 16. As a young adult, Combs continued to commit crimes, each one getting bolder and more violent.

Due to a string of generous judges in the city, Combs had spent very little time in jail for any of his crimes. The phrase most often used by the judges was "troubled childhood" when they placed him on probation after probation, believing that all Combs really needed was a little tough love and some anger management classes.

Before long, Combs had made the city's most wanted list.

As he learned more about Combs, Zane thought he knew what Combs needed.

Anger management wasn't the answer.

Zane was appalled as he listened to the A.D.A present the Commonwealth's evidence against Combs.

During a two-month period the year before, Combs had allegedly committed a string of violent robberies of fast food restaurants. According to the evidence, Combs would stake out the place, or send in an associate to do it. That way, they could determine when the restaurant would make the bank deposits, then rob the place at gunpoint right before the funds were taken to the bank.

At most of the robberies, Combs tied up and blindfolded the cashiers and whoever else was in the store at the time with duct tape. In addition, he wore a ski mask while he and his accomplices robbed the places. While he allegedly roughed up some of his victims during the robberies, no one was seriously hurt.

That was until the last robbery.

On the night of May 23rd of last year, Nicole Montgomery and Walter Fishbeck had the unfortunate distinction of being in the fast-food restaurant Combs chose to rob.

He and his cohorts donned black hoodies and ski masks and entered the restaurant, guns drawn.

During the course of that robbery, Combs thought that either Montgomery of Fishbeck recognized his voice. As a result, he herded the pair into the freezer and promptly proceeded to execute them.

Montgomery was 19 years old, Fishbeck 21. Fishbeck was working at the restaurant part-time, while attending a local college full-time. Montgomery had only begun working there recently when her mother became ill with Alzheimer's.

Video from inside the store's freezer captured the murders. Specifically, the videotape graphically showed how Montgomery's and Fishbeck's bodies convulsed when Combs shot them as they lay facedown on the cold freezer floor.

After the murders, Combs and his associates were so brazen that they turned on the grill and made themselves burgers and fries. One detective even testified that it appeared that Combs was so callous that he even went back into the freezer to get some ice for his soda -- stepping over the bloody bodies as they grew cold on the floor.

The Commonwealth had no eyewitnesses because the suspects all wore masks. However, they were able to lift some of Combs' DNA from off of a plastic straw in front of the restaurant.

In addition, there was a woman who testified that she saw a car carrying several young black men drive quickly out of the parking shortly after the crime. Detectives traced the car's license plate to Combs' deceased aunt.

Moreover, Combs' cell records placed him in the area around the time of the murders. Detectives never recovered a murder weapon when they finally arrested him. However, they did find ammunition in a family member's home which matched the slugs taken from Fishbeck's body. Detectives believe Combs and his cohorts wore gloves during the crime which explained the lack of fingerprints.

Throughout the trial, Combs showed no real emotion. Sitting next to Daria Troy in a suit, Combs was clean-shaven and wore a sharp blue suit. He could pass for a stockbroker or banker.

"Think they'll find him guilty, Judge?" Felice asked, once Zane's staff had assembled back in his chambers.

"If they don't, I will," Zane growled softly.

Felice opened her mouth to respond, but the tone of Zane's answer made her decide otherwise. She had sat through most of the four-day trial and had taken copious notes. She had also noticed the Judge's demeanor grow more and more brooding as the trial went on. He'd barely spoken to his staff and was unusually testy.

"If Combs had been given jail time for his last robbery, he'd probably still be in jail and we wouldn't be here," Ron said as he looked out of the huge bay window of Zane's chambers. "Who was the judge on that case?"

"That damn Janice Murphy," Zane answered contemptuously from behind his desk. "I read the notes of testimony on that case. In fact, I read the whole case file. Combs always had a killer temper, and it was just a matter of time before he actually killed someone. I tell you, if judges in this city were appointed, instead of elected, half of these ACLU and left wing-liberals would not be on the bench."

"You actually got the file on that case, Judge?" Felice said. She finally trusted her mouth to say something to Zane that wouldn't set him off.

That, however, wasn't it.

"You can take your lunch, now, Felice," Zane replied curtly. "I'll see you back at two."

Visibly shaken, Felice quietly rose and walked toward the door. Zane and Ron were left alone in the spacious room.

"Zane, that wasn't necessary," Ron said. "She's a good kid, Zane, you know that."

"I know, I know," Zane said, sighing and rubbing his eyes. "Felice knows I didn't mean it. She's been with me long enough to know how I get when I'm on trial. Maybe I'll get her some flowers."

"I'll pick up some roses for her on my way back from lunch," Ron offered. "I gotta go past the florist anyway."

Ron made sure the chambers were clear.

"Do you think this jury will acquit Combs?" Ron asked.

Zane adjusted his suit jacket beneath his overcoat.

"Can't tell with juries, Ron, you know that. I just hope they do the right thing."

12:00 P.M.

"Detective Siscowicz, I tell you, Gloria Stewart was quite a woman."

Geneva Pickett was like an expert witness, nosy neighbor and historian all rolled into one. For nearly an hour, she had given Sisco choice information on the old South, Gloria Stewart and her life, and the origin of the Scripture cards which had found their way north to his city.

Geneva Pickett and Gloria Stewart attended the same church when they were young girls. Gloria was a few years older than Geneva.

While not best friends, they spoke often, mostly after service. In addition to being a local activist back in Jim Crow-era Reddington, Gloria was also something of a local legend.

According to Geneva, Gloria Stewart was "quite handy with a rifle, and could track an animal better than a bloodhound."

She and her husband Grady had apparently built their home back near the woods of Reddington. Though not very sociable, Gloria and Grady had a small circle of friends, mostly church folk. The Stewarts were thought of as religious fanatics. The Pentecostal revolution had not been received too well in pre-civil rights Reddington.

"What did her husband do, Mrs. Pickett?" Sisco asked, scribbling like a secretary taking shorthand.

"Grady? He drove a truck for a while, then

retired after he was injured in an accident," she recounted. "Wasn't too long after that when he was killed."

"By who?" Sisco asked. He stopped taking notes.

Geneva took a long pause, as if she were at the top of a slope ready to ski down.

"People say it was the Klan that got him for being too outspoken, too uppity. Back then, Klan - well most white folks, period - didn't like Blacks who stood up for themselves. Besides that, it was rumored that Glo and Grady was part of an underground group that did things, you know, caused trouble."

"Like what kind of trouble?" Sisco stopped scribbling.

"Like kidnap and murder some Klansmen. After a young man named Charles Dix got killed, some local Klan members disappeared. A few days later, their bodies turned up off some backwoods road, beaten and tied to a stake. They had apparently been set afire and the swamp animals ate what was left of them. A few of the hermits back there swore they didn't see anything, didn't know anything. The Klan caught one of those hermits and tortured him until he told what he knew: that Gloria was involved in the Klan killings and riling up Black folks."

"Why didn't the Klan just kill Gloria? It seemed like they had no problems killing Black people back then?" Sisco asked.

Despite having a Black partner, Black Marine

buddies and many Black friends, Sisco realized he needed to tread lightly with Geneva Pickett. As a Polish-American, he knew of some past bias against his ancestors, but it was nothing like what Black people in America endured.

As Geneva spoke, Sisco sensed that the wounds of centuries of oppression were still fresh. While Sisco could honestly say he was not racist, he still realized he was not Black. Therefore, he could not even begin to understand the depths of racism's wounds of the old south.

Geneva continued.

"Oh, they tried. Honey, they tried," Geneva sighed. "But, like I told you, Gloria and her husband was good organizers. Some people say they had even organized the people together into some kind of vigilante group."

"Vigilante group?" said Sisco, switching his cell from his left to his right hear. "What did they do?"

"Well, I guess it's safe to talk now, since most of them, as well as most of them Klan is dead and gone. But, from what I was told, Gloria's group would arrange for certain folks to be kidnapped and murdered. You know, members of the Klan, or other whites terrorizing Black folks in the town. Police would find their bodies days later."

"No one ever found out her group was responsible for the murders?" Sisco asked, resuming his writing.

"Oh, I'm sure some of them white people knew,

but I think they was afraid. They knew Gloria and her group was real secretive and could operate in the shadows if need be. They also knew the group members was sworn to secrecy, and wouldn't tell on each other, even if their lives was at stake."

"Were all the Black people there involved?" Sisco asked.

"No, not really. In fact, you still had quite a few Uncle Toms who thought Glo – that's what I called her – was crazy. Those Blacks were still loyal to the whites and didn't want anybody to make trouble. They just figured everyone could just get along, if Blacks knew their place. So, they acted as informants for the whites and Klan. Surprisingly, there was even some whites who hated Jim Crow and helped Glo and her group."

"How'd anyone know who was with Gloria, and who wasn't?" asked Sisco fascinated by the history Geneva Pickett was revealing.

"Well, it was a small town and they all basically knew each other," she said. "Word of mouth travelled faster then the phone in them days. Also, they had other ways. This guy who lived down the road once told me that Gloria's people wore special colored bracelets around their wrists, so they'd know each other. The bracelets looked just like ordinary braided pieces of cord so non-members wouldn't think anything of it."

"Did you think she was a fanatic? Sisco asked.

"Not really," Geneva said. "I knew that she kind

of kept to herself, and she loved her family. I also knew that she was real religious. It was like she could call down God's power when she needed it. Some folks even claimed she and her people could heal the sick and raise the dead. So, I think the Klan, even for all their evilness, didn't want no trouble with Gloria Stewart if they could avoid it."

"Did Gloria and her husband have any kids?" Sisco asked.

"They had two kids, Grady, Jr., and Helen," she replied. "Grady, Jr. met some young gal from Calfornia and moved out west back in '52. Helen stayed in Reddington, and got married to a local businessman, Ted Russell, or something like that. They both had two kids, two little boys. One died of pneumonia when he was a baby. I can't remember their names, though."

"Whatever happened to Helen and Grady, Jr.?" Sisco asked.

"Unfortunately, while the Klan was afraid to touch Gloria, I guess they figured they'd get the next best thing," Geneva said. "They bombed Helen and Ted's house one night. They were killed instantly. Their remaining son wasn't at home, though. Ain't never heard nothing 'bout Grady, Jr., since he went out west."

"What happened to Helen and Ted's remaining son?" Sisco asked, surprised at how his anger level had risen as Geneva told her story.

"Gloria and Grady were watching the boy that

night. After Helen and Ted died, Gloria and Grady raised the boy. He had to be about four when his parents were killed."

"What happened to Gloria and the boy after Grady died?" Sisco asked, trying to follow the family tree.

"Well, depending on who you talk to, Gloria taught the boy how to survive in the backwoods, how to shoot a rifle and other things. In fact, folks think she and the boy may have even killed two of them monsters involved in Emmett Till's murder. Word has it that she and the boy, who was about 15 at the time, stalked Porter Green and Slater Ross over in Tallahatchee County and slaughtered them as they came from a Klan meeting one night. Their bodies were found a few weeks later as the buzzards was feasting on them in the backwoods."

"Wait a minute. Emmett Till was killed in about '55, right?" Sisco was scribbling figures on an old scratchpad. "If the boy was 15 when he and Gloria killed those two, what'd they do? Wait for ten years to slaughter them?"

"Detective, I'm sure you run into folks who have their reasons for waiting on revenge," she said. "Whether they stalk their prey, lay the right bait or trap, or whatever. They takes care of business. That's how Gloria was. She was calculating, cunning and had the patience of Job and the memory of an elephant. That's how Black folks had to be to survive back in the day. We had to smile in your face, while waiting for our chance to cut your heart out. It didn't matter if it took us a lifetime, we'd get our revenge."

"What about her Scripture cards?" Sisco asked.

This was the $64,000,000 question; Sisco saved it for last so he could put it into context.

"Glo always had a Bible around, in the kitchen, the bathroom, the sun porch, wherever. She was constantly teaching her grandson about the Lord. When he was six, the year after his parents were murdered, Gloria gave him a set of little cards with Bible verses on them. Very beautiful. Plastic coated, with a little gold border. She got them right from Hasting Religious Specialties in town on special order."

"How'd you know all of this?" he asked.

"I used to work there part-time in the order department from 1952 to 1956," she said. "I even got her the deal on the cards with my employee discount. They were our special "Glory" series, because their serial number started with a "J" for Jesus."

Sisco couldn't wait to get down to Mississippi. Here was the link to the murders. He had to talk to her in person. He had a final question before he let her go.

"Mrs. Pickett, how many sets of those cards did the company make?" he asked.

"Oh, not many. Not many at all. In fact, in my years at the company, only a few people got special orders of that type. Glo was one of them. I'm sorry I couldn't be much more help than that."

Siscowicz wanted to kiss her. She had provided a key link in their investigation. Now, all he needed to do was match the cards found on the victims with the cards Gloria Stewart had ordered. Geneva was going to locate the paperwork from her old files (she was a pack rat and hated to throw anything away), and then give him a call. He and Luke could fly down early next week to meet her and compare evidence.

Sisco felt the noose tightening around the Scripture Killer's neck. Once he found him, he'd pick his brain.

He may even thank him.

Despite the killer's twisted logic, Sisco had to admit that the guy managed to do something that the Philadelphia Police Department couldn't do: take the fight to the criminals.

2:00 P.M., *same afternoon.*

"All Rise."

Lester had just finished calling the Court to order after lunch. In fact, lunch was cut short because the jury indicated it had reached a verdict in the case of the Commonealth v. Demetrius Combs. Zane was eating in his chambers when Pat informed him.

Zane strode to the bench with determination.

"I don't like it," said Zane to Ron as he hurriedly put on his black robe. "Not a bit. When these juries come back in such a short time, they almost always come back with a 'Not Guilty'."

The 12 jurors and two alternates filed into the Courtroom somberly. None made eye contact with either Zane or the defense table.

"When did they deliberate? During the damn trial?" Ron asked incredulously as he and Zane walked into the courtroom. The jury had already been seated in the jury box.

The courtroom was packed.

Tension and anticipation hung like humidity in the room. From behind the bench, Zane easily picked out the informal seating arrangements in the galley as the victim's families and supporters sat behind the Commonwealth's table to the left, while the defendant's family sat behind the defense table on the right. The victim's families were closer to the jury box.

"Be seated," Zane announced as he sat down. "I understand the jury has reached a verdict?"

"We have, Your Honor," said Barbara McDougal, the jury foreperson.

Zane scanned the faces of the jurors prior to the reading of the verdict and he didn't like what he saw. Most of the jurors wouldn't look at the prosecutor's table. A few made eye contact with the defendant.

"Will the foreperson please rise," Lester said.

A small Irish woman slowly stod up.

"On the charge of murder in the first degree," Lester read, holding the bills of information printed on light blue sheets of paper, "what is your verdict?"

"Not guilty," the woman said softly.

"Praise Jesus!" shrieked Demetrius' mother as she leapt from her seat. A young woman with orange-dyed hair embraced Demetrius' mother.

"Dear God!" said the mother of Walter Fishbeck, one of the slain victims. She wept openly, her shoulders trembling as she was overcome by grief.

Zane fought hard to keep a stoic and impartial look on his face as the foreperson repeated "Not Guilty" to the remaining charges Lester read.

"Mr. Combs," Zane said through pursed lips, "you are free to go." Zane's voice was barely audible amid the Combs' family celebration.

Zane did not thank the jury for their service afterwards.

The courtroom atmosphere was a portrait in contrasts: on one side, jubilation and glee. On the other, shock and disbelief.

Zane left the bench well before Lester officially ended the day's docket of cases.

His demeanor was grim.

"I can't take this much longer, Ron," Zane said back in the robing room. "Damn it! This city is another Sodom and Gomorrah. Doesn't anyone care? Was that jury listening to the same case we were?"

Ron only nodded. He knew it was better to listen when Zane was in one of these moods.

"And, did you see that sick bastard grinning after the verdict like he was named Nobel Prize winner or something?" Zane ranted.

"Zane, you know as well as I do that you'll see this fool again," said Ron, trying to appease Zane. "He'll get picked up again for something else."

"Yeah, but who else will have to die because of it?" Zane looked pensive as he stared out of the huge bay window of his chambers.

"Once again, the wolves are free to prey on the sheep."

4:10 P.M.

Sisco stacked all four cards together in front of him on the table. He leaned back in his chair.

Luke stood next to him at the white board with the mugshots of Rachman, Melnick, Manigault and Baby Mike posted on it. They had gotten a photo of Judge Manigault from the City's Judicial yearbook.

He drew a line connecting the photos using a red magic marker.

Underneath each photo, the detectives had previously written numerous facts and information. They used black ink for that.

He stepped back. Sisco scanned the photos and the rest of the information written on the board.

"Perfect match," said Luke, comparing the cards found on Rachman, in Melnick's car, in Mike's truck and on Judge Manigault's mirror.

Luke handed the small laminated cards inside the plastic ziplock bag to Sisco. He could clearly see the cards' similarities as he laid them out next to each other on the table inside the Homicide Unit.

"Yeah, they look the same to me," Sisco conceded.

"That's three man. Three of the city's worst criminals slaughtered by a vigilante who leaves a Scripture calling card," Luke said. Luke stood next to his partner and examined the pieces of evidence. "What kind of kook does this?"

"Up until Manigault became a part of this equation, I thought we may just be dealing wth your regular vigilante kook," Sisco said. "However, regular kooks don't just sneak into a judge's house – at night – undetected to chop off off a lock of the judge's hair."

"True," Luke nodded. "That took balls. Big balls to roll up into the Judge's own bedroom."

"So we know this person is about law and order," Sisco replied. "He is not afraid to kill and has the ability to remain silent."

Luke stared at the board.

"Military? Ex cop? What you think," he asked Sisco. "He damn sure ain't no amateur."

"Definitely not. I think this guy is too smart to be some regular joe street thug," Sisco replied, "and I really don't see this dude as some psycho."

"I think this cat is some anti-crime crusader. Maybe some disgruntled Town Watch member," Luke said. "And, he's no dummy. Think about it: he knows that taking out some hard-core criminals will give him street cred, take the fools off the street and won't draw a lot of police attention; he figures the cops won't devote a lot of man-power to tracking down the killer."

Sisco turned toward Luke.

"Hell, that makes sense," Sisco said. "Even the community doesn't seem to want to help us. The anonymous crime hotline has been silent on tips about the Scripture Killer."

"This dude probably figured that actually killing Manigault would bring too much heat," Luke said.

"So, he sends the Judge a clear message instead," Sisco agreed. "I could have gotten you."

Luke nodded.

"So, the Scripture cards are simply a smokescreen?" Luke asked. "I mean, those aren't puzzles for us to fgure out, right?"

Sisco picked up the cards again. He flipped them over individually.

"No," Sisco said, "that's a message for the bad guys. It's letting them know God is not too happy."

CHAPTER THIRTY-EIGHT

MARCH 4th, 9:30 A.M.

IS PHILADELPHIA BEING TERRORIZED BY A SERIAL KILLER? THREE MURDERS. THREE SCRIPTURE CARDS. MANY QUESTIONS.

"You see this?" Sisco passed the daily paper to his partner. "The press couldn't even wait for the Department to brief the public on these cases. They had to be the first to get it out there."

Sisco continued to read.

Since the beginning of the year, Philadelphia's murder rate has picked up where it left off from last year's staggering totals.

However, several of the murders may be linked by a key piece of evidence: a small religious card found at each of these particular crime scenes.

Sisco gave Luke the paper, and he read the remainder of the article silently to himself.

Luke subsequently filed the remainder of the night's reports.

"So far, we got three of Philly's worst criminals

chillin' at the morgue, one terrorized anti-cop judge, and four little white cards with Bible verses on them," Luke said.

Sisco nodded in agreement.

"And no real physical evidence," Sisco added. "No fingerprints, no DNA, no nothing."

"And, neither victim, uh, criminal, had any connection to each other, nor were co-defendants in any case," Luke continued.

"At least not that we know of," Sisco added, taking notes on his yellow legal pad.

"We have no witnesses, even less physical evidence. Hell. We don't even have any anonymous tips on the crime hotline."

"But, we got tons of motive," Sisco interjected.

"Copycat crimes?" Luke asked.

"Maybe. But what was the killer copying?" Sisco asked.

"Some vigilante movie, t.v. show, I don't know," Luke said, shaking his head. Sisco tossed his legal pad onto the desk.

Both knew it was going to be another late night.

CHAPTER THIRTY-NINE

MARCH 6th, 11:50 P.M.

The occasion called for some quality stuff, not just any old weed.

He beat his double-murder case last week and he needed to celebrate. So, Demetrius Combs went out yesterday and bought some choice marijuana. He'd brazenly driven up to one of the many open-air drug markets in the city and purchased several kilos of marijuana.

He was free.

No more lawyers, no more court dates, no more talk about pleas and deals. He had hired one of the best lawyers in the city and she'd gotten him off.

It was time to celebrate.

Now, in full party mode, Demetrius picked up a newly-rolled joint and lit it. The pungent herb quickly permeated the air.

"This is what I'm talkin' about!" Combs said, taking a hit of the joint.

Everyone was at his small apartment in Logan

that evening. Among them were: Moochie, Chino, and Nasir. Felix Ross and LeShawn were there as well. Add to that several neighborhood friends, and the number of guests easily topped 30 people. His CD player blasted the latest hip-hop tunes, and the noise level was somewhere between annoying and illegal.

They barely heard the doorbell above the festivities.

"My nigga!" Combs said, greeting Nico Chambers at the door. A compact hoodlum with a square head and crooked teeth, Nico was known around the neighborhood for carjacking and selling car parts for profit. He greeted Combs with a bear hug.

"Told you they couldn't pin that double murder charge on you, didn't I?" Nico shouted over the noise of the party.

"I know, you told me," Combs admitted, as he shut the door. "My mouthpiece said she thought the eyewitnesses weren't credible."

"Well, that and the fact they didn't find the guns on you, right?" Nico added.

"Yeah, that's true, too," Combs laughed.

Partygoers mingled around them.

"You lucky, kid," Nico said, his face suddenly serious. "You almost got the needle bruh."

"Hey, it ain't my fault the A.D.A. didn't do his job right?" Combs replied self-righteously.

"Yo, Boota, was you scared when you knew you had to smoke both of them kids that night in the restaurant?" Nico asked lowering his voice to a more serious pitch.

Combs took a hit of the joint before answering.

"I did what I had to do, know what I'm sayin?" replied Combs replied matter-of-factly. "I'm just a soldier, man. This is a war."

3:30 A.M., next day

Combs glanced at his watch as he parked his money-green Toyota Rav4 in front of his apartment complex. His party had ended at 3:00 a.m., but the food ran out much earlier.

Still hungry, he decided to get some food from the all-night Chinese restaurant a few blocks away. While he could've walked, Combs drove because he didn't want to have to wait to eat.

In any other neighborhood, the neighbors would have called the cops all evening due to the party's rowdiness.

Not here.

Everyone was afraid of Combs because of his notorious reputation. While they may have wanted him out, no one had the heart or courage to take action.

The blaring music coming from Combs' apartment belied the fact that the place was empty. Combs had left his CD player on when he went out.

Just because he could.

He put on his hat, turned on the alarm, and exited the big SUV. He was at his front door in a few steps.

A night of partying and weed-smoking had left Combs buzzing, but not incapacitated. His high tolerance for marijuana was most likely due to his daily use of the drug.

Combs walked through his front door with his bag of food and turned to hang up his jacket in the closet. He couldn't wait to sit down at the kitchen table to feast. He was so busy fumbling with his jacket that he failed to notice that he didn't need his key to open the front door.

He also didn't notice the large tarp-like cloth covering most of the living room furniture and floor.

The first blow found the back of Combs' head. He staggered forward.

"Oh sh –"

He never finished his expletive, as a second blow knocked him face-first into the closet door.

Despite the searing pain in his head, Combs dragged himself to his feet. His hands clumsily felt for the gun in his waistband. He may have been high, but he could still take care of business.

"You won't need that," the intruder said. He was dressed in an olive parka with fur around the hood and opaque latex gloves. A black ski mask covered his face.

The intruder easily disarmed Combs.

"Who the fu --," Combs exclaimed as he looked around for another weapon.

Combs' words were again cut short as the intruder backhanded him.

Rather than risk being knocked down again, Combs began to crawl. Like a drowsy crab, Combs angled toward the front door. The tarp on the floor made it hard to get traction. The marijuana made him feel as if he were in molasses.

The intruder knocked Combs away from the door with a heavy-booted kick in the ribs. The blow nearly lifted Combs off the floor.

"What you want with me, man?" Combs moaned from a fetal position near the entrance to the kitchen. His face was now covered in blood, much of it flowing from his broken nose.

"Is that how Nicole Montgomery and Walter Fishbeck begged for their lives that night," the intruder. He grabded Combs by the neck and dragged him to the middle of the apartment floor.

"I'm innocent man, ain't you hear? My lawyer got me off!" Combs muttered as best he could.

"Innocent! The only innocent people are the two kids you slaughtered!" the intruder responded.

He then emphasized his point with another kick, which caught Combs in the temple.

The intruder went about his work with military precision – no wasted effort.

"What did you do? Get one of your crew to stalk

the young lady who saw you leaving the restaurant after the murder?" the intruder asked.

Combs was so numb from the previous blows that he barely felt the intruder's elbow smash his throat.

Blood gurgled up into his throat.

Combs realized his odds of survival dwindled with every blow, so he decided to make one last rush at the intruder. Half-blind, woozy and bloodied, Combs felt for the mini-dagger he kept in his boot. Summoning up all of his strength, he whipped out the dagger and lunged toward the intruder, who circled Combs.

He managed to get the ski mask off the intruder's face, before a pinpoint left hook dropped Combs like a shot.

"You punk!" the intruder said. "You can't defeat me. You have no idea who I am."

For the next twenty minutes, the intruder masterfully and brutally beat Combs with his bare hands.

The sturdy drop cloth covering the living room floor and some of the furniture was heavily stained with Combs' blood.

When it was over, Combs was unrecognizable.

Unable to speak or move, he could only think of the word mercy. With Combs limp as a rag doll on the floor and nearly choking on his own blood, the intruder calmly went about finishing his handiwork.

He knelt beside Combs, one knee on the tarp, the other knee in Combs' back, pinning him to the floor.

In one swift motion, the intruder removed a lightweight hemp rope from his jacket packet, one end already fashioned into a noose. The noose was around Combs' neck in a matter of seconds.

While Combs lay semi-conscious on the floor, the intruder quickly retrieved one of Combs' kitchen chairs and brought it to the living room. Just below the ceiling in the corner was a large pipe, which ran the length of the room from the corner to the kitchen. The intruder tossed the other end of the hemp rope over the pipe.

The intruder dragged Combs over to the spot where the rope was draped over the pipe. He propped Combs up to a sitting position.

The intruder yanked the free end of the rope. It quickly became taught.

"For your crimes, Demetrius Combs, you must be sentenced to death."

Combs flailed violently as he felt himself rise from the chair. The pain around his neck was incredible. The intruder had reeled in enough rope that before long, Combs' feet were six inches off the floor.

Combs couldn't manage a scream even though his mouth was wide open. So were his eyes. He desperately wished he could raise his hands to get at the rope clawing into his neck, but they were broken. Combs' hands and face turned a dangerous shade of blue.

Before long, Comb's muscles stopped twitching. He swung back and forth silently, his eyes blank and inanimate.

The intruder grabbed the CD remote with his free hand and turned off the blaring music.

He also turned out the lights as he shut the door behind him.

CHAPTER FORTY

MARCH 7th, 8:15 A.M.

"The little bastard didn't even get a chance to spend his first month of freedom at home," Luke said examining the furniture and other items inside Demetrius Combs' apartment.

"I imagine he put up quite a fight," added Sisco. "But, you can't really tell. The place is spotless. Hell, it looks like a realtor came in here and spruced the place up for a buyer."

"How'd they string him up, and not knock over anything?" asked Luke. "From the looks of my man up there, whoever took him out practically tortured him before he strung him up."

The detectives gazed up at the lifeless, battered body hanging from the thick hemp rope. His legs and arms clearly had been broken, and his face was battered. His bulging eyes were no doubt due to the hanging. Medical examiner techs prepared to cut Combs down once they completed their prep work.

The room, marked off by yellow crime scene tape,

was abuzz with officers, detectives and crime scene technicians. It had been nearly four hours since an anonymous call came into Homicide. The call had come from Combs' phone. Sisco and Luke were assigned the job after police found a Scripture card at the crime scene.

Crime scene techs dusted Combs' cell phone for fingerprnts.

"This now makes four bodies," Luke said, fingering the small white card taken from Combs' body. The first officer on the scene found it sticking out of Combs' jacket pocket. This time, the killer had chosen Psalm 94, verse 23 as his message.

He will repay them for their sins and destroy them for their wickedness; the Lord our God will destroy them.

"You guys make sure to get some more door shots," Sisco said, directing the crime scene technicians. The door appeared to have been tampered with. The hemp rope from which Combs hung was solid, expertly-made. Even the knot around his neck was professionally-fashioned. Luke thought it might have been done by someone familiar with tying military knots.

"Nothing else out of place," said Luke.

He finished his tour of the bedroom.

"Nothing missing, nothing misplaced in there. Two laptops in the bedroom," he said. "Wallet still intact with over $100 in it. This room wasn't even touched. This definitely wasn't a robbery."

For all their investigative skill, the detectives would never find out about the old woman living down the hall who, after Combs' murder, had sanitized his apartment spotless of any evidence of the intruder or bodily fluids. They would never know how she and a few older men in the network rolled up the bloody tarp and quietly disposed of it. They would never know how she lived in terror of Combs and how he threatened her and the other residents of the small apartment complex during the time he lived there.

Some, he even physically assaulted.

For all of their high-tech savvy and skill, the detectives would never discover how she and the apartment's maintenance man got fed up enough to enlist the help of an organization so secret and so underground that they could monitor Combs' movements.

These fearful residents ultimately set Combs up to be taken out by an assassin so skilled that the only clue he left behind was a small white card with a scipture verse.

CHAPTER FORTY-ONE

MARCH 9th, 9:00 A.M.

Sisco and Luke sat in Captain Kwan's office with Sgt. Marinovitch and Lt. Gatton.

"Detectives, do we have anything new on the investigation of this Scripture killer?" Captain Kwan.

Sisco spoke first.

"Captain, this guy seems to always be one step ahead of us."

"And he may be having help," Luke chimed in. "We believe this guy may be part of an underground network of vigilantes."

Captain Kwan looked at the Detectives, then at Sergeant Marinovitch. She opened the thick file on her desk.

"What about Torres?" she asked. "That's now four homicides possibly connected to this Bible verse killer. Have we gotten anything new possibly linking Torres to any of the killings?"

"From what we can find, Torres has a lot of bark,

but no real bite," said Luke. "We talked to him, and of course, he didn't give us anything. He was nice to us, though. At this point, no we don't have anything solid on Torres to link him to the murders. In fact, he has a solid alibi for Rachman's murder."

"What about the rest of the homicides we have so far in the city?" Captain Kwan asked.

"According to COMSTAT, murders in Philly have actually gone down during the 3-week period since Rachman was found dead until now. Not counting the four killings we think are connected to this Scripture Killer, there have only been two other unsolved homicides. And both of those were domestic violence situations where the victims knew their killers."

"Not only that," Lucas chimed in, "word on the street is that guys don't want to end up like Rachman, Baby Mike, Melnick, and now Combs. Last week, Sisco and I had two guys surrender to us out of the blue for shootings that happened last year."

Captain Kwan looked up from the file toward Luke.

"When we asked them what made them give themselves up, the guys told us they didn't want to have to watch their back with this killer out here who preys on the bad guys," added Sisco. "They said they were safer locked up."

"I guess hearing about somebody having their nuts crushed, or their neck snapped, will make you change your mind about being on the run,"

Marinovitch said. "At least when you're locked up, you know where to find your enemies."

"Especially, since these guys on the street have no idea who's behind these killings," Kwan added. "Normally if you're a drug dealer or a shooter, you at least know who your enemies are. You figure you're cool as long as you stay away from them. But with this vigilante killer, even these thugs on the streets don't know who to avoid. The vigilante could be anybody, some disgruntled addict, a family member, anybody."

"Hell, it could even be a rogue cop," Sisco said.

"Of course, we've already checked that angle," added Marinovitch, "and that seems a stretch."

"But, you're not sure, right?" Captain Kwan asked.

"Captain, at this point, nothing is certain."

CHAPTER FORTY-TWO

MARCH 11ᵗʰ, 4:32 P.M.

Judge Jack Freidmann had heard that Barbra Streisand was scheduled to sing at this year's Keystone State Bar Association's black-tie gala being held today at the Pavilion Hotel. He'd believe that when he saw it, or rather, her.

He hated going to these functions, but as the President Judge of Philadelphia's Court of Common Pleas, it was almost mandatory. Since he was the one who gave out the city judge's courtroom assignments, this event gave the judges a chance to schmooze with him.

Likewise, it gave Friedmann a chance to lord his power over his peers. At some point, they all knew they had to bow down and kiss the ring.

This afternoon, the Pavilion Hotel was packed with lawyers, judges and significant others. Last year, more than 1,000 people had jammed the Manor Hotel, which hosted the KBA gala.

This year, however, was the Pavilion's turn, and

management spared no expense in hopes of ending the Bar Association's alternating patronage for its yearly gala. In addition to flying in famed Chef Marcel Lateu from the south of France to oversee preparation of the menu, word had it that Barbra Streisand was to make an appearance.

Judge Friedmann spent much of the annual luncheon meeting and greeting some of the region's most-prestigious lawyers and politicians. Even though he was only a common pleas court judge, he still garnered respect from many since being elected Presiding Judge two years ago.

Judge Zane Russell, however, was one who failed to recognize his title.

He was getting to be a fly in Friedman's soup. For quite some time, he had been trying to find a way to rid himself of Zane's arrogance and insubordinate attitude.

While Zane saw himself as a crusader of sorts, Friedmann saw him as a rabble-rouser. In the old days, they could just trump up some charges on Zane, and that would be enough to get him exiled.

These days, however, that was not so easy.

Friedmann had what he sensed was growing support from the defense attorneys' association to do something with Zane. He thought he may have finally found the answer.

CHAPTER FORTY-THREE

MARCH 13ᵗʰ, 10:15 A.M.

"Detective, this is Geneva Pickett, from Reddington, Mississippi. The time is about 9:50 a.m. on Monday. Please call me back. Thank you."

Sisco discovered Mrs. Pickett's voicemail as he checked the messages on his cell phone.

He and Sisco were parked two houses down from a duplex in the city's Sommerdale section. They were waiting to serve an arrest warrant for Benjamin Rafferty, an unemployed carpenter who was wanted for killing his wife and their two month-old son three months earlier. Evidence showed that prior to the killings, Rafferty and his wife had been having marital problems because he thought she was having an affair.

According to the M.E., Rafferty apparently bashed his wife's head in with a blunt object (Sisco guessed a bat, though no murder weapon had been recovered), then drowned the infant in the family tub.

Rafferty disappeared soon after the crime. No one

had seen him or knew of his whereabouts. Numerous anonymous tips, however, flowed in like water since day one. It wasn't long before those tips became consistent: Rafferty was hiding out somewhere in the Northeast at some dinky apartment owned by one of his beer-drinking buddies.

"I think your boy is in there asleep," Luke said, squinting through the binoculars he held. He was focused on the upstairs front bedroom of the duplex.

Luke and Sisco had set up surveillance of the apartment two days ago. The tips were confirmed as Rafferty was seen entering the place late last night. S.W.A.T was in place. Once they secured the apartment, Sisco and Luke would move in for the arrest.

If only it were that simple in reality.

"Luke, Mrs. Pickett called me back. This may be it," said Sisco adjusting the holster on his waist. He also adjusted the light bulletproof vest he wore under his coat. Most homicide detectives didn't bother with vests when serving warrants, as S.W.A.T usually had everything cleaned up and everyone secured before homicide detectives went in.

Sisco, however, had seen too much in his time on the force to take any chances. Even though the margin of error in situations like these was small, it was enough for him to take precautions.

Luke also wore his vest.

"Mrs. Pickett, this is Detective Siscowicz returning your call."

"Yes, hello. Thanks for calling me back."

"No, problem ma'am. You got anything for me?" Sisco had his pad and pen ready.

"I was able to find one of the sample Glory cards. I happened to have some in an old box of things I kept from the company. Like I said, we only made two sets of them. I also remembered something else. Gloria's grandson's name. Zane. Zane Alexander Stewart."

Sisco wrote down all the information.

"I also found out more for you," she continued. "My girlfriend Amelia and I talked about this last week. She was also friends with Gloria, you know."

"Really?" he said.

"Well, Amelia reminded me that her grandson went into the military shortly after he got out of high school. She said she heard through friends that he went on to college and law school somewhere up North, I think she said Philadelphia. She also told me he's now some big-shot politician or judge or something like that."

Sisco was a former Marine, so he was trained not to flinch in the face of bombshells. As a police officer, he expected to engage in gun battles.

But, after hearing Geneva Pickett's revelation, Sisco's training almost went out the window.

"Do you understand what this might mean, Sisco?"

Luke asked, Sisco told Luke what Geneva Pickett said.

Sisco and Luke had been in some high-profile investigations and had arrested some very important people during their careers.

There was the time when Sisco arrested a drunken City Councilman coming out of a notorious strip club following a fight inside.

Eight years ago, a political scandal ensued after Luke (then Detective in Sotuh Philly) investigated and charged a high-profile female state senator who was caught stealing money from her constituents. She was ultmately sentenced to five years in state prison.

But, this was different.

This would be the first time they might have to investigate a high-profile judge or elected official for being a serial killer.

"You think it might be him?" Luke asked. "Gloria Stewart's grandson was named 'Zane Alexander Stewart.'" He looked for any way out other than having to get caught up in investigating a well-known sitting judge – especially a favorite of law enforcement.

"Remember a few weeks ago at Judge Russell's house when he signed that body warrant for us?" Sisco asked.

"Yeah. Ron was there too," Luke responded. "We were talking about their military tattoos or something like that."

"That's the night. Well, when the Judge was signing the warrant, I checked out his high school diploma hanging on the wall with a lot of his other certificates and plaques."

"Yeah, so?" Luke responded.

Sisco paused, then continued.

"Well, his diploma was from Gus Truesdale High School in Reddington, Mississippi. It read Zane Alexander Stewart."

"Damn," Luke replied.

CHAPTER FORTY-FOUR

MARCH 14th, 12:32 P.M.

Zane munched on his chicken salad as he picked through the day's mail. CLE classes, legal correspondence and Bar Association flyers dominated the day's load mail.

He'd started the day with a full load, including a possible jury trial. However, that possiblity quickly diminished when the prosecutor and defense attorney reached a plea deal. Zane recessed the case until after lunch, giving the parties time to discuss the details and fill out the necessary paperwork.

Stuck between another credit card offer and some court paperwork was a letter from the Office of Judge Freidmann, President Judge. Zane noticed the raised gold seal in the upper left corner.

He opened it and scanned the text.

The letter informed him that in thirty days he was being transferred to the Traffic Court's Night

Division pending an investigation into alleged
ethical violations.

****

4:00 P.M.

"What you gon' do, Zane?" Ron asked. "Can't you
appeal his decision or something?"

Ron sat forward in his chair in Zane's chambers.
He held Judge Freidmann's letter like it was a
dirty diaper. He did not think Zane should accept
this without a fight.

"I don't know Ron," Zane said. He sat back in
his chair. "Don't know. Hell, maybe it's time to
just move on."

"Move on? To where? To what?" Ron responded.

Zane stood up and walked over to the large winow
which overlooked City Hall.

"Look, we've done a lot of work here, Ron,"
Zane said. "A lot of good work. We cleaned up a
lot, helped out where we could. Got the citizens
organized. We've done the people's business."

Ron got up and poured himself another cup of
coffee. Black, no cream, no sugar.

"Plus, who knows what other dirty tricks Fiedmann
will try with this ethical investigation? He's got
plenty of clout with the Disciplinary Board," Zane
said.

"But, he don't got nothin' on you Zane!" Ron pleaded. "All a bunch of lies!"

"I know that, and you know that," Zane said. "Hell, Jack knows that. But, he also knows such an investigation involves digging into my past. Not to mention negative press coverage, which could hurt my reputation come re-election time."

"Fight this thing, Zane. Don't take it lying down," Ron said sipping from the cup. "Friedmann will cave in just like he always does. You'll see."

Zane took the letter from Ron and read it again.

"Jack also knows this demotion takes me from the action," Zane said. "I won't be hearing anymore felonies, let alone Homicides. Hell, we'll even have to move our chambers because Night Court is located down on Delaware Avenue. We won't be in the Criminal Justice Center anymore.

Zane looked at Ron. He made sure to keep his voice low, as Marva was eating lunch at her desk just outside the chambers door.

"When you gonna tell the staff?" Ron asked.

"I don't know, Ron," Zane said. "Hell, maybe I ought to just step down from the bench. We've done what we started out to do. We've spread God's Word and we made a difference. In the past 15 years how many of the bad guys have we eliminated? In that time, we helped the Scarlet Chord organize and helped them begin to take back the streets by putting fear into the bad guys. We have fugitives turning themselves in rather than risk ending up like Rachman, Melnick, Hale or Combs. Hell, I understand that since you visited him, Judge Manigault is sending fools to state prison so fast they can't house them all. Who knows how many other fools out there are thinking twice before committing a crime because of us? It may not be much, but it's definitely a start. Now, it's time to move on."

"What you think we ought to do about Friedmann?" Ron asked. His look was one Zane had seen before.

Zane pondered before answering.

"It would draw too much heat," Zane finally answered, shaking his head. "Killing a judge brings major heat. Manigault was easy. We just wanted to send him a message, not hurt him. If we had killed him, we would have gotten the feds' attention even, if we didn't leave a card at the scene."

"So, what are you gonna do, then? Let the citizens down?" Ron asked.

"Look, we always knew it wouldn't last forever," Zane responded. "Remember how we started this whole thing?"

It was Ron's turn to ponder. He walked over to the large window and stood next to Zane.

"Yeah, it was right after my grandson Reno got killed," Ron said. "They gunned him down like a damn dog in the street. My ex-wife came to me and asked me if there was anything I could do. She knew my background and my skills."

Zane just listened.

"That's when I came to you, Zane. Hell, we tracked down and took out bad guys before in the military and then when we got out. I figured maybe we could do the same thing for my grandson."

"It was a pleasure taking him out," Zane said. "The intel we got – between the internet and from our contacts on the street -- on Reno's killer after that horrible jury let him go was more than enough to track him down and kill him."

"Yeah, we did that for Reno," Ron replied. "I had just gotten out of prison, and you were in the D.A.'s office, right? Pulling that one off was a piece of work."

"I was Chief of the D.A.'s Office Homicide Unit at that time," Zane reminded him. "Prosecutor by day, urban vigilante by night."

Zane continued.

"Once we set up that fake website to gather anonymous tips and info on criminals, all we had to do was use our military and professional skills to track them down and do what had to be done."

Zane returned to the table and sat down.

"Now, this thing has gotten so big," Zane continued.

"It's perfect because all we need is the info and the target, and the network don't have to know who we are," Ron replied.

Zane turned back toward Ron.

"However, eventually everything must come to an

end Ron," Zane said. "The Bible says, 'To everything there is a season.' We are the only enforcers in this operation, and we are getting too old for this, my friend. This type of thing is a young man's game."

Ron turned from the window to face Zane. He looked down at his feet.

Zane sat down and rubbed the just-beginning stubble on his face.

"Ron, it seems like I have been chasing bad guys as long as I can remember," Zane said. "I had to change my life for this crusade. I had to start using my real last name, Russell, when I went into the military because of the things I did back in Reddington. I first killed a man when I was 15 years old. After that, killing bad guys became easier."

"And you changed your name when you enlisted so law enforcement couldn't track you down, right?" Ron asked.

Zane nodded in agreement.

"Yes. I wanted to make a brand new start when I left Reddington. When my grandmother died, there was nothing left for me there."

Ron knew Zane was right. Zane always knew what to do.

"Maybe we need to train some new enforcers?" Ron asked.

"Good thought," Zane said, "but who can we trust to do this work? In the beginning, we just wanted to do the work the cops couldn't and the courts wouldn't: bring these demons to true justice."

Ron nodded in agreement.

"While the hard-working citizens appreciated the work we did in the past, once we decided to start leaving the Scripture cards behind, we finally got the devil's attention. We let him and his minions know God's Word still prevails."

"I know. We can still do that, no matter if you're on the bench or not," Ron said.

"True, we could. But, it would be tough," Zane agreed. "Besides, I think the cops may be getting close to us. From what Beck's been telling me, Detectives Lucas and Siscowicz are very good. They'll figure us out before too long."

Ron sat down at the table near Zane just as Zane got up and walked over to the coffee maker. He poured himself a cop.

"Will you finally let Jada know?" Zane asked, without looking at Ron. He knew this was a tough subject, but it had to be broached.

Especially now.

"You know I been going back and forth over that," Ron replied. "I have intentionally stayed out of her life considering what we do. I couldn't take the chance that some thug would hurt her to get at me. It was best this way. Besides I always had eyes on her to make sure she was safe."

"And you did a great job," Zane said. "She would be proud of you. None of us are perfect. You made your mistakes and paid your debt to society. But, you have done a lot of good since then, Ron. You've helped a lot of people my brother."

"I guess if we shutting things down, I could tell her and just leave town," Ron conceded. "I want to show her the picture of her I have on my desk. I think she would like that. Since my ex died after Reno got killed, and then Jada's mother got strung out on drugs, Jada is the only family I really got – other than you Zane."

Zane walked over to Ron and put is hand on his shoulder.

"You are my brother, Ron," Zane said. "You and Beck are my family. You know how I wish my kids would talk to me, but wishing doesn't help. I don't even know if I have any grandchildren. Which is why I say to you: don't miss the opportunity to tell family how you feel about them."

Ron nodded.

"Ron, go to Jada and let her know you are her grandfather."

CHAPTER FORTY-FIVE

MARCH 16th, 10:00 A.M.

Sgt. Marinovitch's small office felt like a cramped elevator. In addition to the sergeant, Sisco and Luke were also present.

All had gotten together for this emergency meeting in light of Sisco and Luke's discovery. The rest of the squad would be briefed later.

Once they determined exactly what they had, they would have to brief Captain Kwan.

"Have either of you spoken to the assigned A.D.A about this new information?" Sgt. Marinovitch asked between sips of bottled water.

"No, we haven't told Beck, yet. We figured we'd keep this hush-hush until we got further direction from you and the Lieutenant. From what we understand, he's pretty tight with Judge Russell."

"You think he'd give the Judge the heads up on our investigation?" Sgt. Marinovitch asked as he leaned forward.

Sisco looked at Luke, then shrugged.

"He might. I'm not sure," Sisco replied.

"Geez," sighed the lieutenant. "That's what we don't need right about now."

"If you don't trust Beck, why don't we just go right to Carlo Ricci?" Marinovitch asked.

"That's definitely an option," Luke answered. "But, what would we tell him? 'Carlo, I think one of your ADA's may compromise our murder investigation. Oh yeah, it just happens to be the Scripture Slayer case, and we think Judge Russell may be the killer?'"

Sisco stepped in.

"Let's hold off on that for now, okay?" Sisco said. "All we're doing is speculating because we have no real evidence on the judge, or that Beck would sabotage our case. Even if what Mrs. Pickett said is true, we couldn't get a judge to sign a search warrant just on that info".

"Not only that, which judge in Philly would be bold enough to sign a search warrant on one of their own?" Luke added.

Sisco agreed with his partner. Their evidence on Judge Russell was thin, at this point. More hunch than solid proof.

Besides, neither detective relished the thought of going over someone's head if it wasn't necessary, especially an A.D.A.

"You guys may be right," replied Sgt. Marinovitch. "Let's just see how this plays out before we bring

Carlo in. He's tough enough to deal with on regular matters."

Luke's cell phone vibrated from his belt. Grabbing it, he hit the talk button.

"What's up?" he answered. After a few moments, he hung up, then turned to the group.

"Judge Russell just resigned from the bench."

CHAPTER FORTY-SIX

MARCH 18th, 11:30 A.M.

"Judge, what do you want to do with all the stuff in those bags?" Beck asked, pointing to a pile of items in Zane's garage.

"Uh, just stack those over there near the door. I'll take them out when I go. There's nothing in them that I really need to keep," Zane replied.

Beck and Zane had been hard at work since early that morning cleaning Zane's garage for the realtors.

Zane's home was one of the nicest in the area, so it should sell in no time. Which was good, because Zane had already put most of his belongings in storage. He had even found an apartment nearby with a month-to-month lease.

It seemed surreal to Beck that Zane was really leaving town. He'd known the judge for over a decade, and Zane had become like a father to him. Despite his repeated requests, Beck thought it odd that Zane still hadn't told him where he was going.

It was just as surreal that Zane stepped down rather than take the traffic court assignment. By stepping down, Zane avoided any investigation into the alleged ethical violations Judge Friedmann gave for his reassignment.

While Friedmann was never Beck's favorite person before this, Beck now considered him an enemy.

"Hungry, yet?" Zane asked as he stacked more boxes.

"Yeah, I guess I could use a bite to eat," Beck said, wiping his hands on his already-dirty sweatpants. "What did you have in mind for lunch?"

"I was thinking maybe some tacos from House of Spain's. How about that?"

"Sounds cool to me, Judge," Beck replied. "You want me to pick them up?"

"No, you relax. We need a break. You've done most of the work, and I appreciate all of your help," Zane said. "It looks totally different now, doesn't it?"

"Yeah, it looks like it should pass inspection. Except for those boxes on the bookshelves up there."

Beck moved toward the shelves.

"Uh, don't worry about those," Zane said, quickly positioning himself between Beck and the shelves. "I'll take care of them before I move out."

Shrugging, Beck headed to the rec room which was attached to the garage.

"What kind of tacos do you want? Beef, pork or chicken?" Zane said, slipping into his coat.

"Chicken tacos for me thanks, with extra salsa and lettuce. I need to eat more vegetables."

"You got it." Zane headed for the door next to the garage. "Go check out the game in the rec room. I think Penn State is playing Michigan. I'll be back in a bit. There are chips in the kitchen cabinet if you're hungry."

"Thanks."

Zane watched Beck leave the garage and walk out to the car.

A few moments later, Beck made himself comfortable on one of the remaining folding chairs in the large recreation room. The rest of the furniture in the room, except for a plasma screen television, had been packed. A full bath was behind the back wall. *Man, all Judge needs is a stove down here, and he never needs to go upstairs,* Beck thought.

During a commercial break, Beck sprinted upstairs to the cabinet with the chips.

He was out of luck.

"Damn, no chips," he said. "I know the judge must keep some snacks around here."

Beck remembered the large can of potato chips he had seen earlier amid the large boxes on the shelf in the garage.

He walked back down to the basement.

Once inside the garage, Beck spotted the can on the top shelf. He moved the small stepladder next to the shelf into position directly underneath the can. He reached the chips in a few steps and lifted the canister off the shelf. Once he retrieved the can, Beck also noticed some large law books between the can and boxes. He grabbed one of them to read during the commercial breaks.

What he didn't realize, however, was that one of the stepladder's legs rested in a small hole in the garage floor. When Beck moved forward, the ladder tilted backward and he lost his footing.

As Beck and the ladder toppled over, he aimed to fall on a stack of large boxes near the shelf.

He hoped that might produce a softer landing.

When he twisted around, his hands swept the can, the books and the boxes next to it off the shelf and onto the floor.

"Damn!" Beck muttered as he rose from the floor.

He assessed the damage. The pain in his shoulder wasn't as bad as the mess he'd made. In addition to some loose papers, and some box tops, there were other small items on the floor. The mess would take some time to clean up.

When Beck picked up a worn rectangular box, several small cards fell on the floor.

Beck picked up a few of the cards. He turned one over and read it.

"What the hell is this?" he muttered.

After a few minutes, Beck forced his legs to move. He jammed two of the cards into his pocket, then worked frantically to stuff the remaining cards back into the box.

He heard a car pull into the driveway.

Beck worked with anxiety-fueled precision as he tried to straighten up the boxes and the shelf.

Zane's house phone rang in the next room throwing Beck into a further panic.

After a few rings, Zane's answering machine clicked on. "Zane, this is Ron. I took care of the thing we talked about. Call me on the cell. It's 1:00 p.m. on Saturday."

Beck sat down heavily on the garage floor, trying to breathe normally. He needed time to sort out these latest events. Sometimes two and two didn't always equal four. Hopefully, this was one of those times.

"I'm back, Beck. Who's winning the game?" Beck heard Zane announce his return and his keys in the garage door.

"Uh, I don't know," Beck lied. "I, ah, I've been going back and forth between the game and boxing," Beck lied.

He feared his face would betray him. Beck quickly sat on one of the chairs and pretended to watch the football game.

"I got us the tacos and peach iced tea," Zane said.

Zane dropped the bag on the table and went upstairs to hang up his coat. Beck looked around quickly, hoping he'd picked up all the cards.

Zane returned and handed Beck a large glass and a plate.

"Any calls?" Zane asked, unwrapping his sandwich.

"Yeah, I think Ron called. I heard it on the machine." Beck said without taking his eyes from the television set.

"Any message?" Zane asked, walking toward the phone.

"Just to call him on the cell," Beck lied.

Stop stammering, man. You're a trial lawyer! Get it together. Beck thought to himself Beck managed to get through the rest of the afternoon.

In fact, by the time the game was over, Beck had convinced himself that his startling discovery was nothing more than coincidence.

That was enough to hang his hopes on.

2:00 P.M.

Beck sweated profusely despite the cold.

Beck knew he needed to see the Rachman file, which was on his desk. The drive to the office after finding the cards at Zane's home was a blur.

Once at his desk, he opened one of the the thick brown accordion folders on top. He pulled out the ziplock baggies containing the small cards. While Detectives Siscowicz and Lucas had taken three of the cards earlier in their investigation, they had since returned them to Beck so he could further study them.

He placed one of the cards he had taken from Zane's home next to the others from the folder.

Beck felt deflated after comparing the cards.

They match perfectly. Same serial number, same insignias. Hell, they're even from the same series, he thought.

He leaned back in his chair and closed his eyes. His mind raced with the endless scenarios facing him. Should he turn over the cards to Carlo? What about Detectives Lucas and Siscowicz? Did he have to start investigating the judge as a suspect?

If he failed to turn over the cards, and Zane turned out to be the killer, Beck could be prosecuted for obstruction of justice. Disbarrment was certain to follow, even if he didn't go to jail.

Who would hire him with a criminal conviction?

I can't believe this is happening, Beck thought.

Beck considered his options.

If he did nothing, maybe things would quiet down. Maybe other evidence would lead to the judge, if he was the real killer. That way, the cards Beck had would be irrelevant.

Once thing was certain: This new evidence was not coincidental. Beck knew too much about the facts to fool himself into that kind of thinking. More importantly, he knew too much about Zane to believe otherwise. Zane was fanatical about religion and justice, strong-willed and physically capable of committing the Scripture crimes.

CHAPTER FORTY-SEVEN

MARCH 20th, 12:00 P.M.

Rather than take the demotion of the Traffic Court assignment, Zane washed his hands of the whole Philadelphia Court of Common Pleas altogether and left town. Instead of taking the local apartment and waiting until his home was sold, Zane let his realtor handle that process and instructed her to contact him if she needed him.

The press coverage surrounding Zane's departure was intense.

Community activists and civic groups loudly protested Zane's demotion. They held press conferences and media events.

Some even called for Judge Friedmann's impeachment.

Ron also left the area. At least, that's what everyone thought, because he hadn't been seen since Zane left.

In the time leading up to Zane's departure, Beck did his best to avoid him for other reasons. After finding the Scripture cards, Beck had no idea what to say to him.

He felt betrayed.

Zane was like a father to him. Zane always preached to him about doing the right thing and avoiding the appearance of evil. To think Zane might be behind the string of gruesome murders of those criminals was more than Beck could handle.

But, if the detectives charged Zane with the murders, Beck, as an officer of the court, was duty-bound to turn the cards over to Homicide.

In contrast to the turmoil surrounding his relationship with Zane, things had gotten much better between him and Serene.

Once he was honest with Serene about his commitment and trust issues, she reassured him that she was committed to their relationship. This quelled his feelings of insecurity.

Beck also began to deal with his anger issues, especially those regarding his dad. He began seeing a therapist who suggested he visit his father in prison.

He followed her advice.

While the first meeting with his father could hardly be described as warm, it was at least a start.

Best of all, Beck's sleep got better. His nightmares subsided to the point where his sessions with Dr. Swanson became few and far between.

"You think the Judge is still going to practice

law?" Beck asked Serene this afternoon as they lounged on her couch.

"I don't know, honey," Serene said, resting her head on Beck's chest. "Wherever he is, I just pray he's doing well."

Beck nodded.

"I just wish he'd call," Beck said. "You know, let us know he's alright. I wonder if he's heard from Ron."

In the weeks since Zane left, Beck had wrestled with a host of emotions. While he couldn't bring himself to believe Zane could be behind the murders, He also found it hard to be angry at Zane if he was the killer.

Most of all, Beck just missed his mentor.

"So much has happened," Beck whispered to Serene as they lay on her couch. "It's too much sometimes."

Serene drew Beck into her arms and held him close. The mood changed somewhere between Serene's gentle caresses and light kisses, and they were swept away by passion they could no longer hold in check.

Promise broken.

ONE YEAR LATER...

EPILOGUE

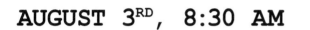

AUGUST 3RD, 8:30 AM

Sisco and Luke had worked their informants hard for the past two weeks trying to get intel on Marco Scarsone.

Earlier in the month he had allegedly shot his girlfriend to death after an argument in their home. Neighbors heard them argue one night, followed by gunshots. While no one saw the murder, several witnesses saw him abruptly leave the house minutes later. In addition, he had not been to work since the argument.

Yesterday, Luke received an anonymous tip that Marco was staying at a motel near Ridge Pike in the Plymouth meeting area in Montgomery County.

With that knowledge, the detectives drove to the hotel. They had already alerted the Plymouth-Whitemarsh police department and their S.W.A.T. team – just to be safe.

"Damn, it's hot already," Luke said, turning up the squad car's air conditioning unit. The unmarked car was plain to look at, but had decent air and heat for a city-issued vehicle.

"Bro, it's been record heat for the past two weeks," Sisco replied as he drove through Chestnut Hill. "Hopefully we'll get some rain to cool us off soon."

Rather than go straight up Germantown Ave, Sisco decided to take a short cut through a few back roads in Chestnut Hill. This would take them to Henry Avenue, them on to Ridge.

As they approached a stately home on a quiet and secluded street, Luke noticed some unfamiliar activity.

"Check that out Sisco," said Luke directing Sisco's attention to the property. "Judge Rusell must have sold that house. I don't see a For Sale sign out front anymore."

Sisco slowed down and glanced to his right.

"I wonder who bought it? They must have some cash," Siso replied.

"I wonder where Judge Russell is?" Luke said.

That was the million dollar question since Zane left the bench abruptly last year amid a cloud of controversy.

"You still think he had something to do with the Scipture killings?" Luke asked.

Sisco didn't answer right away.

"What I think and what we can prove are two different things," he responded. "I mean, we did discover he was Gloria Stewart's grandson and we did determine that those cards came from her collection from Hastings Religious Specialties."

He turned onto Henry Avenue.

"But, that was it. We never got the chance to talk to him or search his property," he said. "And, when Mrs. Pickett died suddenly last year just before we were scheduled to fly down to Mississippi, her info died with her."

Sisco changed lanes as they passed Bells Mills Road.

Luke continued to fiddle with the air conditioning unit. He also reviewed the arrest warrants in the file on his lap.

"You notice we never got any anonymous tips regarding those murders," Sisco said. "Not one. No street intel. Nothing. Didn't that seem strange to you?"

"Hell, it seemed like no one wanted those killings solved but us anyway," Luke said. "Plus, the judge left town quicker than a flash after he got demoted. We had no chance to interview him, even if Captain Kwan had given us the okay."

Sisco accelerated once they passed Hart's Lane.

"To answer your initial question Luke, I can't say if the Judge had anything to do with the killings, but we haven't found any more of those cards since last year. You do the math."

Sisco drove past the Butler Pike intersection.

Traffic was noticeably heavier at this end of Ridge Pike.

"Plus," Sisco continued, "we had some of the baddest thugs just turn themselves in becaue they were afraid of being the next Scripture victim," Sisco reminded him.

"Yeah, I remember that," Luke replied.

Luke turned up the car's police radio. He checked into dispatch to let them know how close they were to their suspect's residence.

"Sisco, maybe it doesn't even matter anymore, bro," Luke said. "Besides, even if we had something on the judge, would you want to be the one to arrest him?"

Sisco pondered as he left turned onto Chemical Road.

"Man, I don't even know what justice looks like anymore," Sisco said.

Luke didn't respond.

The air conditioner finally kicked in, delivering refreshingly cool air to car's cabin. The detectives welcomed the relief from the sticky summer air.

JACKSON MISSISSIPPI

AUGUST 8th 10:30 A.M.

The break came at the right time, Beck thought. Class was grueling enough without having to go straight through.

For the past two days, Beck felt as if he were in law school all over again as he was drilled on cross-exam, direct exam and a wide array of other litigation skills.

This is what made the National Prosecutors Boot Camp so prestigious.

Though it was held in Jackson, Mississippi, prosecutors came from all over the country to hone their skills. Beck was excited that the office chose to send him this year.

The past year had been one of the most difficult times in Beck's life.

Zane, his mentor and father figure, had left Philadelphia with no forwarding address. After finding the Scripture cards in Zane's garage, Beck wasn't sure if he even had anything to say to

Zane. More importantly, Beck's refusal to turn the cards over to his office opened him up to possible obstruction of justice charges.

Without that, the Scripture Killer murders remained unsolved. The fact that no more criminals had been found dead with scripture cards on them since Zane left town was both comforting and unnerving to Beck.

Perhaps the most important change in Beck's life this past year was Aaron, Beck and Serene's nine-month old son. Beck still had a long way to go to patch things up with Serene's parents, as they had deep religious convictions about their baby girl having a child out of wedlock. Serene and Beck had their own convictions as well -- convictions that even their marriage several months ago failed to adequately quell. Beck had drawn closer to God in the ensuing months, a closeness which he eagerly embraced.

* * *

Beck took a moment to reflect on the dizzying events of the past year.

Aaron was born amid the confusion and anguish of the events surrounding Zane and the Scripture cards. However, he was the silver lining in those dark clouds. Beck loved him more than life itself.

Beck also discovered just how much Serene meant to him. While they may have broken their celibacy promise, they had added so much more to their lives.

* * *

The National Prosecutors Association center was the only facility in the country that taught local, state and federal prosecutors the tricks of the trade.

With the latest in courtroom technology, the center offered some of the best trial strategy training anywhere. Top prosecutors from all over the country served as instructors for the week-long training classes.

This morning's lecture was identifying fingerprint patterns and presenting that information at trial.

The past three days of lectures had been educational, but tedious. *If you don't love criminal law before you get here, you'll definitely hate it afterwards* Beck thought.

* * *

"Hi, you're from the Philly D.A.'s office, aren't you?" asked Katrina Derskin, one of the local prosecutors taking the course. She worked in Pearl River County.

Beck nodded, glancing at the name sticker on her suit jacket.

"Katrina, right? Hi, how are you doing?" Beck

offered his hand, which she shook with the standard brawny professional female handshake.

"Great job earlier this week," she said. "I loved your closing argument in the first day's exercise. I thought the story about your ancestor fighting in the Civil War was very effective."

"Thanks a lot. I appreciate that," Beck said. "You never know if your anecdotes really get through to a jury."

"You folks up in Philly sure move a lot of cases, huh?" Katrina said.

"Most definitely," Beck responded, "But that's what we have to do to tackle the volume of cases that go through the criminal justice system. In Common Pleas Court alone, there are somewhere between 50-60,000 criminal cases a year."

Katrina looked impressed.

"Down here, we have our share of cases, but nothing like that. Is it true that Philly is the murder capital of the country?" Katrina asked.

"We've been having our problems, that's for sure. It's crazy. Some days it seems like there are more nuts in Philly than a Planter's jar," he joked.

She laughed as well.

"What about you guys down here?" Beck asked. "I'd be willing to bet we don't own a monopoly on crime, you know what I mean?"

"I've only been in Homicide for six months," she replied, "so I haven't tried that many cases. But, yes, our crime rate is up. As a matter of fact, it seems we have an interesting weirdo in our fair city right now."

"Really?" Beck said.

She nodded. "There's been a number of violent criminals being brutally murdered. One rapist was found hanging in his basement with his testicles crushed."

She now had Beck's full attention.

"It's starting to look like we have a serial killer." Katrina leaned in closer to Beck and whispered, "At each of the past three crime scenes, police found a little white card with a Bible verse on it."

This information hit Beck harder than any left hook or uppercut ever did.

1:00 P.M.

It was all Beck could do to concentrate on the remaining day of training.

Normally, he would look forward to the reception held at the end of the conference. This year, however, he left two days early, booking a stand-by flight home.

By the time Beck had reached the airport, he was feeling somewhat better. He buckled himself into his seat for takeoff. After a cold lemonade, he managed to put the whole matter behind him.

As the plane taxied down the runway, he eased

back into his seat for the two-hour flight to Philly International Airport. The ground fell away in a hurry as the plane climbed to flying altitude.

"Would you like something to eat? Any chips or peanuts?" A sweet-smiling flight attendant stood over Beck. Passengers began to unbuckle as the plane settled into cruising speed.

"No, thanks. I'm okay," he said.

"Let me know if you need anything, alright?"

"Will do." The flight attendant moved down the aisle of the massive jet.

Beck pulled out his wallet and flipped to a small picture of Serene and Aaron in the birthing suite shortly after Aaron's birth. The nurses had cleaned the little fella up, and Serene had given him his first taste of breast milk. Both fell asleep shortly thereafter.

Lying in the bed in the hospital's birthing suite after Aaron was born, Serene was radiant. Beck saw in her Christ's essence – the true spirit of love and tenderness. In Aaron, he saw God's beauty and sacrifice. At that point, he knew there was nothing in this world he wouldn't do for his family.

As for Zane, Beck had made a choice: Zane's secret was safe with him. It was no easy decision, and he'd agonized and prayed over it.

Besides, the criminals who had been killed were some of the cty's worst. They lived and died by the sword, Beck rationalized.

While his oath as a prosecutor nagged at him,

Beck's love for the judge was too great. Zane was like a father to him, and Beck accepted the fact that he might never fully reconcile the confusion within him. If Zane was the Scripture Killer, Beck knew Zane thought he was doing the right thing. In some bizarre way, maybe justice had been served.

Maybe Zane was doing the people's business.

In any event, it wasn't his fight anymore. Perhaps God would work it all out.

He always did. In His own time.

In the meantime, Beck had all he could handle in helping Serene to raise their son, *Zane Alexander Stephens*.

CPSIA information can be obtained
at www.ICGtesting.com
Printed in the USA
BVHW041153111019
560866BV00011B/1021/P

9 781684 706198